IMPOSTORS

IMPOSTORS

SCOTT WESTERFELD

SCHOLASTIC PRESS

Library of Congress Cataloging-in-Publication Data available

ISBN 978-1-338-33550-7

10 9 8 7 6 5 4 3 2 1   18 19 20 21 22

Printed in the U.S.A.   23
First edition, September 2018

Book design by Chris Stengel

To everyone fighting for their right to exist

PART I

HOSTAGE

Regard your soldiers as your children, and they will follow you into the deepest valleys.

—Sun Tzu

KILLER

We're about to die. Probably.

Our best hope is the pulse knife in my hand. It trembles softly, like a bird. That's how my head trainer, Naya, says to hold it.

Gently, careful not to crush it.

Firmly, so it doesn't fly away.

The thing is, my pulse knife really *wants* to fly. It's military grade. Smart as a crow, unruly as a young hawk. Loves a good fight.

It's going to get one. The assassin, twenty meters away, is spraying gunfire from the stage where my sister just gave her first public speech. Her audience, the dignitaries of Shreve, are strewn around the room—dead, faking death, or cowering. Security drones and hovercams are scattered on the floor, knocked out by some kind of jammer.

My sister's huddled next to me, gripping my free hand in both of hers. Her fingernails are deep in my skin.

We're behind a tipped-over table. It's a slab of vat-grown oak, five centimeters thick, but the assassin's got a barrage pistol. We might as well be hiding in a rosebush.

But at least no one can see us together.

We're fifteen years old.

This is the first time anyone's tried to kill us.

My heart is beating slantways, but I'm remembering to breathe. There's something ecstatic about the training kicking in.

Finally, I'm doing what I was born to do.

I'm saving my sister.

The comms are down, but Naya's voice is in my head from a thousand training sessions—*Can you protect Rafia?*

Not unless I take out this attacker.

Then do it.

"Stay here," I say.

Rafi looks up at me. She has a cut above her eye—from the splinters flying everywhere. She keeps touching it in wonder. Her teachers never make her bleed.

She's twenty-six minutes older than me. That's why she gives the speeches and I train with knives.

"Don't leave me, Frey," she whispers.

"I'm always with you." This is what I murmur from the bed beside hers, when she's having nightmares. "Now let go of my hand, Rafi."

She looks into my eyes, finds that unbroken trust we share.

As she lets go, the assassin lets loose again, a roar like the air itself is shredding. But he's spraying randomly, confused. Our father was supposed to be here, and only canceled at the last minute.

Maybe the assassin isn't even thinking about Rafi. He certainly doesn't know about me, my eight years of combat training. My pulse knife.

I make my move.

BODY DOUBLE

Rafi's speech was perfect. Clever and gracious. Unexpected and funny, like when she tells stories in the dark.

The dignitaries loved her.

I listened from the sidelines, hidden, wearing the same dress as her. Everything identical—our faces because we're twins, the rest because we work hard at it. I have more muscle, but Rafi tones her arms to match. When she gains weight, I wear sculpted body armor. We get our haircuts, flash tattoos, and surgeries side by side.

I was standing by to step in and wave to the crowd of randoms outside. Sniper-bait.

I'm her body double. And her last line of defense.

The applause swelled as she finished her speech and headed for the viewing balcony, the brilliant daughter stepping in for the absent leader. Hovercams rose up in a multitude, like sky lanterns on our father's birthday.

We were about to make the switch when the assassin opened fire.

I crawl out from behind cover.

The air is thick with the hot-metal reek of barrage pistol. The rich scents of roast beef and spilled wine. The assassin fires again, the roar thrilling my nerves.

This is what I was born to do.

Another table between me and the assassin is still upright. I crawl through chair legs and dropped silverware, past a spasming body.

On my back, looking up at the splintered table, I feel wine dripping through bullet holes onto my face. It's summer berries and ripe heaven on my tongue—only the best wine for our father's events.

I squeeze the knife, sending it into full pulse. It shrieks in my hand, buzzing and hot, ready to tear the world apart.

I shut my eyes and slice through the table.

Our father burns real wood at his winter hunting lodge. All that smoke trapped in a few logs, enough to rise a kilometer into the sky. A pulse knife at full power shreds things just as fine— molecules ripping, energy spilling out.

A swath of oak, dishes, and food dissolves into a haze of fragments, a thick hot cloud billowing across the room. Sawdust glittering with vaporized glassware.

The assassin stops firing. He can't see.

Me either, but I've already planned my next move.

I scuttle out from beneath the halved table, lungs clenched against the dust. At the edge of the stage, I pull myself up, still blind.

A grinding sound fills the ballroom. The assassin is using the cover of dust to feed his barrage pistol—the weapon uses improvised ammunition to make it smaller, harder to detect.

He's reloading so he can shoot blind and still kill everyone.

My sister is out there in the dust.

The taste of sawdust fills my mouth, along with a hint of vaporized feast. I set my pulse knife to fly at chest height. Hold it like a quivering dart.

And the assassin makes a mistake—

He coughs.

With the slightest nudge the knife flies from my hand, deadly and exuberant. A millisecond later comes a sound I recognize from target practice on pigs' carcasses—the gurgle of tissues, the rattle of bones.

The sawdust is cleared by a new force billowing out from where the knife hit. I see the assassin's legs standing there, nothing above his waist but that sudden blood mist.

For a grisly moment the legs stand alone, then crumple to the stage.

The knife flits back into my hand, warm and slick. The air tastes like iron.

I've just killed someone, but all I think is—

My sister is safe.

My sister is safe.

I drop from the stage, cross to where Rafi still huddles behind the table. She's breathing through a silk napkin, and hands it to me to share.

I stay alert, ready to fight. But the air is filling with the buzz of security drones waking back up. The assassin was wearing the jammer, I guess, so it's mist now too.

Finally, I let my knife go still. I'm starting to shake, and suddenly Rafi is the one thinking straight.

"Backstage, little sister," she whispers. "Before anyone figures out there's two of us."

Right. The dust is clearing, the survivors wiping their eyes. We hustle away through an access door beneath the stage.

We've grown up in this house. Playing hide-and-seek in this ballroom with night-vision lenses, I was always the hunter.

My comms ping back up, and Naya's voice is in my ear:

"We see you, Frey. Does Gemstone need medical?"

This is the first time we've used Rafi's code name in a real attack.

"She's cut," I say. "Over her eye."

9

"Get her to the sub-kitchen. Good work."

That last word sounds strange in my ear. All my training up to this moment might have seemed like work. But this?

This is me, complete.

"Is it over?" I ask Naya.

"Uncertain. Your father's locked down on the other side of the city." Naya's words are sharp with the possibility that this is only the start of something bigger. That at last the rebels are moving in force against our father.

I guide Rafi past stage machinery and lighting drones, to the stairs that lead down. Cleaning drones and cockroaches scuttle out of our way.

Five soldiers—everyone in Security who knows of my existence—meet us in a kitchen cleared of staff. A medic shines a light in Rafi's eyes, cleans and seals her cut, flushes her lungs of smoke and dust.

We move in a tight group toward the secure elevator. The soldiers settle around me and Rafi, hulking in their body armor like protective giants.

The glassy look in my sister's eyes hasn't faded.

"Was that real?" she asks softly.

I take her hand. "Of course."

My trainers have run surprise drills on us a hundred

times, but nothing so public, with dead bodies and barrage pistols.

Rafi touches the wound on her head, like she still can't believe that someone tried to kill her.

"That's nothing," I say. "You're okay."

"What about you, Frey?"

"Not a scratch."

Rafi shakes her head. "No, I mean, did anyone see you—next to *me*?"

I stare into her eyes, her fear cutting into my excitement. What if someone in the ballroom saw us? A body double is worthless if everyone knows they're not the real thing.

Then what would be the point of me?

"No one saw," I tell her. There was too much dust and chaos, too many people wounded and dying. The hovercams were all knocked out.

And what matters is: I've saved my sister. I let the ecstasy of that flood into me.

Nothing will ever feel this good again.

SCAR

"I want a scar," Rafi says.

Our doctor goes quiet.

We've been moved up to the house medical center, where our father takes his longevity treatments. The surfaces glisten, the staff wear white disposables. Rafi and I are lying on tufted leather lounges facing a picture window—a sprawling view of Shreve and beyond, the city rolling off into forest and storm clouds.

Our father isn't back yet, though the city has been quiet. This wasn't a revolution. Just one assassin.

The doctor's assistant is cutting away my fancy dress, checking for any injuries I'm too brain-pumped to feel. She's the only member of Orteg's staff who knows that I exist.

She always seems scared of me. Maybe it's my stream of training injuries. Or maybe it's because if she ever lets slip that I exist, she'll be disappeared. She's never told me her name.

Dr. Orteg leans over Rafi, shining a light on her brow. "Fixing this will only take a minute. It won't hurt."

"I don't care what hurts," she says, knocking his light away. "What I want is a *scar*."

Looks pass between the doctor and his assistant, the caution that descends whenever Rafi's being difficult. Her explosions of temper come without much warning.

Dr. Orteg clears his throat. "I'm sure your father—"

"My father understands exactly why." She arches her neck, sighs dramatically at the ceiling, reminding herself to be patient with lesser beings. "Because they tried to kill *me*."

Silence again. Less fearful, more thoughtful.

Rafia is more popular than our father. No one ever polls the question, but our staff studies the metrics. The way people talk about her, the expressions on their faces, the movements of their eyes. Everything captured by the spy dust shows it's true.

But no one wants to have *that* conversation with our father.

Dr. Orteg looks at me for help, but Rafi's right. The scar won't let anyone forget what happened tonight. What the rebels tried to do to her.

Then it hits me. "Like those old pictures of Tally Youngblood."

Rafi's eyes light up. "Exactly!"

A murmur passes through the room.

No one's seen Tally in years, except her face in random clouds, like she's a saint. Or in shaky hovercam shots. But people still look for her.

13

And she did have that scar, just above her eyebrow. Her first strike against the pretty regime.

"Interesting point, Frey," comes a voice from the doorway. "I'll ask your father."

Standing there is Dona Oliver, his private secretary. Behind her is a bank of screens—the control room, where our father's staff monitors every feed in our city. News, gossip, even the images captured by the spy dust all filter through this tower.

Dr. Orteg gets back to work, looking relieved that the decision is out of his hands now.

Dona turns away from us, whispering into her wrist. She's beautiful in an extravagant way. Big eyes, flawless skin—that crazy-making gorgeousness from the pretty era, back when everyone was perfect. She's never had her beauty surged into something more fashionable. Somehow she carries it without looking like a bubblehead.

Rafi takes a hand mirror from the table between us. "Maybe the scar should be on the left side, where Tally's was. What do you think, little sister?"

I lean across and take her chin gently, give her a long look. "Leave it right where it is. It's perfect."

Her only answer is a little shrug, but she's smiling now. I'm pleased with myself, and that pleasure blends with leftover excitement from the battle downstairs. Sometimes I'm a decent diplomat, even if diplomacy is my sister's job.

The faraway look fades from Dona's face.

"He agrees," she says. "But nothing unsightly, doctor. Make it elegant."

"Only the *best* scars," my sister says, laughing as she eases back into her chair.

It takes a full ten minutes to perfect Rafi's injury. It seems an elegant scar is trickier than none at all.

She's beautiful, as always, but a blemish on her face feels like a mark against me. I should have gotten to her quicker, or spotted the assassin before he had time to open fire at all.

When Dr. Orteg is done, he gives me a troubled look—he has to cut me now.

The same scar exactly.

He picks up a bottle of medspray.

"Wait," I say.

Everyone looks at me. I'm not usually the one giving orders. I was born twenty-six minutes too late for that.

"It's just . . ." The reason isn't clear in my mind, and then it is. "It hurt, didn't it, Rafi?"

"Splinters in my face?" She laughs. "Yeah, a lot."

"Then it should hurt me too."

The others all stare at me, like I'm too shell-shocked to think. But Rafi seems pleased. She loves it when I cause trouble, even if that's her job.

15

"Frey's right," she says. "We should match, inside and out."

The room sharpens a little—a tear in my eye. I love it when Rafi and I think the same way, even after all that work to make us opposites.

"Inside and out," I whisper.

Dr. Orteg shakes his head. "There's no *reason* to do it without anesthetic."

He looks at Dona Oliver.

"Except it's perfect," she says. "Good girl, Frey."

I smile back at her, certain this is the best day of my life.

I'm not even disappointed that she doesn't ask our father for permission to hurt me.

DAMAGE

Half an hour later we're alone in our room, sitting side by side on Rafi's bed. Her wallscreen is set to mirror us.

We keep the lights low, because my head is throbbing. Dr. Orteg had to redo my scar three times before it matched Rafi's.

I didn't let him use the medspray until it was done. I wanted to feel it the same way she did—the sharpness of breaking skin, the warm trickle of my own blood. When we touch our scars, it will be with the same memory of pain.

"We look amazing," she whispers.

That's how she always talks about our looks—in the plural. Like it's not boasting if she includes me too.

And maybe it's true. Our mother was a natural pretty. The only one in the city, Father brags to anyone who'll listen. He says we'll never need a real operation, even when we get old and crumbly, just a touch-up here or there.

But our mix of his glower and our mother's angelic face has always looked disjointed to me. And now this scar.

Like Beauty and the Beast had daughters, and raised them in the wild.

"I don't know if we're pretty," I say. "But we're alive."

"Thanks to you. I just sat there screaming."

I turn to stare at her. "When did you scream?"

"The whole time." She drops her eyes. "Just not out loud."

Rafi was her usual self in front of everyone—bratty and full of swagger. But here alone with me, her voice has gone quiet and serious.

"Doesn't it scare you?" she asks.

I recite what our father always says. "The rebels only hate us because they're jealous of what he's built. That means they're small people, not worth being afraid of."

Rafi shakes her head. "I meant, doesn't it scare you that you *killed* someone?"

The question takes a second to sink in. I've been too brain-rattled to think about it. The sound of the knife churning through the assassin, the taste of his blood in the air.

"In that moment, it's not *me*." My fingers flutter, moving through pulse knife commands. "It's the training—all those hours of practice."

She takes my hand, stills my twitching fingers. "That's what Naya would say. But how did it feel to *you*?"

"Amazing," I say, soft as air. "I'd kill anyone for you, Rafi."

Her eyes stay locked on mine. Her lips barely move, mouthing the shadow of a word—*Anyone?*

My breath catches. I can't believe that she would ask me this, even too softly for spy dust to hear. Because I know exactly who she means.

I dare to give her the barest nod.

Even him.

A smile settling on her face at last, Rafi looks away into the mirror. Those identical faces with identical scars.

"Remember back when we were littlies, and they told us it was a game? Pretending there was only one of us? None of it seemed real."

I nod. "Like a joke we were playing on the world."

"Some joke. It's less funny when someone shoots at you."

"He missed."

She points at her scar. "Speak for yourself."

"That wasn't a bullet, Rafi. Just . . . collateral damage."

She reaches across to touch my brow with careful fingertips. Beneath the tingle of medspray, a dull ache beats in time with my heartbeat.

"So what's this?"

I turn away, but Rafi's still there in the mirror.

"That's not damage," I say. "That's me, always part of you."

She squeezes my hand, and I feel that certainty I always had as a littlie. That I'm more than expendable. More than a body double.

"This isn't normal," she whispers. "This secret. People don't raise their kids to take a bullet."

"But I saved you."

Rafi doesn't know how amazing this feels. How those years of training, all that work and pain, flowing through me now like lightning.

She turns away for a moment.

"One day I'll save you too."

THE SOFTEST THING

Naya is trying to hurt me.

She's coming at me with a *bō*, a long bamboo staff with metal tips. It's one her favorite weapons—it spins in her hands, stirring the cool air of the training room.

It's a whole year after the assassination attempt, and there haven't been any attacks on our family since. But they train me harder than ever.

Lately, it's all been improvised weapons. I never go anywhere without my pulse knife, but Naya wants me ready for anything.

The weapons table is full of random junk—a handscreen, a scarf, a vase of flowers, a fireplace poker. I'm supposed to grab something to protect myself.

The poker can't be right. Too obvious, too heavy and slow to block that wheeling staff.

The vase would shatter—and I'm barefoot. No thanks.

Scarves can strangle, bind, and trap. But I'd have to get close to use it, and the spinning *bō* is longer than I am tall.

So I grab the handscreen and fling it edgewise at Naya.

For a glorious moment it's a flying blade, flashing sharp and deadly. I almost worry it'll hurt her. But a flick of the *bō* shatters it into a spray of safety glass.

Naya barely squints as the shards rain past her.

I grab the vase and tip it onto the mat. Maybe I can make her slip.

But there's no water in the vase, just dried flowers. Petals scatter, like she's getting married.

Maybe I'm being too clever. As she closes in, I grab for the—

Whap.

The *bō* cracks down on the back of my hand, and agony erupts. Anatomy classes spill like fire through my head—all those nerves in the hand, laced around all those delicate bones.

The best way to take down a bigger opponent is to break a finger.

I'm sinking to my knees, clutching my wrist.

"Your turn." Naya throws me the staff.

It clatters to the floor. The pain is fizzing up my arm, filling my head. Red sparks fly at the edge of my vision.

"Get up," she says. "Fights don't stop when you get hurt."

"But I think it's—"

"Stand and *fight*." She means it.

All my trainers have been brain-missing lately. Eager to make me bleed, to break bones. But this is the first time Naya's forced me to keep fighting after hurting me this bad.

I stagger to my feet, clutching the staff in my left hand.

"Get your weapon moving, Frey."

I put my broken hand on the staff, and for a moment it's too painful to think. Then I remember—all the power of the *bō* comes from the back hand, the front only guides the staff.

I get the weapon spinning, barely.

"Faster."

It's impossible, but I try anyway. If I pass out from the pain, at least this will be over.

Naya darts forward to the table, then rolls back out of reach, the scarf in her hands. She ties a quick knot at one end.

Of course—the correct answer is always the softest, fluffiest thing on the table.

She flicks the scarf into the slow gyre of my staff. It tangles, jerks the *bō* from my grasp. The jolt to my broken hand is so painful I almost throw up.

"The best way to blunt a force is to tangle it," Naya says.

This was the point of today's lesson, I suppose—a parable to make me wiser. But it's hard to learn anything when it hurts too much to breathe.

Five minutes later, while the autodoc is knitting my metacarpals back together, our father summons me.

Naya doesn't look surprised. Just shakes her head.

"You aren't ready."

I stare at her. "For what?"

"It's not my place to tell you."

"Are we going someplace?"

She hesitates, then nods.

"So there's a *reason* for this." I wave my good hand at the wreckage in the room. The shattered glass of the handscreen, the strewn petals, the scarf still tangled with the bamboo staff.

"There's always a reason, Frey. Did you think we were doing this for fun?"

Fun? I almost laugh. The autodoc is making a grinding sound, like the beautiful steel contraption in my father's office that dribbles out coffee on command. I distantly feel my bones being restitched and reshaped.

It makes me twitch.

Then it hits me—

Improvised weapons. All month long.

Wherever Rafi and I are going, I won't be taking my knife.

Naya and I take the private elevator up—only people who know about me are allowed to use it. There are special hallways for me too, marked with red stripes for the highest-clearance members of staff.

When we were little, sometimes Rafi would hide in our room and let me wander the house. When I was dressed like her, I could go anywhere I wanted. But freedom was never really-happy-making, because I was always alone.

So we made up a better game. We pretended we lived in a dungeon with monsters roaming the halls. Sneaking into the nonsecure corridors, we'd spy on the staff at work, careful not to be seen.

Luckily, we got caught by Naya before anyone else. Furious, she explained what would happen to someone who saw us together, if they didn't already know about me.

After that, the game wasn't fun anymore.

But I miss having time for games.

My hand is wrapped in a cold-sleeve to keep the swelling down. The bones are knitted, but the tissues deep inside feel wrong. Like always after a fresh training injury, I keep imagining something torn in there, too small for the autodoc to catch.

When the elevator arrives outside our father's office, Rafi and her assistant are waiting. Father never sees me without my older sister in the room. Bonding too closely with his spare daughter would be sloppy.

Rafi takes in my sweatpants and flushed face, the cold-sleeve around my hand.

"You smell like effort," she says—part of her act is making everything look effortless. But she offers a little shrug of sympathy. "At least he'll be able to tell us apart."

This makes me smile.

Once when we were ten years old, we dressed up to fool him, Rafi in workout gear and me in a pinafore. She spent a solid hour getting my makeup right, me squirming the whole time.

Our father didn't spot the deception, but Dona did. She didn't let us ride our hoverboards for a month. But it was worth it for those moments of power over our father—knowing something that he didn't.

Now he keeps us waiting.

Naya checks the readout on my cold-sleeve while Rafi's assistant lists what parties she's attending tonight. Nothing too public, so I'll stay here, making up for the training hours lost to this broken hand.

Normally I'd be happy to stay home. But after a month of heavy workouts, I need a night at a dance club. One of the big places, where I get to leave the family suite and take Rafi's place on the floor.

I'm a better dancer than my sister. Not when it comes to ballet or ballroom, of course. But jostling in a crowd of sweaty strangers is more like combat than anything she's studied.

When her assistant is finished, Rafi looks at me.

"Do you know why we're here, little sister?"

I shake my head. She looks disappointed, and gives me one of her old hand signals. The ones we started using when we realized they were always watching us.

Follow my lead.

As if I ever do anything else.

The doors to the office open, and Dona Oliver is standing there.

"Your father will see you now."

Our father's office is the highest floor of the tower, which he built the old-fashioned way, with a skeleton of steel. He doesn't trust hoverstruts, just metal and stone.

From two hundred meters in the sky, the city looks puny. The distant forest blurs into a mottle of green. But the clouds still loom large, hunkering in the distance, unconquerable.

My sister curtsies, and I nod my head. Our father's staring off into an airscreen, giving no sign he's paying attention.

"You girls have noticed the change in your routine?" Dona begins.

"Hard to miss," Rafi says. "You've been sending me to *all* the parties, and look at poor Frey. Someone's broken her!"

"It's been challenging, I'm sure," Dona says. "But necessary."

Rafi turns to our father. "This is about the Palafox deal, right?"

Still looking off into the airscreen, he smiles to himself.

I don't know what deal they're talking about. Business and politics aren't my job. All I know is that the Palafoxes are the first family of Victoria. A smaller, weaker city, four hundred kilometers south of Shreve. Not a military threat.

"Very good, Rafia." Dona gives my sister a measured smile. "We're almost done with the agreement. Next month, Victoria's salvage operations will merge with ours."

"You mean, we'll handle security," Rafi says. "Protect them from the rebels while they pick through the ruins."

The Rusty ruins—so this is about steel.

This is history that every littlie knows. Centuries ago, there were people called the Rusties, who loved metal. They dug mines, poisoned rivers, and tore down entire mountains to get it. They used the metal to build their cities, their cars, their tools, and—of course—the weapons they annihilated each other with.

Now all that's left of the Rusties is their ruins. The bones of the old world are their legacy to us.

Turns out, picking through those dead cities to recycle Rusty metal is much easier than digging it out of the ground. Our father loves to build, and he's close to exhausting all the ruins near Shreve.

So he wants to make a deal. Protection for metal.

Dona Oliver is still smiling, but Rafi's expression makes me nervous. That twitch in her eye, like she's about to have a tantrum.

"Why would the Palafoxes trust *you*?" she says, straight to our father's face. My breath catches, and Dona's expression draws tight.

He doesn't seem angry, though. It's another moment before his eyes drop from the airscreen to take us both in—me sweaty and injured, my sister sharp and focused.

A knife with two edges.

"A good question from a clever girl. Why would they trust us to drop an army in their ruins?" He smiles again. "The answer is, they don't."

My heart pulses in my right hand.

No one trusts our father. They all remember what he did to his allies here in Shreve, once he got what he wanted from them. They're all nobodies now, like they never existed.

Our father makes his own reality.

"The Palafoxes want a token of good faith," he says. "A guarantee that we'll give their ruins back once the rebels have been driven away."

My sister's eyes are bright, like she's working up tears.

"Daddy. Don't do this."

"They insisted." His voice softens. "It has to be something we'd never risk losing. Something more important to us than anything else in the world. Something exquisite."

"You can't!" Rafi shouts. "I won't *let* you!"

Dread silence falls, like it does whenever she raises her voice to him. Dona looks like she wants to disappear. And it dawns on me what they're talking about—sending my sister to the Palafoxes as a hostage.

She's the collateral for the deal. If our father keeps the ruins, the Palafoxes keep Rafi.

The world tilts a little beneath my feet. We've never been separated for more than a few days.

"Those are the terms," he says. "The Palafoxes insisted."

"But they'll know!" Rafi takes a step closer to his desk, her voice raw. "She'll never fool them!"

That's when my pain-addled brain grasps the rest of it. Rafi's been out socializing, building her face rank, making it clear that she's indispensable to our father's leadership. But I've been the one training with improvised weapons, because no one lets a hostage keep a pulse knife.

She's not going to be the collateral.

I am.

The world tilts a little farther.

"Frey can handle this," Dona says.

Rafi wheels on her. "In what universe? This isn't a bunch of randoms asking for autographs—it's another first family!"

"We'll train her," Dona says.

"In a *month*? She doesn't know how to dress, how to eat. She barely knows how to hold a conversation!"

Rafi's words sting, even if she's trying to protect me.

"It's true," Dona relents. "This isn't something our training program has anticipated."

"Because *none* of you understand." Rafi turns to our father. "The other families aren't as soft as you think, Daddy. The Palafoxes will eat her alive!"

I stare at Rafi, wondering how soft she thinks *I* am. She can't keep me locked in our room forever.

But no one asks my opinion. No one even looks at me. They're all so used to pretending I don't exist.

And that makes me say, "I can do it."

Silence again, like they'd forgotten I could speak.

"I've been imitating you for sixteen years, Rafi. This is what I was *born* to do."

My sister stares at me in disbelief. She wants to argue, but her momentum is broken by my betrayal.

Our father gives me an appraising smile.

"Good girl." His eyes drift away again. "It's decided."

Relieved, Dona hustles us out of the office.

"Come along. There's a lot of work ahead, Frey. Your French lessons start tonight."

"French?" I ask. "But Victoria's down south. Why not Spanish?"

Rafi sighs, wiping her tears away. "Their oldest son goes to school in Genève. Or didn't you know that?"

I shake my head. Because I didn't know the Palafoxes had a son. I didn't even know people spoke French in Genève.

I don't know anything.

Rafi gives me a dark little smile.

"*T'es dans la merde,*" she says.

Despite my woeful French, I have a pretty good idea what that means.

MACHIAVELLI

"Ton accent est terrible," Rafi says.

I am aware.

"Encore," she commands, and the sim starts over.

I try—I really do—but halfway through the exercise, my tongue gets tangled. The nice man in the airscreen looks confused. He's wearing a beret and the Paris Hoverdrome sits behind him, because this simulation is designed for littlies.

Bored by my failure, Rafi jumps in to finish the exercise. Effortlessly. Flawlessly. Too quickly to help me.

The man in the beret is happy again.

Je le déteste.

My sister learns languages all day, every day. When she points at something with two fingers, the cyrano in her ear whispers the French word for it—three fingers for German. She has human tutors in both tongues, to learn native gestures and expressions, so she won't look like some random taught by a machine.

Of *course* she's better than me at this. All that time I was learning how to fight, Rafi was learning how to be witty and worldly and wise.

She waves her hand in disgust, and the airscreen fades. Her temper has been flaring since the meeting with our father.

"I can't *believe* you've forgotten, Frey!"

Rafi taught me secondhand French when we were littlies. So I could make small talk in receiving lines without making her look foolish. But my irregular verbs didn't have to be correct for that.

Irregular verbs are bogus.

"No one's going to test me, Rafi. I bet the Palafoxes don't even know you speak French!"

"They'll know everything about me. Remember our trip to Montré?"

She waves a hand, and the airscreen pops back on—Rafi on a newsfeed, smiling, posing with children in school uniforms in a hovering garden of snow. She looks confident and charming, not like someone murdering the local grammar.

My memories of that trip aren't about schoolkids. I hid in our private suite while my sister and father met with famous people. Then I took her place in front of polite crowds, wearing vat-grown furs over body armor. Sniper bait in the snow.

Traveling isn't much fun for me. Just as much hiding, a lot less space.

I flop back on my bed. "So it's your fault for showing off."

"It's your fault for telling him you wanted to go!"

"What I say doesn't matter." I stare at Rafi, daring her to deny it.

She looks away. "Fine. It's *his* fault. If people trusted him, the Palafoxes wouldn't need a hostage."

I can only shrug. That's just the way it is—the way *he* is.

And the brave part of me that spoke up in front of our father really wants to do this.

Rafi doesn't understand. She gets to charm people every day, making sure the citizens of Shreve love as well as fear us. But all my years of training have only been relevant for two minutes and four seconds—the time it took me to save her life.

"I need to do this, Rafi."

Her answer is a whisper. "To *help* him? He doesn't even see you."

I turn away, stung again. These are things that she never says out loud.

"I want to feel useful."

She sighs. "You don't hate him as much as I do."

This is an old accusation. But it's easier for Rafi to hate our father—he recognizes her existence.

"I won't be gone forever. Two months to secure the ruins, Dona says."

"'Secure the ruins'? If you want to fool the Palafoxes, at least stop talking like a military advisor." Rafi goes to the window to glare down at the garden. "Why people are fighting over Rusty garbage is beyond me."

"Everyone needs metal. We can't go back to digging holes in the ground."

"Because when the Rusties did, they almost destroyed the world," she recites. "Maybe the pretty regime had the right idea. If everyone was still a bubblehead, there wouldn't be all this fighting."

I laugh at this, because she's probably kidding.

The pretty regime ended just before Rafi and I were born. Back then, everyone had an operation when they turned sixteen. It made you beautiful, but also had a secret purpose—it changed the way you thought.

Pretties never questioned authority, always consumed their fair share of resources and no more. Cities used only the power generated by their solar footprint, and recycled every scrap of metal. The Rusty ruins were left alone, a strategic reserve, so that humanity would never have to strip-mine the earth again.

But then a girl called Tally Youngblood became the first rebel. She brought the pretty regime down, and suddenly everyone had to think for themselves. It was called the mind-rain, all those bubbleheads waking up at once. All those cities hungry and ready to expand.

Freedom has a way of destroying things.

People like our father seized power in the chaos. They began to build new structures, whole new cities, starting a race for metal. Now the ruins aren't just reminders of the Rusties' excesses—they're invitations to start it all again.

Tally may be missing, but there are still rebels out there who think the ruins should be left alone.

"You'd hate being a bubblehead," I argue. "They had brain damage!"

Rafi shrugs. "But they were happy all the time. They didn't have to worry about getting shot at. They didn't have wars."

"They were too *dumb* to have wars!"

She shakes her head. "Repartee like that won't impress your hosts."

"I'll just be quiet. They can't *make* me be witty."

"You think wit is your problem?" Rafi starts counting on her fingers. "You don't know which designs everyone's wearing. You don't know the latest scandals—who doesn't get invited to parties anymore, or why. You've never even had to change the subject in an awkward conversation!"

I stand up to look out the window of our room, my hands twitching.

"I love you, little sister," Rafi says softly. "But you're not normal. Instead of clothes and music, you talk about escape routes and improvised weapons. And you eat like a barbarian."

She's said all this before—that growing up as a body double made me different. But always fondly, because I wasn't like her rich, bratty friends. The way she's saying it now just makes me feel lonely.

The thing is, I can smile like Rafi, move like her, mimic her expressions. Read a speech from an eyescreen with her pauses and inflections. We even hoverboard with the same stance.

But I don't know *people* like she does. She can talk to anyone—dignitaries, soldiers, randoms in a receiving line—with perfect ease. She has a hundred friends I've never really met. I've just memorized their faces so I know who to wave to on the dance floor. She has a whole life I've only seen slivers of, like I'm spying on a party through a keyhole.

Maybe that's why I want to go to Victoria. To have my own party for once.

I stick out my lower lip. "I'll just pout the whole time, and they'll never know the difference. Two months is your average sulk."

Rafi's resting sulk face is my masterpiece, but she doesn't even crack a smile.

"You have to be the perfect guest, Frey. It's a disaster for both families if anyone figures out you're a hostage."

"Who'd believe it? I mean, has anyone ever *done* this before?"

"Not for about seven hundred years. Which you'd know if you'd read Machiavelli." Her voice goes softer. "But this is Dad we're talking about. Do you think maybe he . . ."

She hesitates, then whispers the magic words.

"Sensei Noriko."

We go to the bathroom and turn on all the taps, loud and hot, steaming the room up in case of stray spy dust. We wait there silently, watching as the mirror fogs.

Sensei Noriko was Rafi's etiquette tutor. She taught my sister all the subtle refinements I never needed to know—how to eat properly, how to use a fan, how to sit at a tea ceremony. She didn't know about me.

Then, when we were nine, Rafi declared that my curtsying needed some serious work. So I pretended to be my sister for one lesson.

Noriko had an amazing eye for movement, and knew immediately that something was wrong with me. She was about to call Rafi's head tutor, which would have only made things worse. So I admitted who I was—*what* I was.

Someone must have been watching, because Sensei Noriko never came to teach again.

Rafi and I were twelve before we ever said aloud what probably happened to her. Since then, the words *Sensei Noriko* remind us that our secrets are dangerous.

Once the steam is thick, Rafi leans close and whispers, "What if he planned this way back when we were born? Hiding you this whole time, in case he ever needed to guarantee a deal?"

A shudder goes through me.

On the newsfeeds outside our city, people always wonder if our father plans everything, or just makes it up as he goes along. Nobody can predict his next move, because he does things no one else would.

Like this hostage exchange. Like me.

But Rafi can't be right.

"It's because of our brother," I say softly. "You know that."

She looks away into the steam.

Before we were born, when the mind-rain was spilling across the world, our father was just another politician. But even back then, some people already thought he was dangerous.

Our brother, Seanan, was only seven years old. Someone—they never found out who—kidnapped him, trying to force Father to resign his council seat. When he refused, no one ever saw Seanan again.

So he raised me as a body double, a last defense against the people who hate this family.

"That's exactly what I mean," Rafi says. "What if Dad's setting up the same situation again? His child in someone else's hands, so they think they can control him. Except they can't. And this time, he can't lose."

I stare at her—he *can* lose.

He can lose me.

"Sending a hostage wasn't his idea," I hiss. "The Palafoxes insisted on it!"

Rafi raises an eyebrow. It's one expression of hers I've never been able to master—wary and wise. She leans forward.

"And who told you that, little sister?" she whispers in my ear.

CYRANO

The next month is a blur.

Language lessons. Dance lessons.

Lessons on the history of the mind-rain. On the Palafoxes, and how they rose to become the first family of Victoria. On the nature-loving rebels who try to keep them from salvaging the Rusty ruins nearby.

Riding lessons. What-to-wear-for-dinner lessons.

How to talk to serving drones. How to ping a heartfelt apology. The polite ways to block surveillance in someone else's home. Lessons on small talk, body language, giving clever toasts at dinner parties. And, of course, which forks to use when. (Turns out, I *do* eat like a barbarian.)

I never realized my sister had to work so hard, to know so much. And all of it on top of being trained how to escape from an unfamiliar city and get home through the wilderness, in case something goes wrong with our father's deal.

It leaves me too tired to worry about being separated from Rafi and my pulse knife. About being an impostor for two months.

Tired as I am, my big sister and I stay awake the night before I leave.

"You can't get assassinated while I'm not here to save you," I tell her. "It's not allowed."

Rafi rolls her eyes at me, angles away on her hoverboard. "Not much chance of that. While you're off having adventures, I'll be stuck here, hiding!"

"For two whole months?" I catch up with her, making sure she sees my shocked face. "How will you survive?"

She doesn't get the joke. Or doesn't show it.

We reach the edge of our father's property, where the clear-cutting stops and the forest rears up like a dark tsunami.

Rafi doesn't slow down, plunging into the upper branches. She banks hard right, dodging through the trees, keeping low on her board so the garlands of kudzu don't knock her off.

I follow, knees bent, keeping close watch on the lights on my board. We have to stay at the edge of the forest, where our lifters can keep hold of the property's magnetics.

Branches lash my face and hands. I set my eyescreen to night vision, and Rafi becomes a zigzag of body heat against the cool blue forest. When we whip hard around a tree trunk, my crash bracelets purr on my wrists—they think I'm about to fall.

A flock of birds scatters before Rafi's approach, pearly white in night vision. We climb through the flutter-storm of their wings, reaching the limit of our lifters just as the treetops open onto sky.

Rafi comes to a trembling halt.

"Careful." I point down—only one light flickers on her board.

She doesn't look. Her eyes are on our home, a black tower in the flat sea of manicured gardens and softly lit pathways. A couple of security drones bob on the horizon, keeping watch on us, on the forest.

"You're the one who has to be careful, little sister."

"I'll be fine." I reach out and pull her closer to the property. Another light sputters to life on her board. "I've trained for this my whole life."

"You're loving this." Her voice is bitter. "You *want* to get away from me."

"I hate leaving you, Rafi. But I'm totally done with all this training. All that stuff you know is *boring*." This doesn't convince her, so I add a little of the truth. "Maybe it'll be nice, living out in the open for a while. You'll see what it's like for me, hiding all the time."

Rafi lets her board drift closer, reaches out to take my shoulders. "When I'm in charge, you won't have to hide."

My mouth goes dry. This is something she's never said before. It's not something I think about.

But our father's on his second round of life extension, when even the best crumbly surge starts to crack around the eyes.

Hard as it is to believe, he has to die sometime.

"I'll tell the whole city about you." Rafi's voice is the barest whisper, even though there's no spy dust out here over the forest. "I'll explain how it was *you* waving to the crowds. That *you* were the brave one when the assassin tried to kill us."

I manage a smile. But the thought of everyone knowing our secret makes my stomach clench.

"Won't they be mad at us for tricking them?"

She shakes her head. "It's not our fault."

A weight lifts from me, like it does every time she says that.

Maybe I won't always be one of our father's deceptions.

"I'm going to give you something," Rafi says. "My cyrano."

"Already got one." I've been training with it, learning to listen to the quiet prompts without looking distracted. It sits in my ear, helping with etiquette and putting names to faces. It even corrects my irregular verbs.

"Not like this one." With a tug, she pulls a glistening curve of metal from behind her ear.

I frown. "Mine's a lot smaller."

"Yeah, but mine's smarter. It scans the news, makes

44

assessments, translates on the fly. In the wild, it can pick up satellite feeds." Rafi smiles. "But it's totally passive. Never transmits. No one will ever spot that it's there."

She hands the cyrano to me. It's warm in my hand.

"How come you never told me about this?"

"I mostly don't wear it." She breathes out through her teeth. "It's only got one voice setting. It sounds like *him*."

I almost drop the cyrano, let it fall down into the darkness of the trees. But this is the only way Rafi has of protecting me.

"Thank you." It curls up behind my ear, warm and buzzing.

"Just come home," she says.

We stay there all night above the trees, fragile on our trembling hoverboards, talking about how things will change when he's gone.

RUINS

Five hovercars full of soldiers take me to Victoria.

They aren't city cars, flying on silent magnetics. They're military grade, with lifting fans to keep their armored bulk in the sky. The engine roar drowns out everything inside the cabin, and our rotor wash incises the desert below, a traveling sandstorm.

You're late for an appointment, my father's voice whispers in my ear. *Lunch with the Palafoxes.*

It's just Rafi's cyrano, but it startles me. I hardly slept last night.

My clothes feel wrong on my body. I've dressed like Rafi a thousand times before, but it's different without her sitting here next to me. Like they're really *my* clothes now.

Why are we late?

I turn to the soldier in the next jumpseat. She's taller than me, broad across the shoulders, her body surged into a fighting machine.

The cyrano reminds me her name:

Sergeant Tani Slidell. She commands this unit.

"Shouldn't we be there by now?" I yell over the engine noise.

She glances to the right—checking an eyescreen.

"Eight minutes, miss. We're taking a detour over the ruins."

I look out the closest window, a rectangle of ten-centimeter-thick ferroglass. The mountains are to the west, bright red in the high sun.

The rebels hide in those mountains, always watching the ruins for opportunities to harry and attack the Palafoxes' salvage operations. The point of traveling in force was to get me to Victoria safe and quick.

"Why the detour?" The engine vibration rattles my voice.

"Orders, miss. A little recon."

I twitch every time they call me *miss*. No one on this trip— the soldiers, the pilots, the diplomatic staff—knows I'm an impostor, or even a hostage. The newsfeeds are calling this a friendly visit, cementing an alliance of two first families.

It's safer like this—no one can give me away. But it feels lonely.

I've always shared my secrets with Rafi. And now she's three hundred klicks away—farther than she's ever been before.

So is my pulse knife.

Out the window, the ruins are drawing closer, a dark patch on the desert. An ancient skyscraper stands tall, its skeleton picked clean by hovering salvage drones. The rest of the dead city lies in a jumble at its feet, metal spires jutting from the sand. Sentry drones bob in the wind, studded with armaments.

The hovercar's engines drop into a sudden silence. The vibration's aftershock ripples across my skin.

"We're on magnetics now, miss," Sergeant Slidell explains.

Right. Plenty of metal down there. No need for lifting fans.

Metal is what this fight is all about.

In the last month, I've learned a lot more about the rebels. They say they're following Tally Youngblood's oath, fighting anything that threatens the wild. They say the new cities are being built too fast, and that recycling the ruins only brings us closer to the day that strip mining starts again. They think we'll all turn back into Rusties soon, knocking down mountains, burning down forests, and poisoning the air.

The first families promise that the rebels are wrong. That they'll stop building new cities once the ruins are depleted. They say the wild is safe.

But everyone knows that promises aren't sacred anymore. And Tally herself isn't around to weigh in.

I look out the window again. Can two months really be long enough to strip all this bare?

The lights in the cabin turn yellow.

"Ready stations!" Slidell calls out, then turns to me. "Just a precaution, miss. The rebels aren't dangerous."

I shake my head. "If they weren't dangerous, the Palafoxes wouldn't need us here."

Slidell nods, surprised that Rafi knows anything about

such matters. She thinks I've been studying irregular verbs all my life.

"True, miss. But we're not like those Palafox wimps." She pulls back a bolt on the side of her rifle. An airscreen comes alive above its optics, showing internal temperature and ammo count. "We come ready to fight. The rebels know that."

"You think they're scared of us?"

"Not as much as they will be. But they won't mess with five of our best gunships."

I stare out the window again. The ruins are below us now, spread out across the desert like broken toys.

"Time to arrival?" I murmur.

Eleven minutes, the cyrano says.

Slidell just said eight minutes. We must be angling away from Victoria, closer to the mountains. That fact, and the sound of my father's voice, jog a memory in my brain.

I remember being twelve, Naya fitting me for my first body armor, teaching me how to duck and cover, how to suture my own wounds. And I realized that I wasn't just my sister's guardian, but also a way to draw fire.

"Is there any extra armor for me?" I ask.

Slidell stares at me, confused.

Then a distant *boom* sounds, and the hovercar rattles around us. The air smells wrong.

Alarms begin to ring.

JUMP

The alarm sounds like a bird being strangled to death, over and over.

The cabin lights are flashing, the soldiers clipping themselves into bungee jackets. Slidell thrusts a tangle of straps at me.

"You know how to use this?"

Nervous laughter spills out of my mouth. Rafi and I spent a whole summer playing with bungee jackets, taking turns jumping out the eleventh-story window of our bedroom. Pretend fire drills.

"Like a parachute," I say. "As long as there's enough metal for the magnetics to catch you."

I press the jacket to my chest and push the red button. The smart-plastic straps come to life, weaving around my arms and legs. A moment later they're clicking into place.

I hear the rising hum of a battery charging, then a green light on my shoulder flickers to life. If we need to jump, I'm ready.

My heart is drumming inside my chest. I'm here again, in the place I found the last time someone tried to kill me.

That ecstasy. That purpose.

But one thing's missing—there's no Rafi to save this time.

Only myself. Because my father knows that I can handle this.

And I see his plan in full. The detour over the ruins—a trap for the rebels, a target to lure them out and show the world that Shreve's military can handle them.

Around me, everything is a blur. The soldiers checking weapons, strapping on equipment. The dazzle-camo of their armor dances, trying to adapt to the flashing lights.

It's all too dizzy-making. I look out the window—slender white columns are rising into the air around us.

"What's that?" I whisper.

Anti-hovercraft defenses, my cyrano replies.

All at once, the tips of the columns blossom, spreading out like sudden spiderwebs against the sky.

One shoots straight at us—

It smacks the side of the hovercar with a sharp, wet sound. The view out the window jerks left.

We're caught.

The car skews sideways. Soldiers slip across the metal floor, grabbing hand straps. Slidell stands over me, a protective wall of armor.

I cling to the window frame. The strand that hit us is some kind of smart plastic—it's crawling around the outside of the car, seeking a way in. One tendril winds its way out to a lifting fan. There, it splits into a hundred filaments, wrapping the rotors in white.

With no lifters, we're trapped over the ruins. We start to spiral down, pulled earthward by the white strand.

The cabin lights turn solid red.

For the first time, the faces around me look scared.

I should be scared too. But this is like my dreams about the assassin. Time slows down, and I become a spot of rapture in the chaos.

My father has put me here on purpose. It's my job to get myself out.

"Abandon ship!" Slidell calls out. "Me and Gemstone first!"

The soldiers make way for us, pressing against the cabin walls.

The hovercar is spinning now, earth and sky cycling past the windows every few seconds. A door irises open at the tail end, spilling a hot rushing wind inside.

I can barely keep my feet, but Slidell drags me to the door.

Outside is a writhing white mass of webbing. The soldiers' rifles erupt, the thunder bone-rattling in the cramped cabin. They slice the smart plastic into fluttering ribbons.

The landscape rushes past outside, closer with every second.

"Hold on to me!" Slidell cries, and pulls me out into the void.

We tumble in the vertigo of free fall, my stomach lurching.

We're gyrating through the air, thrown slantways by the hover-car's spin.

Slidell's armored gauntlet spits and hisses—compressed air shooting out in little jolts to steady our fall. She gets our spin under control.

For a moment I can see everything clearly. The soldiers spilling out behind us like a string of pearls, turning blue as their dazzle-camo matches the sky. Two more hovercars in the distance, caught in the aerial webs, spinning madly. Flashes of light on the horizon, a low continuous rumble, like the frantic end of a fireworks show. Tracers streaking past us—rebel fire from the ground.

The ruins splay out below us, rushing closer.

Then something roars past overhead—another car in our formation, trying to get away from the white spiderwebs.

The wash of its rotors pushes me and Slidell down, hard. Suddenly the jagged, ruined city is coming up too fast.

My jacket light turns yellow.

Alert, my cyrano says. *The jacket reports that you are too heavy.*

It's Slidell holding on to me—her body armor, her weapons, all that equipment. Her jacket is rated for that much weight. Mine isn't.

"Let go!" I scream.

"It's okay, miss. I've got you!"

"No! It's just that . . ." There's no time to explain that mono-pole magnetics don't work well in tandem. All I know is that the ground is rushing up at us, much too fast. "Let go!"

When she doesn't, I pull myself into a ball and slam my heels into her chest. One foot slips off the armor and catches her chin, jerking her head back.

She lets go.

I'm spinning again, unable to control my fall. The sky, the ground, it's all a dizzy-making blur around me.

But the light on my bungee jacket turns green again.

The *snap* of the harness comes seconds later. It digs into my thighs and under my arms, halting me as fast as it can.

Below is the skeleton of an ancient building the color of rust, scoured by centuries of sandstorms. Coming at me.

I cover my face.

The bungee jacket jerks sideways, angling me away from the metal beams. I hit a sand dune, skid down a slope for a few skin-scraping seconds. Then I'm pulled up again, hover-bouncing into the air.

I'm bruised, the bungee jacket's straps deep in my flesh. But I'm alive.

A hissing wall of armor flies at me. Wraps around me.

It's Slidell, her gauntlets spitting air to guide her bounce. She angles us down again, going to ground behind the skeleton of the fallen building.

I land on my feet this time, settling into the sand.

"Sorry about kicking you," I say.

She rubs her jaw. "Everyone panics their first jump, miss."

I'm about to say that this isn't my first jump when a shadow passes overhead, and we duck.

But it's just another soldier—

No—the body of one, limbs hanging limp, hoverbouncing to a halt in shattered armor. We may have survived the fall, but the rebels are still shooting at us.

I stare at the dead body. Something's gone wrong.

That could have been me.

CODE

"I have Gemstone!" Slidell shouts into her throat mike. "Muster on my mark!"

We're under the cover of the fallen Rusty building, a sky-scraper half-stripped of its metal, wilting under its own unsupported weight. Projectiles fly overhead—our remaining hovercars hitting the rebels from a safe distance. The sky is laced with white spiderwebs, dotted with more of my father's soldiers bailing out, firing as they fall.

I'm in the clothes I was supposed to wear to meet the Palafoxes. Rafi spent an hour choosing this coral silk shirt from the depths of her closet, matching it with sandals. She explained that the ensemble was respectful, but friendly. Perfect for break-fast or a light lunch, never dinner.

It's not body armor, and I feel naked.

More bodies of soldiers float in the air. The rebels must be stronger than we expected. I have to get under cover until help arrives.

The dune slopes away beneath the shadows of the ruin. I slide lower, sand flowing around my feet.

The air is cooler down here. It's dark, echoing with size. The sand mutes the rattle of the firefight outside.

I've never been to a ruin before, but this place is somehow familiar. Everything blocky and square, every line straight. My father builds in this Rusty style, with powerful grids of steel.

"Miss Rafia!" Slidell calls from above. "Please stay close."

My father will have planned this part out too—the heroic rescue, every insult to him transformed into a victory.

My father makes his own reality. Sometimes with force.

"It's okay," I tell the sergeant. "Reinforcements are coming."

"Of course, miss. But Shreve's over an hour away!"

"Sooner than that," I murmur in the dark. There's no way he would leave me in danger for that long.

The bungee jacket has a signal light, and I switch it on. Shadows dance in all directions. The space is even bigger than I thought.

The bottom wall of the ancient fallen building forms the ceiling of this subterranean chamber. Sand filters down whenever a *boom* sounds outside. It's not stable.

Maybe not the smartest place to be in a battle.

But people have sheltered here before. Empty food packs litter the ground, and dark patches show where campfires burned.

There's something written on a beam overhead. Not in cluttered Rusty letters, but with the clean strokes of a spray gun.

She's not coming to save us.

There's more, but it's all random symbols.

"Rafia!" Slidell comes scrambling down behind me. Her camo matches the shadows, shifting from sand and rust to black. "My squad's assembled. We're going to move you to safety."

I'm already safe. Help is coming.

There's no way my father would sacrifice me for a single victory against the rebels.

"Do you know what those symbols mean?" I move my light across the ceiling.

Unknown, my cyrano says.

Slidell glances up, thinking I mean her.

"Rebel code, looks like. This must have been a base, before the Palafoxes drove them into the mountains." She looks around. "Bad choice—all that sand could come down any second. Let's get you out of here."

I hesitate, still looking up at the symbols, not obeying at first. I've been acting like Rafi all day, and I'm starting to feel like her. Like nobody gives me orders.

Instead, I give consent.

"Okay. Let's go."

Slidell leads me back up the dune, into the sunlight. Five more soldiers are up here, crouched in a ring around us.

"That's the rendezvous point." Slidell points at the tallest building in the ruin—the skyscraper. "It's the best place to hold out."

"Isn't moving through this firefight dangerous?"

"Only for a few minutes, miss. But then we're safe. We'll wait there for reinforcements."

"A few minutes?" I shake my head. "They'll be here before then."

"Miss Rafia," Slidell says, her voice sharp for the first time. "Shreve is an hour away by hovercar!"

I lock eyes with her, mustering every gram of my sister in my blood.

It's not just for myself—I'm responsible for these soldiers, my protectors. And we're safer hunkering here a few more minutes than scrambling through the ruins, drawing fire.

I'm certain that my father expected this attack to happen.

Wanted it to happen.

"We stay," I command.

Slidell glares at me. She's ten years older, five centimeters taller, looming in the bulk of her body armor. My head spins with all the ways she can win this—inject me with some sedative in her medpack, bind my wrists with those zip ties on her belt. Or just haul me kicking and screaming across the ruined city.

Of course, she's expecting defenseless Rafi.

Slidell moves forward, reaching for my arm—

My battle reflexes ignite.

I grab her wrist and pull, sending her staggering past me. Then I launch a kick to the side of her knee. Her body armor saves her ligaments from tearing, but she goes down in pain.

"What the—"

I turn away from Slidell, facing her confused soldiers.

"We stay *here*." I'm a fearsome mix of Rafi and Frey, imperious and lethal. "Those are my father's orders."

They look back and forth between me and their sergeant, terrified of making the wrong choice. I keep my back to Slidell, daring her to attack me again.

For a nervous-making moment, this could go either way.

But then the soldiers' eyes all rise up to the sky.

"Ten o'clock!" one calls, and they all hit the ground.

I turn to see a shower of meteors coming down, a score of objects burning across the sky.

"What are they?" I ask Slidell.

"Suborbital insertion drones," she answers. "But the rebels don't have low orbit. And neither do we!"

"Yes, we do," I say. "Just sit tight."

She glares at me, angry and confused, wondering if she should take me down. But I keep my gaze steady at the sky, showing no uncertainty.

Over the last month, Naya has told me about my father quietly waking up the old war machines. Waiting for an excuse to use them.

No—*engineering* an excuse.

The ecstasy comes back, the bubble of my father's will settling over me again. I was right. He has it all under control. Despite the rebels' unexpected firepower, I'm safe again.

A sequence of *boom*s rattles the ancient ruins—the suborbital craft punching through the sound barrier. They're falling from the edge of space, coming in so fast that an envelope of air burns around them. They slice through the rebels' anti-hovercraft webs like knives through smoke.

Reentry chutes pop and unfurl, bringing the meteors to a sudden halt. Then their glowing heat shields split apart and heavy battle drones tumble out, bristling with weapons.

They start firing as they fall.

Slidell pulls her eyes from the spectacle and stares at me again.

I am nothing that she thought I was.

"You *knew* about this?"

"Not exactly," I admit. "But I know more every day."

FIRST SON

The next morning, I have breakfast with the Palafoxes.

Three generations of them—mother, grandmother, and son—join me at a small iron table on a sunlit balcony. The serving drones are painted with flowers and dancing skeletons. The coffee is strong and sweet.

I'm in one of Rafi's favorite outfits: a sky-blue dress fringed with dragonfly wings. Harvested from real insects, of course, not printed by a hole in the wall. My luggage escaped the battle untouched, but the silk shirt was a write-off.

Eleven soldiers died as well.

I can't think about that now—it's too brain-spinning. The rebels took more casualties than we did, of course. The newsfeeds are abuzz with the attack, and with the revelation that my father's suborbital forces can strike anywhere in the world.

But eleven soldiers.

"Such an outrage," Zefina Palafox keeps saying. "It's a miracle you weren't hurt."

"I was never scared." My voice trembles a little, which doesn't sound like Rafi. I need to keep control.

"Of course not." Zefina pats my hand. "We all remember that unpleasantness last year. You were very brave then too."

I give her a fearless smile.

Zefina is the grande dame of the clan. Eighty-six years old, with the classic crumbly surge of the pretty era—white hair, rosy cheeks, sparkling eyes. She greeted me yesterday afternoon when I arrived, still dirty and in shock, and put me to bed.

"Maybe we should talk about something else," Aribella Palafox gently commands. She's Zefina's daughter, the leader of the city of Victoria. My father's equal. "We mustn't let this spoil your visit, Rafia."

"Of course not." I cut myself a large bite of mango, as if the rebels can't stop me from enjoying breakfast.

The cyrano whispers: *Fork in the left hand, knife in the right. Bring the food to your mouth, not the other way around.*

Aribella notices when I reach up and pull out the cyrano. I don't care if she sees—lots of people wear cyranos—and I don't care if I eat like a barbarian. I can't stand my father's voice in my ear right now.

Eleven soldiers.

I smile back at Aribella. She's beautiful. Not in the old-fashioned way—her pretty surgery has been fully reversed. Her glamour resides in her expression, in her certainty that she was born to rule.

Looking at her, I can understand why so many cities wanted leaders after the mind-rain. Not another parliament, council, or committee. But a singular figure to guide them through the chaos of humanity waking up. Like Rusty celebrities or royal houses.

I can almost forget that I'm her prisoner.

"Do you hunt, Rafia?"

We all turn to a boy my age, Col Palafox. This is the first thing he's said since we were introduced. He's worn a wary expression the whole time, glancing at his coffee like it might be poisoned.

"I'm sure Rafia has better things to do," Aribella says.

I don't argue. Aribella's not about to let her hostage out with a weapon, an all-terrain hoverboard, and her son.

Col's eyes drop to his food again.

It's fine with me if he doesn't want to talk. He's the older of the two Palafox sons, the one who knows French. A few of my grammar-missing verbs and he'll start wondering.

Rafi and I have been studying what the feeds say about Col. That he's thoughtful, a bit boring and studious. He's never been part of Rafi's social scene. But he's still the person here most like her—the young heir of a first family. If anyone can spot that my dazzling socialite act is bogus, it's him.

He looks older in person than on the public feeds. His shoulders are broader, his dark eyes sadder, and he's more handsome too. But that's just another reason not to talk to him. Rafi is famous for charming girls and boys with equal ease, and I've never so much as flirted with a stranger.

"You have a lovely home," I say, to fill the untidy silence. Rafi told me to use this when I don't know what else to say, even though it's banal.

Zefina perks up. "You should have a tour! Why don't you show Rafia around after breakfast, Col?"

Aribella nods, like she's giving permission. "An excellent idea. You haven't spoken French with a real person since you got home."

Col looks miserable.

I share his pain.

FAKE JUNGLE

The Palafox home really is lovely.

While my father's estate is shuttered and dark, everything here opens onto light and air. Rooms spill onto balconies and terraces, skylights slant the hallways with morning sun, all of it surrounding a tree-filled courtyard as big as two soccer fields.

This jungle is where Col takes me first, on a path of hovering stones, down through swaying fronds and storms of tiny wings. I can't tell if the butterflies are gene-spliced or natural, or what keeps them from fluttering away into the open sky.

Safety drones hover near us in case we fall. The long drop to the ground makes my wrists itch for crash bracelets.

"Are you trying to make me nervous, Col?"

He shrugs. "Don't tell me a girl who faces down rebels and assassins is afraid of heights."

"I meant the butterflies. They're carnivorous, right?"

For the first time, Col gives me a thin smile. I shouldn't be making brain-missing jokes. He might joke back to me in French, and my cyrano's still in my pocket. I don't want my father whispering cues in my ear.

But Col doesn't answer, just leads me down.

The rocky ground of the courtyard is damp. Pale green lichen covers everything, dotted with red sprays of flyspeck flowers. This is more a habitat than a garden, like a slice of the wild here in the city.

I wonder if there's a way from the treetops up onto the roof, an escape route in case I need it. Col probably knows, but I can't just ask him. He's standing with one hand out, dead still, waiting for a butterfly to land.

Whenever Rafi wants to get someone talking, she teases them.

"For a tour guide, you don't say much."

He lowers his hand. "We're standing in a simulation of the Reserva de la Biosfera El Cielo."

Maybe I should put the cyrano back in. But that was Spanish, not French.

"The Biosphere of Heaven," he translates. "It's a cloud forest fifty klicks southwest of here. It's been a nature preserve since Rusty times. My family still protects it."

"A cloud forest? That sounds made up."

Col shrugs. "It's a jungle on a mountain, high enough for the trees to strip moisture from passing clouds—rain on demand. The old jungles made their own weather."

"*Now* you sound like a tour guide."

"I'm famously boring," he says.

He also flashes a hand sign: *They're watching us.*

For a moment I only stare dumbly. How does he know Rafi's private signals? She was taught them by the kids at a private dance school in Diego. But Col Palafox goes to school an ocean away.

Maybe the signs are universal, carried around the globe by misbehaving kids shuffling from school to school. Or maybe *They're watching us* is so useful that it's the same everywhere.

Rafi would know all this. I'm already missing her.

Col's staring at me now, and I nod to show that I saw his signal. That I'm just like him, a spoiled kid—not a body double, not a trained killer.

He gives me his first real smile.

A rushing sound comes from overhead—like a passing hovercar. I jerk my eyes up, ready to take cover.

"That's just the hourly storm," Col says. "The real Reserva collects three meters of rainfall a year."

A mist is descending, so fine that the butterflies don't seem to care. I can't see the sprayers anywhere.

"So jungles really do make their own weather."

Another smile. "Let's get you out of the rain."

I shrug. "This dress is laced with wicking nanos. Even after full immersion, it'll be clean and dry in five minutes."

He stares at me—that was *not* how Rafi talks about her

clothes. She'd be worried about the dragonfly wings drooping, her hair getting wet.

"Okay," Col says. "But there's something I want to show you. It's in the original building, five hundred years old."

He makes another hand sign. I don't know this one, but I can guess.

A building that old has to be made of stone—the walls not smart enough to listen in on us. They don't have spy dust here in Victoria.

"That sounds lovely," I say.

Col goes quiet again, leading me out of the misting jungle and into a hallway lined with frescoes. More skulls and flowers, a background landscape like the desert I flew across yesterday.

I'm quietly pleased with myself. So far, Col has no idea that I'm not Rafi. That I've never gone to fancy parties or designed my own clothes.

But we haven't really talked yet—and now he wants privacy. What if it's to discuss secret spoiled-kid business, full of gossip I know nothing about?

Rafi warned me that making friends with Col could only get me into trouble. I should say I'm tired and go back to my room. I'm supposed to be gathering an escape kit, just in case.

But when I open my mouth to make excuses, nothing comes out. Other than my sister, I've never had a friend before.

And what if Col tells me something useful?

He leads me deeper into the family home.

The old building is the gloomiest part of House Palafox.

Col takes me there through a door with a retina lock, then down a hallway with uneven walls. Hints of the morning sun leak through high, barred windows. There are no bright murals here, just the cool gray silence of stone.

"What was this?" I ask. "A castle?"

"A monastery," Col says, then goes quiet again. He's still not much of a tour guide.

Rafi would probably know this, but I ask, "What's a monastery?"

"Like a dorm, for pre-Rusties who were really serious about religion." He runs his hand along the rough surface of the wall. "The monks who lived here took vows to ignore the outside world."

"Monks? Like the Shaolin fighting style?"

I manage to keep from blurting out that I've studied it myself. But Col still raises an eyebrow, matching Rafi's expression when she judges me for talking like a military advisor.

"Kind of. These monks were more into calligraphy than beating people up."

I slip my cyrano back in, give it a tap.

Calligraphy is the art of decorative handwriting.

"Wonderful," I say in Rafi's mocking tone. "So you're going to show me your handwriting collection?"

"Sorry to disappoint you, but we don't have anything that old. We keep the family antiques here. You might find the collection . . . interesting."

He leads me around another corner, into a low-ceilinged room crowded with glass cases.

The cases are full of weaponry, Rusty-era and even older. Swords, rifles, body armor made of metal scales, a crossbow.

I try not to look too excited, but then my eyes fall on the smallest case—it holds a pulse knife. An original, from the last days of chaos, before the pretty regime brought peace.

It's less sophisticated than mine back at home, but more reliable. The sort of military hardware that might still work after a hundred years.

I reach out to touch the case.

It feels like ferroglass, maybe a centimeter thick. Hard to break, but not impossible, and we're surrounded by dumb stone walls.

The Palafoxes are bubbleheads. They keep their weapons collection in the easiest part of the house to steal from.

Of course, they think I'm Rafi, who's never stolen anything in her life.

"You have some lovely toys," I murmur.

"This is my favorite." He guides me to another case, points at the hunting bow inside.

It's not an antique. Nanotech, collapsible nanotech polymers, laser-sighted. The arrows are fletched with smart feathers and have an assortment of high-tech heads—airburst tips to take down birds, explosives for big game.

Back in the pretty regime, people didn't kill animals. This weapon was made after the mind-rain.

"That's mine," Col says. "It usually lives on my wall."

"What's it doing down here?"

"Jefa personally came and took it away. She locked it up, along with my hoverboard." He stares at me. "Yesterday, right before you arrived. She didn't explain why."

"Who's Jefa?"

"That's what my brother and I call our mother. For obvious reasons."

It means "boss," my cyrano whispers.

So that's why Col brought up hunting at breakfast. He's trying to figure out why she locked up his bow. He has no idea I'm a hostage.

It's time to turn back into Rafi.

I give him a big sigh. "Maybe she doesn't want you showing off your boring hobbies to guests."

"Maybe." Col's eyes fall to the case. "Or maybe she thinks I don't know what this is all about. Your little 'holiday' with my family."

A tremor goes through me—*has* he figured it out?

He's waiting for me to say something. And I'm pretty sure *You have a lovely home* isn't going to cut it.

"Our parents want our families to be allies," I say carefully.

"Exactly." He sighs. "But you'd think they could be more subtle about it. *Why don't you show Rafia around, Col?*"

It takes a moment for the gears in my head to mesh. But finally they do.

"Oh," I say.

"Right. Like you didn't know."

I shake my head. I'm not lying.

Rafi and I should've figured it out before I left home, but we were too worried about table manners and irregular verbs to realize what Grandma Palafox must be thinking.

"Your family," I say. "They want us to . . . get together?"

Col snorts with disgust. "*My* family? Like your father isn't thinking the same thing?"

I don't have an answer. My father doesn't want that kind of alliance or he'd have sent the real Rafia, not her brain-missing body double.

He just wants to humiliate the rebels, take his cut of metal from Victoria's ruins, and leave.

All of us missed this possibility.

"I can't *believe* Jefa," Col keeps going. "I've spent my whole life studying, preparing to help her lead the city. And now she wants to marry me off to some . . ." He comes to a halt, throws his hands in the air.

"Some *what*, exactly?"

Col sputters a moment, then says, "The whole thing's medieval!"

A laugh spills out of me. It's so much more medieval than he knows.

His dark eyes flash. "You think this is funny?"

I shake my head. Aribella *knows* I'm a hostage, not a guest. But she seemed enthusiastic about this little house tour.

Is she trying to outflank my father? Getting Rafi into her home, then using her son to secure an alliance?

"It's just that I didn't know, Col. That's the truth."

He studies me a moment longer. Then he starts pacing, waving his arms.

"Last winter, when the rebels were about to push us out of the ruins, everyone was saying we couldn't let your forces in to help. That we could never trust your father to leave again, once he saw how much metal we're salvaging. Then suddenly the deal was made, except *you* came along with it, and no one would say why. Like everyone was playing a game and I didn't know the rules!"

"Yeah. I know that feeling."

"My mother cut me out of the decision completely. And the most annoying thing is, it took me till this morning to figure out why!"

I nod. "Hide a plan till it's ripe for execution and it's more likely to succeed."

He turns to me. "Did you just quote Machiavelli at me?"

"I've been reading him a lot lately."

Col looks me up and down, and I realize that I'm standing

wrong. Not with Rafi's ballet poise, but in the combat stance that Naya makes me hold in classes. Weight on the balls of my feet, ready to fight.

"You're not what I'd thought you'd be, Rafia."

I should say something to contradict Col. Act like my sister on the newsfeeds—imperious, bratty, always finding weaknesses and nipping at them.

But instead I ask, "How do you mean?"

"Your parties. Your temper tantrums. I was expecting a bubble-head socialite, frankly."

I stare at him, a little offended for Rafi. She's no bubblehead, except when she's pretending. *She* was the one who got me read-ing Machiavelli.

But it's also flattering, because Col isn't seeing Rafi—he's see-ing me. At least, the parts of me that are poking out of my disguise.

The whole thing makes me dizzy.

But dizzy Frey doesn't know what to say, so I let sarcastic Rafi take over. "Sorry to disappoint you, Col. I'll try to be more bubbleheaded."

"Trust me, it's a relief. Especially if my family's going to keep throwing us together."

Right, they are. And Col's already realized that I'm not the Rafi everyone sees on the feeds—he's smart enough to figure out more. A friendship with him is risky.

But there are also advantages. He spotted something that even my big sister missed—the Palafoxes are seeking an alliance of blood.

I need someone who can tell me how this family thinks.

"Forget our parents," I say. "Let's make our own alliance."

He raises an eyebrow. "Something short of marriage, I presume?"

That makes me laugh. "*Way* short. We don't even have to like each other, if we don't want to."

"So I don't have to be your tour guide?"

I nod, and in a fit of brilliance reply, "And I don't have to be your French study partner!"

"*Comme il faut*," he says.

As is proper, my father's voice translates.

I smile. "It's decided, then. We're allies."

He holds out his hand. "Not pawns for our families."

We shake on it. But it feels like a promise I can't keep.

I was born to be a pawn.

VICTORIA

A few days after my arrival, Col takes me out to see his city.

I'm excited to be outside. Until now it's all been formal dinners with the dignitaries of Victoria, lunches with the Palafoxes. Stilted conversation and too much rich food for calorie purgers to burn off. What I need is a good training session with Naya, but a long hike in the city will do.

Col and I walk on the street like randoms. No body armor, just half a dozen wardens blending into the crowd around us. A single drone hovers up among the pigeons. It's probably only there to make sure I don't run.

The weird thing is, I'm more free as a hostage here than as a second daughter back home. House Palafox has no special corridors or elevators. No spy dust in the air.

I've always wanted to feel what it was like in Rafi's skin, but this is something she's never done—walking down a street with normal people at arm's length.

They mostly ignore us, but a few walk straight past the wardens to introduce themselves to Col, the first son of the city. He jokes effortlessly with them, using the same banter over and over, managing to sound each time like the words just popped into his head.

Naya warned me that in Victoria I might be exposed like this. A lot of cities work this way—the wealthy and powerful walking freely among randoms. But it's strange to see it in real life.

It makes me twitchy. Like everyone can see through my disguise.

Col acts like it's perfectly natural, of course. And the people of Victoria seem to adore their first son.

They ask about his schoolwork, his botany, his archery. All the reasons that my sister's friends ignore him—his studiousness, his boring hobbies—are celebrated here.

Which is odd, because Victoria isn't boring or studious at all. It's acutely alive.

Kids zip past on hoverboards at speeds that would get them jailed back at home. Drones flit just above the rooftops, carrying not only official cargo, but groceries, shopping, folded laundry, as if every random gets their own air fleet here. And it's not just the traffic that's wild and uncontrolled. People seem to wear whatever they want—bright colors, flash tattoos, and surgeries that would never pass the censors back in Shreve.

Even the buildings are bursting with life. The hoverstrut architecture drifts overhead, airy and fantastical. And down here at street level, the adobe houses are painted in sunset oranges and yellows, or the radiant blues of a low flame.

But strangest to me are the animals. The flocks of pigeons against the sky, the imperious cats strutting the rooftops.

I point at a chicken scuttling underfoot, its feathers as gaudy as the houses.

"What are *they* for?"

Col gives me a questioning look.

"Wild animals aren't allowed in Shreve," I explain. "Some birds get in, of course. But nothing like *that*."

"The chickens aren't wild, exactly." Col switches to his tour-guide voice. "They're tagged with transmitters so the city can monitor the ecosystem. They make for good pest control."

"Why not just spray?"

"We're old-fashioned here. When my little brother's home from school, he goes out every morning to collect eggs."

"To *eat*? From birds that eat *bugs*?" I shake my head. "This whole city's like something from the Rusty era, or whatever was before that!"

"The pre-Rusties," Col says, laughing.

"Whatever," I say. "But it's beautiful."

His laughter fades, and he gives me a curious look.

"Really, Rafia? Shreve's so much bigger and newer than Victoria, I thought you'd be bored. Might you actually be *charmed* by our little town?"

I don't answer right away. The real Rafi would be bored. Or at least she'd pretend to be, because older, smaller cities are passé compared to the bold new constructions of the mind-rain. But I don't want to offend Col. He's my ally now.

And after a lifetime of hiding, training, and carefully scripted appearances, it's hard not to be entranced by all this street life swirling around me. All these smells and sounds are overwhelming. As is the fact that I could choose any street to walk down next.

But the most confusing part isn't my own freedom—it's everyone else's. Victoria seems like a city entirely out of control.

"I'm not bored at all, Col. If anything, it's too much, walking around in the open like this. It feels . . . precarious."

He studies me. "More precarious than having assassins shoot at you?"

"I have bodyguards in Shreve. Here, there's just a few wardens. You don't even have spy dust!"

"It's illegal."

"I know, but . . ." My tutors explained how privacy is an obsession in Victoria. The city scrubs its data every day, forgetting where everyone went, what they pinged each other, what they made with their holes in the wall.

Back home in Shreve, the air is full of machines. When you shine a flashlight in the dark, most of those floating specks are spy dust, nanocameras taking a hundred pictures a second in all directions, along with the tiny microphones, transmitters, batteries, and repeaters that support them.

If the wardens in Shreve want to know what happened at a certain place and time, they just call it up on the city interface. They can watch from any angle, replay any sound but the softest whisper—unless Dona's people have censored it to hide my father's secrets, of course. Like me.

"It just feels unsafe, Col. What if there's a murder? How do you solve *any* crimes?"

"Crimes got solved before dust was invented, you know. We use DNA, fingerprints, eyewitnesses." He shrugs. "And, I don't know, logic?"

"Sounds like a lot of trouble, when you could just *watch* what happened."

"People don't like being spied on. Besides, we haven't had an unsolved murder since the mind-rain."

I lower my voice a little. "But how does your family keep control?"

He looks at me through narrowed eyes.

"We don't *keep control*. We lead."

"Are you being smug?"

"Usually." He watches a dog run past, chasing a pair of cats. "My mother does a good job. So people don't try to get rid of us."

I come to a halt and stare at him. "Are you saying someone tried to kill me because my father was doing a *bad job*?"

"Your father's different," he answers calmly. "You know that."

I stand there in the cool shade of an adobe wall, gathering my thoughts. I don't have an answer, because I don't really know why I'm arguing. Is this me pretending to be Rafi, who always upholds the family name in public? Or do I just hate being judged?

"I'm sorry you can't walk around like this at home," Col says. "The violence must be tough."

There's that smugness again.

"Don't talk to me about violence," I say. "You mother's borrowing my father's army."

"Borrowing, because we don't have a big standing army of our own. Half our soldiers have other jobs. Don't you see the difference?"

"Not really."

He sighs. *"Il n'est pire sourd que celui qui ne veut pas entendre."*

No one's as deaf as one who doesn't want to listen, my cyrano translates.

French proverbs? Perfect. Rafi would be *so* much better at this than me. She could probably spit some fancy saying back at him.

I try to remember what my tutors have been teaching me about the debates of the new era. About whether the first families, with their all-knowing dust and ancient weapons, have grown too powerful.

But why would anyone want to be ruled by a family that was *weak*?

I notice that the wardens have formed a loose circle around me and Col, facing outward, standing with their arms crossed. The crowd is giving us a wide berth while we argue.

I remember Rafi saying that the Palafoxes aren't soft. Their power is in the air around us. Gentle but firm.

They just don't like to admit it.

"Maybe you don't know everything about your own family," I say.

Col considers this a moment, then nods.

"You're right. I never thought Jefa would let Shreve's forces in. Or cut me out of the decision. Or try to marry me off like some bubblehead." His voice goes quieter. "And I still can't figure out why she locked up my hunting bow."

I don't bother to explain. Allies or not, Col doesn't need to know that I'm a hostage. All he really wants is his hunting bow, if only to push back against Aribella for treating him like breeding stock.

Maybe I can use this.

"Here's a question." I step a little closer, whispering, "How often does anyone go down to the monastery?"

"Hardly ever. Even cleaning drones aren't allowed—Jefa says they wear away the stone."

"Then maybe I can get your hunting bow back, if you find something for me."

His eyes widen. "What?"

"You can't tell your mother what I'm about to ask for. Promise?"

"Of course."

I wonder whether to trust him. Back home, my father's office is full of sensors that track heartbeat, skin temperature, the subtle motions of the eyes—every telltale that someone might be lying.

But out here on the street, all I have to go on is Col's unwavering gaze back at me.

Somehow it's enough.

"Do you know what a pulse charger looks like?"

BALL GOWN

A week later, the Palafoxes throw a welcome bash for me.

The newsfeeds are ablaze with it. Every high-face-rank family in Victoria is invited. Everyone wants to meet the plucky girl who survived an assassination *and* a rebel attack. Every kicker with a feed is speculating on how long I'll stay in the city. On how I'm getting along with my hosts. On whether our families' alliance has been strengthened by this shared war against the rebels.

People speculate about me and Col too.

Our intense conversation on the street was caught by a few private cams, but the gossip varies depending on the source. Were we arguing? Flirting? Performing for the cameras?

The whole city is starting to wonder if my visit here is more than a vacation.

It's the afternoon of the ball, and I'm still trying on virtual outfits in my bedroom wallscreen.

I've tried the hole in the wall's standard designs, but they're
too basic for Rafi to wear. My fingers flex and twitch, picking
from endless menus of styles and options. Customize, refine,
specify in a hundred ways—but I'm just guessing.

Every attempt winds up with another disaster.

What if Grandma Zefina, curious about what I'm wearing
tonight, is watching? She must wonder why the always stylish
Rafi is suddenly so lost.

This is what I get for wanting to leave home, to be my own
person. I'm finally getting to have my own party, and it's a
nightmare.

Rafi was right—I don't know how to dress, or flirt, or make
conversation. Which is fine for a few stilted dinner parties. But
now the whole world is going to see how fashion-missing I am.
How *everything*-missing.

Like I'm only half a person.

My sister's cyrano isn't helping. It's full of protocol tips, not
fashion advice—something Rafi would never need.

I'd give anything for her help right now. But the Palafoxes
might find it strange if I called home to ask myself for fashion
advice.

But then, as I'm staring at my fifteenth absolute wreck of an outfit, the cyrano hisses softly in my ear—

A secret ping from home. The first since I've arrived.

The cyrano can't send signals out or House Palafox security will catch them. But it can scan the public newsfeeds for incoming hidden messages. They're encrypted in images of my father, official vids of him waving to a crowd or signing a document. Strewn across those billions of pixels are tiny, random-seeming shifts of color, information buried in a hundred devious layers of math for my cyrano to decode.

I don't react at first, in case anyone's watching. Instead, I discard my latest design with a disgusted Rafi sigh, flop on my bed, and stare at the ceiling. Only then do I reach up and tap the cyrano to play the message.

It's a recording of my sister's voice.

Frey! Hope you're okay, or at least muddling along.

But mostly, I hope you're listening to this right away. You have to nail this party tonight. Have you seen our face rank lately? Since the rebel attack, we're top hundred. And I don't mean locally—that's our global rank, Frey.

People from all over are going to be watching this bash.

You better look amazing.

I wish I could interrupt Rafi and tell her this isn't helping. My nerves are bad enough without imagining a worldwide audience. All those people watching me and Col, ready to gossip . . .

Then it hits me—Rafi said *our* face rank. That's new. It was always her fame, not mine. But the rebels were shooting at *me*, I guess, so it's only fair to get some credit.

It's lucky you've got a very clever big sister.

Pause this until you're in front of a wallscreen. Then do exactly as I say.

I jump up from the bed, stand in front of the screen. Ready to obey.

Okay, call up the Seft. Do you even know what that is? Standard European Fashion Timeline, duh. You call it by making two fists, thumbs on the inside. Like you're about to punch someone, I guess.

Except you'd break a thumb if you hit someone that way.

Now scroll to the mid-2040s, the A-frame dresses. Not that you know what that means, but I assume you know what the letter A looks like? Hah.

See that one near the middle, with the lace collar? Select it and open Options. Not the littlie menu with four choices—put on your big girl pants and use the advanced list.

Yeah, I know. There's, like, a hundred submenus. And this is only the beginning.

But never fear, big sister's here . . .

I follow along, barely keeping up with her narration. She's racing, guiding me through the bottomless specificities of fashion. The whole time I can imagine her talking to herself in our bedroom, in front of the wallscreen we've shared since we were littlies. It feels like I'm there beside her, back at home.

But as Rafi whispers in my ear, weaving this dress for my body—for *our* body—it starts to feel like these are my own thoughts flowing through my head. *My* skills navigating the centuries of styles and trends, the measure of my hips, arms, shoulders.

Anyone snooping must think my lost fashion genius has come rushing back, full force.

When Rafi's recording finally ends, the wallscreen shows me wrapped in spiral coils of gunmetal lace, the dress beneath in subtle gradients of reflective black. Gray gloves up to my elbows, dark tulle with an iridescent oil-slick sheen peeking out from beneath my hem.

The hole in the wall says fabrication will take three hours. I didn't know *anything* took that long for a nano-forge to make. I'll barely have time to dress before the bash.

And already I'm impatient. I usually don't care what Rafi and I wear. But having watched this creation emerge from a thousand swift, skillful choices, I'm eager to become that girl in the dress.

No, not a dress. A ball gown.

A ping sounds in the room.

"Rafia?" It's Aribella Palafox, my host—my captor. The timing is so perfect, she must've been watching. "If you're free, perhaps we could chat about tonight."

"That would be lovely." I slip the cyrano off. Aribella runs a whole city from her office—it'll be packed with sensors.

And suddenly I'm Frey again, not the princess in the beautiful dress. Frey, who doesn't know what to wear, what fork to use. Or how to chat with her host about a party that will be watched across the world.

"Would now be convenient?" she asks.

I nod, not trusting the steadiness of my voice.

Greeting me at her office door, Aribella takes my hands in hers.

"Let me look at you, Rafia."

She steps back, studying me. Is she imagining the ball gown, making sure I'll be elegant enough for her bash tonight? Or is she wondering if I seem somehow different in real life?

Rafi's voice has been in my ear all afternoon, so her stance, her cool expression, come naturally. But Aribella's scrutiny is still nervous-making. I look past her to the tall windows of the office, which are full of light and motion. House Palafox doesn't lurk on the edge of the wild like my father's tower; it sits in the center of town, Aribella's office looking out across the city she rules.

Victoria is all open terraces and hoverstruts, a fairy kingdom compared to squat, stolid Shreve. A pre-Rusty cathedral rises in the distance, its stone spire dappled with sunlight reflected from floating glass buildings. Drones flit past the windows, their cargos bright with flowers and fruit, scattering the ever-present pigeons before them.

Like the town, Aribella's office is full of color. There's no desk, no dominating wallscreen. Just the circle of red velvet couches that she guides me to.

We sit close, our knees almost touching.

"I must confess," she says. "I took a peek at your gown for tonight, and it's perfect. I'll make sure Col wears something to match."

With all the newsfeed buzz about me and him, Aribella wants to play up the rumors. To show the city that her family can secure an alliance with my father.

"Col's been very kind to me," I say.

"Of course, he has—you're so lovely, Rafia." She leans closer, looking me over again. "And no surgery at all?"

For a moment, I don't know how to answer. Back in the pretty regime, looks weren't something to brag about. But now every city has its own customs.

"My nose could be smaller," I say—Rafi's complaint since she was a littlie. "But Father won't let me change it."

Aribella gives me a sympathetic smile. "He's always talking about your mother, the natural pretty. Maybe he wants to see her in your face."

"I don't remember her."

"Of course not." She reaches up to smooth my hair. Her

touch is unexpectedly gentle. "Everyone knows the story—your father taking what he wants."

I'm not sure what to say to that. If our father didn't take what he wanted, Rafi and I wouldn't exist.

When my brother, Seanan, was abducted, my mother resisted the kidnappers. She was shot four times, and as she lay dying on the operating table, Father told the doctors to harvest her eggs so he could have more children with her.

My father makes his own reality. Sometimes with force. Sometimes with technology.

He snatched me and Rafi from oblivion.

I repeat what Dona Oliver always says: "He loved my mother too much to let her go."

"That's what I'm counting on." Aribella turns to face the windows. "I'm gambling my city's safety that he'd never endanger his own blood."

A tremble of relief travels through me—at last, we aren't pretending anymore. I'm a captive here, not a guest. Collateral for my father's good behavior.

Aribella misinterprets my shiver. "You must think I'm dreadful, taking a child hostage."

"You didn't take me." I sit a little straighter. "I came of my own free will."

"Well, that's a relief, Rafia. I was worried your father wouldn't tell you, which might have left us with . . . an awkward conversation."

I almost laugh at that. "He's not afraid of delivering bad news."

"Your father does enjoy a crisis. But he's been as good as his word on this deal. So far."

"Of course." The feeds are saying that the rebels are faltering already. Retreating under the combined forces of Victoria and Shreve. "My family doesn't shy away from a fight."

"No, you don't." Aribella looks at the scar above my eye. "In fact, I heard a rumor, from someone who was there that day, when that awful man tried to kill you."

My body goes tense. Dona's security people scrutinized every angle of spy-dust data, hunting for anyone who might have seen me and Rafi together. But with all the smoke and confusion, they were never certain.

I shrug. "There are a lot of rumors about that day."

"I never believed this one, until I met you." Aribella leans closer. "Did *you* kill the assassin?"

Rafi would deny it, or simply laugh it away. But with my other, bigger secret always lurking, I want to admit this truth. And maybe impressing Aribella matters to me now.

"Yes. I killed him."

I'm not sure what to expect, but her warm smile surprises me.

"Thank you for trusting me, Rafia." She gently takes my right wrist. "Is your hand better?"

I stare at her. "My hand?"

"We were worried that there might be something hidden

under your skin." Aribella looks away, a little embarrassed. "A tracker, perhaps. It seemed prudent to scan you."

"Right." My father's security uses millimeter-wave radar to make sure his guests aren't carrying weapons. "But I don't have any implants, except for my eyes."

"No. But we noticed that the bones in your right hand were recently broken."

"Fell off my hoverboard."

Aribella shakes her head.

"That's what we thought, till we looked a little closer." She touches my shoulder. "There's an old dislocation here, and more breaks in your left wrist, your right knee. And scar tissue in the muscles all over your body. My physician says he's never seen so many training injuries. Or such high-quality vision implants. Your body doesn't lie, Rafia."

My fists curl. The Palafoxes might not have an army to match my father's, but they're just as smart as he is.

We knew they'd check my DNA—it matches Rafi's, of course. But how can I keep any secrets from them if they scan me while I sleep?

Maybe more of the truth will distract her.

"My brother's kidnapping still haunts my father. So he made sure I could defend myself."

"That's very sad." She takes my hand again and looks into my eyes with a kind of pity. "But you should know something, Rafia.

94

Whatever deal I've made with your father, I would never hurt you."

I stare at her, unbelieving.

"This has to stay our little secret, of course," she says. "For the sake of peace, I'll pretend to stand by my threats. But you'll always be safe under my roof. I swear to you."

Why is she telling me this? The hostage deal doesn't work unless my father fears the worst. Unless she's trying to get me on her side . . .

But she's also scared of me. She locked up Col's hunting bow, even before she found the marks of training on my bones.

Suddenly I know what she needs to hear.

"I'll never hurt anyone in your family, Aribella. I promise."

With a warm smile, she leans across to hug me. She smells like the garden in the center of House Palafox, fresh and alive—and powerful, like she makes her own rain.

"Thank you, Rafi." Aribella releases me and stands. "We have to trust each other."

"Of course." Until she finds out I'm not my father's real heir. Do you have to keep promises to impostors?

"I notice you haven't pinged home," she says softly.

I hesitate, wondering how to explain that there's no one in Shreve I can talk to. Rafi's friends would know I wasn't her in five minutes, and my father's never had a real conversation with me.

The only person I want to talk to is my sister, and we can't let the Palafoxes know there's two of us.

"I've been so busy. Maybe after the party."

"Of course. We should both be getting ready, I suppose." Aribella straightens, smiles. "Everybody will be watching tonight."

I stand up, nodding. Everybody's always watching me.

PARTY

The Palafoxes know how to throw a bash.

The sky above the city is bright with explosions. Sharp little crackles scatter against the night, white and sudden. Willows of blue embers bloom, taking endless minutes to shimmer away. Vast scarlet umbrellas burn stately overhead.

Inside House Palafox, safety flames ripple on the curtains, tumble down the gaudy columns lining the entryway. Even the music sets the air on fire, the instruments of the brass band sparking from their bells.

The ballroom has expanded all day, its walls sliding grandly across the parquet floors. The party swells to fill the giant space, a long line of hovercars spilling out a thousand guests, all in more vibrant colors than anyone wears at a bash in Shreve.

At first, Rafi's ball gown feels dull. But as the crowd grows, the black and gray begins to stand out against this rainbow of fabric and flame. And Col looks perfect next to me. His midnight suit shines like dark metal, glinting with the sparks raining from the ceiling and the sky. His necktie is a nanoscreen, showing images of rolling ocean waves at night.

"Smile for the hovercams," he says. We're on a balcony above the throng, raising glasses of champagne. "Spoiled brats aren't permitted to be glum."

I hide my mouth behind my bubbly. "You know people read lips, right?"

"Not here." He gestures at the falling sparks. "Those shimmer at the exact speed of hovercam frame rates. Rattles the image just enough for privacy."

"Clever," I say.

"Necessary."

Again, the Victorians and their privacy obsession. But there's something electric about knowing that our words are hidden, even with a million people watching.

Rafi must be among them. She's watched me out in public before, of course, at nightclubs and in big crowds. But always from a private suite, not from back in our bedroom. I wonder if she's happy for me, finally getting the attention she always promised I would. Or is she only jealous of me now?

A friend of Col's joins us on the balcony, and the cyrano whispers in my ear.

Yandre Marin, eldest child of a famous couple. Their father is a popular novelist, their mother a leader in the political opposition here.

I don't know what a *novelist* is, except that it must be old-fashioned. Victorians are smug about keeping crumbly pastimes alive, from calligraphy to kayaking.

But Yandre's mother is an opposition leader? In Shreve, no one invites their political enemies to parties.

I smile and curtsy, admiring Yandre's long blue dress, its hem wreathed with flowers stitched in gold. A flash tattoo on their bare shoulder pulses with the music.

"Welcome to Victoria," Yandre says, bowing in return. "I hope you won't judge us all by your boring host."

"Boring!" Col protests. "Did you miss the part where we welcomed her with rebels?"

"You never welcome *me* with rebels!" Yandre looks my way, waiting for Rafi's famous wit to manifest.

My sister would say something bubbly, making light of the attack. I understand the theory of jokes like this, turning an uncomfortable topic into humor, but I haven't had much practice. The cyrano is silent.

Col steps in. "Your family practically *are* rebels, Yandre. Besides, you're just here to drink Jefa's champagne."

"And for my weekly dose of dullness." Yandre turns to me. "Has he given you the cloud forest lecture yet?"

"The first day," I manage. Which is only marginally bubbly.

They're still waiting for me to be funny. So I open my mouth, hoping that nothing too brain-missing comes out . . .

"'She's not coming to save us.'"

Yandre frowns, pushing their long black hair over one ear. "Pardon?"

I have no idea why, out of all the madness of that day, those words stuck. But now I have to explain.

"During the attack, we took cover under a Rusty building. There was an abandoned camp down there, with rebel code all over the ceiling. The only thing we could read was, 'She's not coming to save us.'"

"I wonder who *she* is," Yandre says. "Our patron saint, Victoria? She was forced into a marriage with a heathen. Not unlike your predicament, Rafia."

"Don't be brain-missing," Col says. "The rebels don't care about pre-Rusty sky-gods."

"A saint isn't a god, silly boy. And our city *is* named after her."

Col sighs. "I hate it when that happens."

"You hate what?" Yandre says with a laugh. "When your hover-car crash-lands in a cryptic rebel base? Is that a thing?"

"No. When you hear a snatch of someone else's conversation, and it sounds mysterious and significant"—Col watches as a glittering sparkler falls past the balcony—"but you never find out what it means."

"You're so deep, chico." Yandre rolls their eyes and turns to me. "I'll ask my little brother. He's a bit of a rebel—*not* the kind that shoots at visiting celebrities, of course. But he might know that slogan."

I smile back at them. "Thank you."

"Speaking of your brother," Col says quietly. "Did he find what I asked for?"

Yandre nods. "I hid it under the daybed in the west room—Grandma Zefina let me in to fix my dress. But why you need a pulse charger is beyond me."

I take another swig to hide my expression.

"We just do." Col grins at me. "We can sneak it down to the old building tonight."

I stare at him. "With a million people watching? We'd need a pretty big diversion."

Yandre takes us both by the arms, and laughs.

"This is Victoria, my dear. Parties are their own diversion."

SWEAR

An hour later, the diversion arrives.

There's no warning, no ping from the city interface about taking cover. Just a sudden barrage from all directions.

The first one hits Yandre, a blur of motion in the corner of my eye, a *pop* as scarlet powder streaks their blue dress. I startle, but Col and Yandre only laugh.

Then something hits my shoulder. I barely feel it—the outer shell is some kind of aerogel, light as a puff of air. It breaks and scatters luminous green powder across my ball gown.

Overhead, the air is crisscrossed with projectiles.

"What the hell?"

"Cascarones," Col says. "To ruffle up the bash a little. It's a tradition that dates back to the pre-Rusty festival of—"

A bolt of brilliant blue streaks his forehead.

"Oh so perfect," Yandre manages through their laughter.

The projectiles are hitting everyone. Pinging into champagne flutes, marking dresses, suits, hats, faces with colored powder. The party redoubles in energy around us, and the musicians switch to a faster tempo.

Dancing erupts in the milling crowd.

"Come on," Col says, taking my hand. "It'll take a minute for the hovercams to find cover."

Yandre raises their glass as we slip away. "Have fun, you two."

Col leads me to the edge of the crowd, then along the ballroom's back wall. Cascarones smack and pop around us. Another hits me, a soft kiss between my shoulder blades.

We reach the corner, and Col opens a hidden door.

"If anyone asks, you wanted to clean up."

I almost protest this cover story—I *like* the vivid streaks on my ball gown. But Rafi would hate her design being marred by random colors.

She must be glued to the feeds right now, wondering where I am. Has she guessed that I've snuck away with Col? Will it hurt her face rank to be associated with someone as boring and studious as him?

He leads me through the door into a narrow space, stuffed with the extra furniture crowded out by the expansion of the ballroom. He pulls a flare from his pocket, snaps its top. A bright flickering erupts, and safety sparks cascade down my ball gown. Of course—like the fireworks outside, the flare pulses, dazzling any watching cams.

Col weaves among chairs, couches, reading desks, heading straight for a daybed in the corner. Kneeling, he pulls out an object wrapped in white plastic.

He hands it to me. "Is this what you need?"

The charger feels bulky, old-fashioned. But so was the pulse knife.

"It should work."

Col smiles. His eyes are bright, and there's a trickle of sweat channeling the blue powder on his face. I wonder if this is the first time he's snuck around in his own house.

"Do we have time?" I whisper.

He nods. "When Yandre tells people we snuck out together, no one will come looking."

"Oh. Right." Rafi would make a joke about now.

I've got nothing.

"Sorry," Col says, looking embarrassed

Then I remember one of Rafi's famous lines.

"If I cared what people said, they'd only gossip more."

The impersonation was perfect, even the wearily raised eyebrow to drive it home. But Col just frowns at me, then leads me to another door.

Minutes later we're running along the stone wall at the edge of the old building. Once we're past the retina lock, Col drops the flare and grinds it out under his heel. He leads me down a dark hallway into the weapons room.

I cross to the case that holds the pulse knife and drop to my knees. It doesn't take long to find the right spot—on the bottom, just beneath the knife.

With a squeeze, the charger wakes up, clinging to the case with magnetics. It detects the knife and begins a charge cycle, pulsing fast and featherlight.

"So how does it work?" Col asks.

I stand and face him. "Once the knife's charged, it can free itself. Then we use it to open the case with your bow."

"That'll make a mess, right?"

"Like a bomb hit." I shrug. "But you said no one comes down here."

"Hardly ever." He gives his hunting bow a look of longing. "How much time?"

"To fully charge? A day or so. Tomorrow night, we can sneak back and tell the knife to cut its way out—if it still works."

Col comes closer, staring down through the ferroglass.

I hold my hand out above the knife and make the *come to me* gesture—middle and ring fingers together, the others splayed.

For a moment the knife does nothing. But then a pale red light appears on its hilt.

"See that? It wants to jump into my hand. But it doesn't have enough juice."

"And it can cut through ferroglass?"

I grin at him. "Like sponge cake."

"Okay," he says. "But there's something you're not telling me."

The words yank my attention away from the knife. He's staring at me, his dark eyes intense.

I put on Rafi's amused voice. "Whatever do you mean?"

"Something's different. This isn't you."

Of course. The real Rafi wouldn't leave a global audience to help someone steal a hunting bow. She wouldn't spend all night talking to one boy, with a thousand other guests to charm. And she certainly wouldn't stand here explaining how pulse knives work.

Col knows I'm not her.

An escape plan flashes through my head—an open-handed strike to his temple. Then breaking into the case somehow and fleeing with the pulse knife and the charger. The party upstairs will give me a few hours of cover.

But why would Col accuse me *here*, where no one can help him?

He's waiting for an answer. The real Rafia would have one.

Not me.

"On the feeds," he says, "when you act like a spoiled littlie, I get now that it's all a joke. That you're making *fun* of people like us."

My racing heart settles a little.

"It's fun," I tell him, "making fun of spoiled brats."

"Then why are you down here? There's a hundred hover-cams up there, all of them begging for it, and you didn't do your act. What's different now, Rafia?"

Say something. Say anything.

I touch my cyrano, hoping for something useful.

Col Palafox. He's the eldest son of the Victorian first family.

The idiot machine thinks I've forgotten his name. My father's voice, mocking me.

"Why did my mother lock up my bow?" Col asks. "Is she scared of you?"

"Yes," I say, grateful for anything.

He's waiting for more, but I finally see a way out. To keep him from understanding my big secret, I have to give him a smaller one.

"Your mother can't know I told you this." All my anxiety is in my voice.

"Told me what?"

"I'm a hostage here."

Col doesn't react. Like he doesn't even know the word.

"I'm a prisoner," I say. "A guarantee that my father's forces won't take over the ruins."

His voice is uncertain in the darkness. "And my mother agreed to this?"

A strange urge to defend Aribella hits me. "She doesn't like it either. And she's promised not to hurt me, Col."

A bitter laugh forces its way out of him. "How nice for you. And she's always saying we're different from the other first families. I can't *believe* her!"

He looks angry enough to storm upstairs and confront Aribella right now. That argument could go wrong for me in a hundred ways.

I take hold of his arm. "She can't find out that I told you."

"Of course not, but . . ." Col stares at me, uncertain. "Your father letting this happen, I halfway believe. But why did *you* agree to it?"

I have to look away. Col will never understand that I didn't have a choice.

"I don't want our cities to fight. With me here, they won't."

"That's very brave of you." I can't tell if he's sarcastic or serious.

"I should have told you sooner. I'm sorry."

He takes my right hand. Something electric goes through those knitted bones. "Don't apologize, Rafi. And don't worry. I'll make sure Jefa keeps her promise."

He touches his lips to my hand. Just for a moment.

"*J'en mettrais ma main au feu*," he says.

I'm staring at my hand, at his lips.

The cyrano translates in my ear—*I put my hand in the fire.*

What do they mean, those words? That kiss? Is this how they seal promises in Victoria? Or is it the start of something else?

I don't know anything about kissing.

His dark eyes lock with mine. No one looks at me this intently, except Naya, when she's sizing up my weaknesses. I feel measured, scanned, defenseless.

Then Col lets go and turns toward the hallway.

"We should get back to the party," he says.

I nod dumbly. Suddenly that swirl of music, fire, and projectiles seems safer than being alone with him.

TELL ME EVERYTHING

A strange thing has happened overnight—I'm popular here.

Everyone expected bratty, sophisticated Rafia at the party, but they got me instead. All those guests and hovercams to charm, and I paid attention only to Col. Like some random, brain-missing with a sudden crush.

And then, when that rain of cascarones came down, the two of us disappeared for half an hour.

Rafi's global face rank has dipped a little this morning; pairing off with the host is boring by her standards. But here in Victoria the audience was thrilled to see Col Palafox, their thoughtful first-family son, turn a dazzling socialite into a bubblehead.

Watching the social feeds discuss this makes me twitchy— now that they're about *me* instead of Rafi. All that focus on my ball gown, my posture, my hair. All that speculation about what's going on with me and Col, when I don't even know myself.

How does Rafi stand all this attention? How does she remember who she really is, underneath all the layers of fashion and rumors and gossip? No wonder she has those temper tantrums.

I wonder if she ever wants to trade lives with me, if only for the chance to punch something.

I switch to the news. Here in Victoria, I can watch the global feeds instead of Shreve propaganda. It's weird how everything is laid out in such a matter-of-fact way, without the music or eye-dazzling headlines.

My father's forces sortied into the mountains last night, destroying a rebel camp a hundred klicks from the ruins. Maybe this will all be over soon and I can go home.

Of course, I can't count on that. So while I listen, I work on my escape kit.

I've been gathering useful things, leaving them around the room, ready to be swept up if I have to run. So far it's dried fruit brought back from meals, a few plastic bags for collecting rainwater, my self-cleaning sweats, a firestarter. This morning's work is adding an improvised weapon to the mix—a sharp-edged light fixture that I loosen from the wall as I pretend to stretch.

A pulse knife would be better.

My head still throbs and buzzes from the party. I miss training. I'm going soft here in Victoria. Naya will kill me if I come back home over my fighting weight. But calorie purger pills make me jittery, and I'm jittery enough already.

Of course, Aribella already knows I'm dangerous, so maybe it doesn't matter if I do some pushups.

Halfway into my workout, my cyrano pings—another hidden message from Rafi.

I tap it and keep exercising.

You're killing me, Frey.

It's bad enough my dress got ruined, but did you have to make me look like such a face-missing wallflower! And crushing on Col Palafox? Really? What if he speaks French to you?

Or have you two been too busy to talk?

Ugh. Don't tell me.

*By which I mean, yes—*definitely *tell me.*

A grin creeps onto my face. Rafi sounds almost jealous.

She's stuck in hiding, of course, with no parties of her own. But the thought of her living vicariously through *my* social life is the most brain-missing thing ever.

Out the window, a flock of pigeons wheels around the distant cathedral spire, exuberant and playful. My hand tingles where Col kissed me.

Is this what it feels like to have my own life?

That's what kills me, Frey—that you can't even tell me what's going on. If you're getting clothes-missing for the first time ever without your big sister there to counsel you, it's an outrage.

I take a slow breath.

Clothes-missing? That's a laugh. Col's lips barely brushed my hand.

If Rafi were here, she could figure out what's actually going on between me and him. *Allies* is the only word we've said out loud. Is that more or less than *friends?*

But he kissed my hand . . .

I should research what that means here in Victoria, just ask the city interface about local romance customs.

But Palafox security would notice—that doesn't sound like something Rafi would have to ask. She'd just know.

Throw me a clue, Frey. If you and that boy have shared so much as a meaningful look, wear the scarlet jacket today—the one with too many buttons on the sleeves. But if there's nothing going on, wear my white jacket.

Red for passion. White for lonely and cold. Surely you can remember that.

Send me a sign, Frey. Entertain me—I'm going crazy here!

But really, I hope it's the white jacket. I mean, really. He's the first boy you've ever talked to!

Love you, little sister. But take it from your sensei—you don't know anything yet.

The recording ends, and the last words ring in my ears.

Sensei. That's not a word she would ever use casually. Not since Noriko disappeared.

Rafi's trying to send me a message that no one else would catch, something deadly important. But I can't figure it out.

She's right. I don't know anything.

And suddenly it's all so embarrassing. Was my father listening while she recorded it? Does he care what's going on between me and Col?

Which is probably *nothing*. Col's lips on the back of my hand must be some crumbly Victorian tradition, like calligraphy or novel writing.

But the look he gave me after . . .

There's a knock at the door. Not a ping, knuckles on wood.

"Come in."

The door swings open, and it's Col.

He gives me a puzzled look. I'm in pajamas, my hair frazzled, sweaty. Hardly a state Rafi would receive visitors in.

Now that I've started telling people my secrets, the rest of my act is falling apart.

"I thought we'd tour the roof garden before lunch," he says, making the hand sign for *We're being watched*.

"That sounds lovely, Col. I'll be dressed in . . . forty minutes?"

He nods, looking reassured.

That, at least, was a very Rafi thing to say.

SPINES

The roof of House Palafox is covered with sharp things—antennae slicing into the sky, the spinning blades of windmills, a garden full of cactuses.

The succulents come in all sizes, from spiky soccer balls to three-meter, splay-armed giants. Some are abloom with tiny flowers, surrounded by sizzling galaxies of bees.

"*Les murs n'ont pas d'oreilles,*" Col says.

The walls don't have ears, my cyrano translates.

I look around. No security drones, no smart walls. Unless one of the bees is a nanocam, he's probably right.

No newsfeed hovercams either. Which is good, because I haven't chosen a jacket yet.

Like my sister said, I don't know anything.

Col gestures toward my ear. "That's listening, isn't it?"

I shrug. "It's just a cyrano. I'm terrible at names."

"Jefa says the house scanners can't crack it, which means it's serious tech." He gives me a look. "It could be reporting back to your father."

I roll my eyes. I know more about spyware than romance.

"It's strictly passive. Your house security would notice if it started transmitting. But if it makes you happy." I drop the cyrano in my pocket.

Col doesn't know it's always listening.

We stand there in awkward silence for a moment.

"The party was lovely," I say.

Col gives me a sheepish smile. "Jefa was pleased. No complaints about us disappearing."

So Aribella is okay with something happening between me and Col. Or at least she's fine with the rest of the city thinking there is.

But what does Col think?

That tingle is still there where he kissed me.

Naya's voice pops into my head. *So many nerves in the hand— it's the best way to take down a stronger foe.*

I know how to break fingers. But not how to kiss someone.

"Yandre pinged me this morning," Col says. "They talked to their brother, the rebel sympathizer, about that slogan—'She's not coming to save us.' Turns out *she* is Tally Youngblood."

A little tremor rolls through me. The rebels have their own saint, of course. "But what does it mean?"

"Exactly what it says. Tally's not coming back. We have to save ourselves."

That's not news to me.

I turn away, looking around the rooftop, mapping the shape of the building against the layout of the floors below.

Making escape plans is something I know all about.

A few of the trees in the courtyard garden have grown higher than the roofline. It wouldn't be too hard to climb up here from the garden.

"You think the knife is charged yet?" Col asks.

"Too soon. Do you miss hunting that much?"

"I miss people not taking my stuff." He gazes off at the mountains. "But sure. I like surviving off the land, being connected to the wild."

I laugh. "You connect to nature by *eating* it? I hope the same doesn't apply to your friends."

"Is that what we are?"

Right. We've only said *allies* so far.

Col is giving me one of his intense looks, which must mean something. But who knows what? I've never really made a friend before. I've only ever had one, and she's my twin sister.

"If you want to be friends, sure."

"Great." He nods a little and turns away.

Somehow I'm doing this wrong.

"Speaking of eating nature: These *nopales* are tasty." He's switched into his tour guide voice, pointing to a cluster of flat-armed cactuses, like oblong dinner plates covered with red flowers. "They're on the lunch menu today."

"Not exactly hungry-making." I reach out and touch one of the cactuses, expecting it to stab me—and it does. "Ow. Why does everything up here have spikes?"

"Spines," Col corrects me. "Furry ones to keep insects away. Big needle ones for mammals like me and you."

"So a cactus is afraid of *everything*?"

Col looks at me meaningfully. "When you've got water in the desert, you have to protect yourself."

He's talking about the ruins, of course. Metal is the thing that every city wants, like water in a desert.

"What kind of spines does your family have?" I ask.

"Sharp ones. This morning, I asked Jefa what she'll do if your father refuses to leave our ruins."

I frown. "She didn't mention throwing me in a dungeon, I hope?"

"No. She's still keeping that a secret from me. But she said we have some surprises in store for your father. He's not the only one waking up old weapons."

"That'll only make things worse."

"For him."

I shake my head. "Whenever things don't go his way, he escalates. When he's caught in a lie, he tells a bigger one. When someone resists, he hits them harder."

When someone took his child, he made two more.

"We're not afraid of him," Col says.

"Then why does your mother need me as a hostage?"

"To save lives. We don't *want* to fight." He looks off at the mountains. "Even if the first families don't fight all-out Rusty wars, soldiers still die. By having you here, Jefa's trying to show your father another way. Negotiation instead of violence."

So Aribella thinks she's playing my father.

"She scares me a little," I say.

"*Très drôle*. Considering who your father is."

"*Je suppose*," I manage, pleased that I didn't need my cyrano. *Drôle* means the same in French as it does in English.

Col thinks I'm funny.

"There's something you might want to see," he says.

"Is it edible and spiny?"

Col smiles, leading me to the western edge of the roof, facing the mountains. "The best view of the city."

It's not. We're looking down a jumble of narrow alleyways, through a part of Victoria that's old and earth-bound. No soaring fairy-tale towers or bright colors.

But it's the perfect neighborhood to disappear into.

Col glances down at a plastic box at our feet, marked with the fire escape symbol. Bungee jackets.

A tangle of thoughts goes through my head. He's helping me make escape plans. He really *is* an ally.

Or maybe something more. After all, he's betraying his own family for me.

"I don't know what to say."

Col shrugs. "No one should be a prisoner just because of who their father is."

The strange thing is, I've never felt like a prisoner here in Victoria. Before I came here, my whole life was spent behind locked doors and impenetrable walls. A prisoner is what I've always been.

It's like Col knows that somehow, and he wants to save me.

He leans over the parapet. "That long alley leads to the edge of the city, with a few twists and turns."

"Thank you."

"It's the least I can do." Col looks like he's about to say something more—but he turns away. "I should dress for lunch. We'll be on the south terrace. With all the gossip about last night, there'll be newscams snooping around."

So whatever I wear will be in the feeds, and Rafi will be watching with keen eyes. But I don't know which jacket. Not yet.

And I don't know why she said *sensei*.

We head back down to my room in uncertain silence, everything unsaid still lingering between us.

At my door I hesitate. "It's nice to have a friend here."

Col doesn't answer, just gives me another silent look. We're back inside, where the house can hear us, so maybe he can't say what he's thinking. But I can't resist asking.

"What is it?" I whisper.

"Nothing," he says softly. "Just . . . *parfois je me perds dans tes yeux.*"

Crap. That's too much French all at once. I have no idea what it means.

Was it a clue about an escape route? Something droll about the lunch menu?

I give him one of Rafi's looks of amusement.

"That's . . . lovely."

"Ah, sorry," Col says. He takes a step back, his expression darkening.

He's apologizing. I've messed something up.

But I can't confess how terrible my French is. I've spilled enough of my secrets to the Palafoxes.

Col is walking away, and I say nothing.

Once the door's shut, I pull the cyrano from my pocket, praying it caught whatever he said. I head to the bathroom and turn on all the taps.

"Replay last sixty seconds," I whisper.

His words are there at the edge of hearing. But I still don't know what they mean.

"Translate?" I plead, and it's awful to hear it in my father's voice.

Sometimes I get lost in your eyes.

I stand there, steam building around me, not caring if Palafox security wonders what this is all about. What matters is what I do next.

That look of amusement on my face after he said the words—he must have thought I'd turned back into Rafi. Arch and superior and too detached for any sentiment so simple and so sweet.

I have to fix this.

"Ping Col Palafox," I say to the room.

"Message content?" the room asks.

My heart is racing. "The message is, 'Me too.' End and send."

Then I go to the closet and stare at the red jacket.

I should wear it for lunch—my still-racing heart is proof of that. But do I really want Rafi knowing what's going on in my head?

What if she laughs at me? That would be too much to bear. And Dona will be watching closely too, maybe even my father. They don't want me compromised by some brain-missing crush.

But Rafi's my big sister, and she asked for a sign. She said the word *sensei*, so I knew how important it was.

I have to share this with her.

I reach for the red jacket.

FLY

That night I wake up to a screaming sound.

It's a dream at first—my bed scanning me with bright shafts of light. But instead of scars and healed bones, the scanner finds a weapon buried inside me. A knife hidden in my chest, pulsing quick.

And that's where the dream shifts into a nightmare—an alarm shrieks, an ice pick of sound that I can't shut out, even with my hands over my ears. As sharp and hard as anger, the alarm penetrates my body, rattles my bones, lances my frenzied heart.

Finally I sputter awake, look around in a panic. The screaming doesn't stop, as if I'm still dreaming.

Then I realize it's the cyrano, jittering on my bedside table.

It must be malfunctioning.

"Quiet!" I tell it.

The noise shuts off.

I pick it up, hesitantly put it in my ear—if the shrieking starts again, it'll deafen me. But it speaks calmly now.

Emergency message.

I tap it, and my sister's voice rushes into my head.

I'm so sorry, Frey. He wouldn't let me warn you until now. It's because you wore that stupid red jacket. How could you be so brain-missing?

After what I said, couldn't you tell you were supposed to wear the white *one?*

How could you not know it was a test? That he made me do it?

Now he thinks you'll put Col before him. That you won't follow orders. That you'll warn them!

I sit up in bed. Warn them about what?

He's moved up the timetable—we're pushing the Palafoxes out of the ruins tonight.

The attack starts in two minutes.

My eyes blink, trying to resolve meaning in the darkness. It's like being in the dream again. My body lanced by scanning rays, my heart vibrating fast as a pulse knife.

I take slow breaths to calm myself. I have an escape kit. This is something I know how to do. Something I've been getting ready for my whole life.

But all my reflexes and training falter when it hits me—

My father only thinks I'm worth two minutes' warning.

I cling to my sister's voice.

All you have to do is get to the ruins, Frey. We'll take control of them first, like everyone expects.

Come in from the south, on foot. The soldiers won't dare shoot. They still think you're me.

You'll be fine. You can do this.

Yes—escaping, fighting my way out. I'm Frey, the one who uses her fists.

This is the only thing I know how to do.

I spring up from the bed, jump into my sweats and running shoes and jacket. Shove my stolen dried fruit, firestarter, and plastic bags into the pockets. A desperate idea hits me, and I grab the tulle lining of my ball gown.

With one kick, the loosened light fixture flies off the wall. It fits in my hand perfectly, metal edges glinting in the dark.

The house security must have heard my cyrano screaming, and they've seen my curious behavior. They'll be sending someone up to check on me.

If my father had given me more time, I could've gotten ready quietly, stealthily. But he doesn't trust me anymore.

Because I wore the red jacket, like a lovelorn bubblehead. Like someone whose social life is more important than her mission.

Focus.

The door pings.

"Excuse me, Rafia." A male voice comes into the room. "This is Warden Renold. I'd like to have a word with—"

I open the door and punch him hard in the face, my improvised weapon giving the blow extra weight. He topples backward, hits the ground.

My hand screams with pain. It's been so long since I hit anything.

I kick the warden once in the stomach to make sure he stays down. They'll come in numbers now, but the security barracks are all the way downstairs. It's the drones I have to worry about.

But I have a plan for that.

I run for the billiard room, which has a window overlooking the courtyard. Close enough to the tallest tree to jump—maybe.

On the way, I tear the ball gown lining into pieces. I aim the firestarter at the strips of tulle, tossing them at curtains and pieces of furniture. The hallways start to fill with smoke.

Halfway to the billiard room, a drone comes down the hall. But it zooms right past me, spraying fire-foam. Alarms are ringing in every direction, a thousand sensors calling for its attention.

Someone could reset the drones' priorities to focus on me instead of the fires, but by now my father's attack has started in the Rusty ruins. Palafox security has bigger things to worry about than one runaway rich kid.

They only have to underestimate me for a few more minutes.

In the billiard room, I spill two racks of balls in front of the door. Grab a pool cue off the wall.

One swing of the cue smashes the window to pieces, glittering shards scattering out into the night. It's old-fashioned glass, not safety polymer, so I sweep the cue back and forth to clear the window frame.

Stepping out into the dark, I realize that the tree branch is farther away than I thought.

My stomach does a little flip. The ground is nothing but blackness below. A few stars sparkle through the jungle canopy.

A clatter of balls sounds behind me—a warden coming in, losing her footing. I leap at her, the cue spinning like a lopsided *bō* in my hands. She raises some kind of stunner, but the heavy end of the cue knocks it from her grip. When she blocks my swing at her temple, I follow with a thrust to her stomach.

She's down.

But more will come. I have to make the jump.

Flinging the cue aside, I run for the window, wishing I had crash bracelets.

The cool night wraps around me. My hands grab for the tree branch, palms slapping against smooth bark and holding for a moment. But my momentum carries my feet out, and my fingers slip.

I fall in ringing silence, but only for a second—a lower branch hits my midsection like a body tackle, knocking the breath from my lungs.

The branch bows under my weight, and the rattle of leaves comes from all directions, the flutter of wings. My crash landing sending a host of creatures stampeding through the canopy.

Somehow I hold on.

But the window of the billiard room is right there, gaping open, shining light out on me.

Sucking in shallow, painful breaths, I start to climb. Up into the darkness of the dense treetops, the crisscross of vines pricked with stars.

This is what I was made for, but somehow the ecstasy of combat isn't kicking in. Breathing is agony after the gut-punch of landing on the branch.

The gut-punch of Father sacrificing me . . .

Rafi was right. Since they stole Seanan from him, my father has wanted to scream at the world, *Take my child! I don't care!*

He's trading me for a pile of metal. I was just a distraction, a way to give the Palafoxes a false sense of security.

This is what I was made for—throwing away.

I hear voices from the open window below and freeze.

A man in a warden's uniform leans out. He scans the upper branches quickly, then gives the ground below a hard look. The lighting along the paths is flickering on.

Two drones waft into position behind the warden, and he sends them out the window with a jerk of his hand. They descend into the garden.

Why can't they see me? My body heat must stick out like a brush fire against this cool jungle.

Setting my eyescreen to night vision, I realize why—the canopy is full of living things. Flocks of birds and scurrying creatures, a lively host all around me.

But if the warden looks harder, he'll recognize my shape.

I start climbing again, careful not to shake the leaves. The sharp outline of rooftop against open sky is almost within reach, but the branch beneath me bends under my weight as I go farther out.

Then I hear a sound against all the alarms and shouting below. A slithering.

And I remember what Dr. Orteg jokingly warned me about when he put my eyes in—

Snakes are cold-blooded, matching the temperature of their environment. They're invisible in heat vision.

And they don't like being stepped on.

SNAKE

The sound is soft, like the rasp of a dry tongue against the bark, mixed with the faint rattle of leaves.

Which direction is it coming from?

The branches are crowded together up here, and other sounds distract my ears. The garden below is full of wardens and drones.

Someone's going to spot me up here soon.

I reach out to take the next branch, hoping my fingers close on bark, not scales.

The branch feels thick enough to hold my weight, and I swing across. Hanging there, I listen. The slithering sounds closer now.

But I can't focus on the snake. A dozen armed soldiers and a house full of security drones are after me.

I hoist myself up, wrapping my legs around the branch.

The roof is so close. As I shimmy upward, the leaves rattle, but I don't care about noise. I just want to put my feet on solid ground.

Then the slithering sound comes again. I freeze. Switch off my useless night vision.

There it is ahead of me. Scales glinting in the moonlight, sinuous and coiling.

Two black eyes like dots of oil.

It stares at me with boundless patience, paralyzing me. I hang like that for an endless time, barely breathing, dimly aware that my muscles are starting to burn.

Sooner or later, I'll fall.

It's a drone that saves me, the little red-and-green running lights whirring up into the corner of my vision. Only a meter away, the barrel of its little stunner is pointed right at my face.

"Don't move," it says. "We don't want to hurt you, but we will if we have to."

Hurt me? If it hits me with the stunner, I'll tumble all the way to the ground. Maybe that fact will make the operator hesitant.

I don't even have a weapon. So I improvise one, my reflexes overriding my fear.

I reach out to grab the tail end of the snake and fling it at the drone. It hits with a *smack* and tightens its coils around the little machine. The drone tips over, its lifters fighting the shifting weight.

But the startled creature won't let go, and together they tumble away through the leaves.

I'm already scrambling for the roof. Noise doesn't matter anymore. If I can only get to those bungee jackets and hurl myself into the night.

This branch is just close enough for my fingers to reach the roof edge. I swing across, my feet scrabbling on rough stone.

A heave of my burning muscles hauls me up and onto the parapet. Solid stone feels like salvation, but I don't have time to rest. I roll from the parapet wall onto . . .

Needles. Spines.

The edge of the cactus garden.

A thousand pinpricks pull a ragged gasp from my lips. I launch myself from the cactus bed and onto the gravel rooftop.

My jacket is pinned to me, a hundred little hooks still in my skin. I pull it off, tearing spines with it.

"Stop right there," comes a familiar voice.

Another drone, two meters from me.

"You don't have to fight us," it says, speaking with Aribella's voice. My father's forces are invading the ruins, and she's focusing on *me*.

Why do I matter so much?

Because she doesn't realize that my father has thrown me away.

"You can't escape, Rafia."

She's probably right. There are no weapons for me to grab. My jacket lies at my feet—maybe I could throw it at the drone, but I'm exhausted, my muscles screaming.

"You have nothing to fear from us," Aribella says.

I want so badly to believe her, to think that *someone* is on my side.

"Okay," I murmur, and raise my hands. "I give up."

"Very good, Rafia. I knew you were a smart—"

Something slams into the drone, lighting up the night with sparks and flame.

I stumble away, hands across my eyes, almost falling back into the cactuses again. My eyes pulsing with leftover explosion, I can see someone at the far parapet, the dark mountains framed behind him.

He's holding a hunting bow.

"Come on!" Col calls. "I've only got two more explosive arrows."

He glitters in the starlight, because he's covered with ferro-glass dust.

My pulse knife is on his belt.

ESCAPE

I run across the roof and wrap my arms around him.

Col holds me for a moment, then pulls back, frowning.

"Ouch! Why are you so *pointy*?"

"Sorry. Took a roll in your cactuses." The spines in my nightshirt are still prickling me all over. "How did you get up here?"

"The stairs," he says.

Of course—the roof is a fire escape. When the house smelled smoke, it opened all the doors, security lockdown or not.

I could have taken the stairs.

"Couldn't sleep," Col says. "So I went down to the old building and called the knife, like you showed me."

He coughs once, and a little sparkling cloud lifts from him. I should probably tell him that breathing ferroglass dust is a bad idea.

I splay my hand, ring and middle fingers together. The knife jumps from his belt and into my palm. With it trembling in my hand, it's like a missing part of me has returned.

"When the alarms went off, I thought I was busted," he says. "But it wasn't me. Your father hit our forces in the ruins."

"I didn't know he would do this, I swear."

"You're not him, Rafi. But we should hide you until we figure out what Jefa plans to—"

His voice drops away, and he pushes me backward, clearing space to notch another arrow on his bowstring.

I spin around. Three more drones are lofting up from the garden.

"Save your arrows, Col," I say, and throw my knife sideways.

It takes a sweeping course around the roof. Hits the rightmost drone on the side, turns it into metal and plastic fragments, then continues on to plow through the other two.

A moment later it's back in my hand, humming with delight, as warm as fresh bread.

"Whoa." Col stares at me, only now realizing the power of the weapon he's given me.

I kneel and pull open the box of bungee jackets. "They'll send more drones. Let's get these on."

"Um, Rafi?"

I look up. Col snaps his fingers and rises into the air.

He's standing on a hoverboard.

Smugly.

"I liberated all my hunting gear," he says. "Thought you could use a ride."

I stand back up, staring at his board. It's all-terrain, with lifting fans and solar panels. Not fast, but perfect for crossing the wild.

There's so much I want to say, but all I've got is "Thank you."

Col folds his bow, collapsing its hingeless nanotech polymers down to the shape and size of a boomerang.

"Step on."

I climb up behind him, and the board rises higher into the air and over the parapet. The jumble of the city opens up below us, my stomach clenching.

"No crash bracelets?" I ask.

He shrugs. "I was in a hurry."

"Wait—why are *you* coming?"

"I'll take you to the edge of town." Col angles us forward, gaining speed over the rooftops. "If anyone chases us, they won't shoot at me."

Of course—he's the beloved first son of Victoria.

And this way we don't have to say good-bye yet.

"Tell them I took you hostage," I say, holding on to him as we gain speed. "So you won't get in trouble."

"Or I can tell Jefa the truth—she shouldn't use people's children for collateral."

"Sure," I say. "Telling the truth is one way."

We bend our knees together as the board drops into the alley behind House Palafox, leaving the alarms of war behind.

ESCALATION

We zoom down the alley, ten meters above empty streets.

Looking back over my shoulder, I see no signs of pursuit. Maybe they know that Col's with me—there's no way to shoot the board down without killing us both.

Or maybe they've got too much else to deal with.

It's hitting at last, the ecstasy of combat. With my arms wrapped around Col, our weight leaning together into the turns, that rapture of unquestioned reflex and purpose comes over me.

But then, as we peak above the rooftops for a moment, I catch a glimpse of the night sky streaked with flames ahead—my father's suborbitals coming down in the distant ruins. Jagged forks of lightning reach up from the earth, contesting with them.

Our families are at war.

More soldiers will die tonight.

"I'm so sorry," I murmur into Col's shoulder.

"You tried to stop this by coming here! It's Jefa's fault for trusting him."

Col thinks I came here of my own free will. That my presence had some chance of making my father stay his hand. But I was disposable, a way to make the Palafoxes drop their guard.

All that training in escape and improvised weapons wasn't as a last resort. It was always the plan to leave me exposed in enemy territory.

All my life, I thought my sister and I were a knife with two edges. But she was all that mattered, and I was just a bullet to be fired and forgotten.

What if I was fooling myself along with everyone else?

We fly until we reach an industrial belt at the edge of the city. The buildings are windowless and square, and the roads swarm with self-driving trucks.

The factories down there must be shifting gears, ready to produce drones and battle armor. Aribella plans to retake the ruins.

She doesn't know my father.

"We're close to the city's edge," Col says.

The hoverboard slows. Past the factory lights I see the dark expanse of the desert.

I've camped in the wild before, but the thought of going out there alone makes me nervous.

At home, Rafi was always there in the next bed. Even as a hostage, there's always been a house full of people around me.

The thought of making my lonely way out into that blackness makes my stomach twist.

Before this moment, I had no idea I was afraid to be alone. Of course, I didn't know about the snake thing either, until I came face-to-face with one.

A shudder goes through me.

"You can take my jacket," Col says. "It's heated."

"Thank you."

The board comes to a halt, and he turns around to face me.

I look down at myself. I'm a mess, my nightshirt dotted with cactus spines.

Col shrugs his jacket off. "You can't make it all the way to Shreve on one charge. But this board has solar panels."

"It's okay. They'll pick me up in the ruins."

He turns, frowns at the streaks of light in the west.

"Don't be so sure about that. You could be walking into a battle."

I let out of sigh. People always think the fight will be fair, but it never is.

"I'll be fine, as long as I've got my knife." The board shifts a little beneath our feet. "Thank you for helping me escape, Col."

He drapes his jacket around my shoulders. It's warm, but not as warm as being in his arms.

"Why did your father do this?" Col asks. "How could he risk losing you?"

I could tell him what I've realized at last—that risking me was always the plan. My father used me to lure the rebels out. He warned me to be ready to escape. My whole life I've been disposable.

But that confession can't be the last thing I say to him.

So I make up a lie. "Something must have gone wrong. An accident. Friendly fire . . ."

He nods. "This can't last long. Wars between cities never do. I'll ping you as soon as I can."

I look away. Col won't be able to ping me, because my sister will get her name back once I'm home. As far as the global interface is concerned, Frey doesn't exist.

"Just remember," he says. "This fight has nothing to do with us."

It has everything to do with me, the impostor who tricked the Palafoxes into trusting my father.

"I'll miss you," I say.

"Me too, Rafi."

He takes my shoulders then and leans forward.

The warmth of his lips on mine sets the air humming, like my skin when a rainstorm is on its way. There's a rushing in my head, and in it I hear my own name instead of hers, as if this kiss is the first thing that really belongs to me alone. And I know exactly how to kiss him back, like I've been practicing my whole life for this.

But then my father's voice whispers in my ear—

Emergency message.

I startle, pulling back.

Col stares at me. "What?"

I tap my cyrano, and my sister's voice starts crying—

Get out of that house! Now, Frey!

Out a window! Kill anyone in your way!

In thirty seconds it won't matter!

I look up into Col's dark eyes, hoping I'm wrong.

Knowing I'm right.

Aribella wasn't lying that she had a surprise for my father up her sleeve. His forces have been repulsed in the ruins. This fight is harder than he expected.

And when that happens, he only knows one way to respond.

"I'm so sorry," I whisper.

"Oh." Col turns away, the back of his hand against his lips. "I thought you wanted me to kiss you."

He doesn't understand. He can't hear Rafi in my ears.

He's going to escalate.

I swear I didn't know about this.

Just get out, Frey. Get out!

I open my mouth to explain, but Rafi's message hasn't come in time. From the north, a speck of light shrieks across the sky, faster than anything I've ever seen.

It leaves a trace, a wavering trail of plasma, the air itself on fire . . .

And plunges deep into the heart of Victoria.

My father makes his own reality. Sometimes with force. Sometimes with atrocity.

The flash reaches us first, then a *boom* that ripples the air, setting us wavering for a moment on the hoverboard.

From the center of the distant city, a dark fist of smoke begins to rise.

Col stands there, his eyes wide.

There's no room inside me to feel anything but resolve. I need to protect him now, with an urgency that feels like hunger.

"We have to move," I say softly. "He'll hit the factories next."

"But that's my . . ." Col starts, and his words shudder to a halt.

I turn him gently away from the column of smoke rising from his home, and lean forward to urge our hoverboard deeper into the darkness.

PART II

ALLIANCE

If injury must be done to a man,
it should be so severe that
his vengeance need not be feared.

—Niccolò Machiavelli

ANVILS

More missiles hit as we fly away.

They come as shrieks of light across the heavens, arcing down to earth in the city behind us. Flashes kindle the horizon, followed by tardy thunder that sets our hoverboard shuddering.

The missiles leave glowing streaks in their wake, until the sky is sliced to pieces. There's a smell like ozone and burned plastic. My eyes sting.

I try to breathe away the shock, to wrap my mind around my father's strategy.

The strikes are hitting the periphery of Victoria, focused on the factory belt. At least they're not destroying more of the city center—all that life and color, those fragile, hovering buildings.

"What's happening?" Col keeps asking in disbelief. None of this makes sense to him. This is not normal.

When we're far enough away from Victoria, I ease to a halt over the dark trees and turn to face him, the board unsteady beneath us.

"Aribella was right—your family's forces were stronger than my father expected. So he hit back where you were most vulnerable. It's what I tried to say yesterday. He always escalates."

Col drags his eyes from the spectacle behind us, faces me.

"*This* is what you meant? An attack on the city? On my *family*? You didn't say anything about . . ."

He flings out an arm at Victoria. A dozen columns of smoke rise from its periphery, but none as high as the black tower rising from its center.

House Palafox, now smoke and dust.

I don't want to see it. But even when I close my eyes, the traces of missiles are burned into my vision.

"It's always the same, Col. Back home, the newsfeeds thought they could report what was happening, until he shut them down. The elected council thought they were in charge, until they weren't. His allies thought they could pull him back if he went too far. But he astounds *everyone*."

"That was all in Shreve." Col turns to face his home again. "No one's done anything like *this* in three hundred years!"

It's true. No one's bombed a population center since the Rusties. The first families never attack one another directly.

"The unthinkable is what he's best at, Col."

"My mother." His voice drops away.

"The attack started out in the ruins." I sound like I'm trying to convince myself. "She might have been headed there."

"Maybe. But Abuela wouldn't have left home."

Grandmother, my father whispers in my ear.

"We don't know anything yet, Col."

He turns on me, suddenly pleading. "But *you* were there too! Why would he risk killing you?"

"To show that he could."

Col just stares at me. There's no way he can understand all this at once. It's taken me sixteen years to see how my father's mind works.

But I try to explain.

"He wanted to show the world that nobody can win against him, no matter what cards they hold. Proving that he could throw me away was just as important as taking the ruins."

As I speak, my chest tightens. The spreading smoke is catching up with us.

"The other cities will fear him even more now. They'll know there's no weapon he won't use. No one he won't hurt."

Something clicks in Col's stunned expression.

"My little brother—we have to warn him!"

I look back at the burning city. The wind is stretching the columns of smoke inland toward the mountains, angling their shape. Like a host of vast black anvils has dropped from the sky.

"He knows already, Col. This will be on all the feeds."

"But Teo needs to know that he's not safe. And that I'm still alive!"

Col is shaking, and I take hold of his arms.

"He's at a boarding school, right? How many other important families send their kids there?"

"I don't know. A hundred?"

I hold him tighter. "My father can't attack a place like that. He wants the other cities divided. Nothing will unify them like their own children getting hurt."

Col steadies himself. "So there's a limit."

"He can't have the whole world turn on him at once." My voice rasps from the smoke.

There's a pause. Col is staring at me.

"How can you think this way? How can you even begin to understand him?"

I don't have an answer for that. But my brain is still whirring.

To the rest of the world, my father risked his only daughter. But even if I never make it home, he's still got Rafi. He can reveal her in a day or so. Concoct some story about her daring escape. Yet another chance to prove that he always wins.

This was all a dreadful magic trick—a city aflame, the Palafoxes dead, but his own daughter appears.

But first he has to wait to see if I'm okay. If two identical daughters show up, the story of his victory gets messy.

And that's when I realize—I have a small measure of power over my father.

He doesn't know I'm alive. There must be some way to use this. But only if I stay hidden instead of going home.

The smoke is getting thicker. Ash flutters down around us.

"We should keep moving," I say.

Col looks out into the darkness. "Where?"

I shake my head. All I know is that I'm not going to the ruins. There will be no rescue by my father's forces. No triumphant return home for his brilliant warrior-daughter.

The leash around my neck is gone.

TRUST ME

"You told me something," Col says. "Right before the missile hit my house."

I look up from the fire. It's the best we could do—a pile of damp leaves and twigs that it took us ages to light. The night is cold, and we're still wet, though the rain has stopped. Neither of us has spoken in an hour.

"I don't remember." All I know is, he was kissing me just before the missile hit. Something was flickering to life between us, but my father's atrocity has torn it all away.

Col's gaze is sharp in the firelight. Tears have left streaks in the smoke and ash on his face.

"You said, 'They'll pick me up at the ruins.' You had an escape plan worked out with your father."

I take a shuddering breath, then nod.

"And all this stuff." Col points at what's left of my escape kit—the firestarter, the plastic bags collecting rain from the dripping trees. "Do you always have a getaway bag ready?"

"When I'm a hostage? Yes."

His expression doesn't soften. Now that the shock has sunk in, he's had time to wonder how much I knew about my father's plans.

Something starts to crumble inside my chest.

Col is all I have left. If he stops trusting me, neither of us will survive.

"You got onto the roof so fast," he says. "Wide awake and ready to run. You knew the attack was coming, didn't you?"

There's no way through this but the truth.

"Aribella was right about my cyrano." I take it out of my pocket. The metal glows dully in the firelight. "It scans for hidden messages in Shreve's public feeds, encoded in the pixels. A warning came, telling me to run."

"Kill it," Col says.

I stare at the cyrano.

There's no city interface out here, and it's not like I need etiquette tips. But the device is my last link to Rafi. There's no other way for her to get a message to me. No more warnings. No more advice from my big sister.

But every second I hesitate costs me Col's trust.

I drop the cyrano in the fire.

For the first time in my life, Rafi and I are truly separated.

And yet, as the smell of burned circuitry rises up, relief floods through me. My father's voice is gone from my ear forever.

I've traded my sister for freedom.

Col still stares at me like an enemy. "So why didn't you warn us?"

"They only gave me two minutes' head start."

He shakes his head. "Two minutes? Why would they cut it so close?"

"Because . . ."

I wore the red jacket. A game between me and my sister, while my father was planning murder.

But it's too unbelievable, that I'm a spare daughter, nothing but a decoy. That having a crush on Col meant I could be thrown away.

As unbelievable as the fact that two hours ago Col was kissing me, and now he thinks I betrayed him.

Something turns hard in my throat.

"My father couldn't risk an earlier warning. If you caught me trying to run, you might guess what was coming."

Col looks down into the fire. "Or maybe you wanted everything to happen exactly as it did."

"What do you mean?"

"The whole time you were in my home, Rafia, you weren't your usual self. You were someone I could be friends with. You gained my trust. And once the attack was on its way, you got us both to safety just in time." Col looks around at the darkness.

"And now we're out here alone, a hundred klicks from my city's forces."

"Col, helping me escape was *your* idea! You showed me those bungee jackets on the roof!"

He leans back from the fire, his expression unchanged.

Logic doesn't matter. He doesn't trust me anymore.

"Your father," he says, then spits into the fire. "He wants to wrap this war up quickly, right? That's much easier if you bring me to him. A hostage, so the rest of my city surrenders. A puppet to put in charge of Victoria."

"Never." I reach out and take his hand. "I knew about the attack *two minutes* before you did. All my prep was just in case something went wrong. And I never thought he'd . . ."

Kill your mother. Your grandmother.

Destroy your home.

Set your city on fire.

Col pulls his hand away from me, and my heart tears a little.

There's only one way to convince him.

I point two fingers, and the pulse knife jumps up from beside me. It hovers in the air, trembling and eager, aimed at his face.

Ready to kill.

"Col. If I really wanted to take you to my father, do you think I'd have to *trick* you?"

He stares straight at the knife, like he doesn't care what happens next. Like he's daring me to turn him into mist.

But then he says, "Save the battery. I forgot the pulse charger."

I close my fist, and the knife drops back to the ground.

My nightshirt feels cold and damp. A few cactus spines are still caught in it—all that remains of House Palafox's gardens. That jungle full of life. Those butterflies.

We sit there in silence, until I gather the nerve to ask . . .

"Do we still have an alliance? Or do you think I killed your family?"

He's silent, thinking. The leaves are dripping. The wet wood in the fire hisses softly.

I can't just sit here, so I move toward him across the darkness. But I don't know how to do this—how to touch someone this way. I don't know anything.

When my trembling hand falls on his shoulder, he flinches. A sob racks his body.

"There must have been *something* I could've done to stop this. But I made it worse by trusting you."

"This isn't your fault, Col." My sister's mantra.

"I should have *forced* my mother to listen—"

"It's not her fault either. It's him. It's always him."

Col starts to shiver, and I pull him closer to the fire. My workout sweats have wicked away the rain, but his clothes are still wet.

I look up—no stars, no moon, no aircraft. Just the choking darkness of a city burned and thrown into the air.

Too much smoke for anyone to see our little fire. I grab the last handful of the kindling and throw it on the pile. It hisses like a wet, angry cat.

"They must think we're dead," Col says. "We should keep it that way."

I hold his gaze across the fire. It's a good idea, but there's one problem.

Rafi's still at home, safe and sound. Once my father is certain that I'm dead, he'll reveal her to the world—and Col will know I was always an impostor, sent to make his family drop their guard.

He'll know I've been lying to him all along.

But I can't tell him the truth about myself tonight. His world is already shaken enough.

"Good idea," I say.

"If he thinks I'm dead, your father won't look for me. We can move easier if we aren't being hunted."

"Move? Where are we headed, anyway? Is there someone who can protect you?"

"I don't want protection. I want revenge."

A surge of exhaustion rises in me. Col still hasn't learned that with my father, there is no winning.

"Listen, Col. Whatever military Victoria has left, it's not enough to beat him. You'll only get more of your people killed!"

"I know," he says.

"The other first families won't help either. They'll feel sorry for you, and they'll embargo Shreve for a while. Someone might give you asylum, as long as you keep your head down. But no city will risk all-out war with him!"

"Then I'll work with people who have no cities. Who've always hated him. And who already have their own army."

I shake my head. "Who the hell is that?"

Col leans back from the fire and gives me a cold smile.

"I'm going to join the rebels."

OVERKILL

The next morning, I'm watching Col sleep.

He's curled in on himself. The fire is spent and my clothes, my hands, and the inside of my head all smell like smoke. And yet the sky is blue, finally clear of smoke from the attack on Victoria.

It's weird, but even after everything that's happened, I'm still thinking about our kiss. It was my first real kiss. And that look in his eyes . . .

He'll never look at me that way again. Or trust me. Not once he finds out that I was at the center of my father's plans against his family.

Col doesn't even know my real name. And every time I think about telling him, I think of Sensei Noriko, which is enough to shut my mouth.

Still, we need to have this conversation soon, before the real Rafi shows up in the feeds.

"Let's kill a rabbit," Col says when he wakes up.

"Sounds good." Finding the rebels might take a while, and I'm starving.

We drink our rainwater, pack up our meager camp, and hike to the edge of the forest. We leave the hoverboard out in the sun, its solar panels unfolded.

Col leads me along the boundary between trees and prairie, his hunting bow in his hand. We keep to the forest shadows, peering out into the tall sunlit grass.

"There are two kinds of rabbits here," he says, somehow still a tour guide. "The ones with small ears are volcano rabbits. Not enough fat to be worth eating."

"*Volcano* rabbits? Really?"

Col shrugs. "Nature doesn't care what you call it. We're hunting the cottontails—the ones with big ears."

"Okay. But this is your show. My knife doesn't do rabbits."

"Too slow?"

I snort. "It can break the sound barrier. But it's overkill—unless you know how to cook rabbit mist."

He gives the knife a look. "What's that thing actually *for*?"

"For when people try to kill me. If I have to get out of a room, it cuts through a wall. If I need cover, it turns furniture into dust clouds."

"No wonder Jefa had it locked up." Col's eyes go from the knife to me. "How do you know so much about ancient weapons?"

There's no answer for that except the truth.

"I know about *all* weapons, Col. I've been learning how to kill since I was seven."

He looks at me. "Did you say *seven*?"

"Years old, yeah."

And I can tell from his eyes—the way he sees me just changed.

Col knew right away that I wasn't the temperamental socialite of Rafi's feeds. He liked me because I was someone unexpected, someone who'd tricked the whole world. But now he's seeing a deeper me—the trained killer—and I'm starting to scare him.

"After I join the rebels, where will you go?" he asks out of nowhere.

I stare at him. "What do you mean?"

"There's no way the rebels will trust you, Rafi. Because of who you are."

"Who *I* am? Your family has been at war with them for years!"

"They never tried to kill me."

I take a slow breath. Going to sleep last night, I kept thinking about that—Col wants to join the people who attacked my convoy only two weeks ago.

"Maybe they were waiting for the right time. Are you *sure* you want to join them, Col?"

He shrugs. "It won't be easy, getting them to trust me. But there must be Victorian forces out here, still loyal to my family, still ready to fight. The rebels and I can help each other."

Without Col, I have nowhere to go . . . except home.

"But we agreed to be allies," I say.

He turns away, embarrassed.

"That was back when I thought our parents were trying to set us up. This is deadly serious. The rebels will believe that I hate your father, Rafi, because of what he did to my family. But why would they trust *you*?"

"Because I'm . . ." Not Rafi. But my lips won't say the words.

I don't know what will happen when I unleash this secret. Do I really exist outside of this lie?

"Because you're a trained killer?" Col shakes his head. "That's just another reason not to let you get too close."

"But I'm not—" Even thinking the words makes me start to unravel. "I'm really—"

Col's hand goes up for silence. He's staring into the forest, and I can hear the faintest stirring of the leaves.

"Jaguar," he whispers.

I close my mouth, relieved. A wild predator seems safer than telling him the truth.

"The Rusties almost wiped out the big cats," he says softly. "But they're everywhere now."

"So it's okay to eat one?"

Col gives me a pained look. "Really?"

"What? We're starving!"

"People don't eat cats, Rafi. How do you not know that?"

I shrug. My father eats what he wants. Whether or not it's on the menu. Or the endangered list.

"We follow it," Col explains. "It's probably stalking something we *can* eat."

We push along the edge of the forest. Col moves in perfect silence, but I'm clumsy and loud. I've been trained to fight in ballrooms, tight corridors, and stairways, but not the wild.

Col comes to a halt, and the bow unfolds in his hand. Its nanotech polymers spread like wings; the string shivers taut. He stares out into the grassland, at something I can't see.

When I switch to heat vision, a white blob twitches out there against the sun-warmed rocks. The rabbit's ears stick up like antennae.

In the cooler forest to our right, the sinuous curve of the jaguar lurks on a branch. It's watching us, probably wondering if we're a threat.

How deadly are these big cats? I know in theory that the wild can kill you, but no animal is worse than an assassin with a barrage pistol.

Then I remember the snake, invisible and almost silent, and I shudder.

Beside me, Col notches an arrow. Then he stands there unmoving for endless seconds.

When he strikes, it's all one motion—drawing the bow, aiming, letting the arrow fly. It flits through the tall grass, and an instant later the cottontail explodes into motion, its hind legs scrabbling. But it's like a pinned insect, the fluttering taking it nowhere.

As Col runs forward, I turn to watch the jaguar, my knife ready. But it's already disappearing deeper into the trees, graceful and unhurried.

I switch off my heat vision and catch up with Col as he's breaking the rabbit's neck. He holds the limp body up by its ears, a look of satisfaction on his face.

"I don't have anything to skin this," he says. "Can that weapon cut like a regular knife?"

"It's not very sharp when it's turned off. But sure."

Col looks up into the sky. "Think we can risk a fire?"

I close my eyes and listen. Last night, we fell asleep to booms in the distance—explosions, gunfire, suborbitals entering the atmosphere. But today is silent, the Victorians either defeated or in hiding.

My father must think we're dead, or that I'm headed toward the ruins on foot, hoping to be rescued. He has no reason to look for me this far down the coast.

And my stomach is rumbling now.

"Might as well," I say. "Unless you want to eat it raw."

CONFESSION

"This is amazing, Col."

The rabbit really is good. It's harder to chew than vat-grown meat, but the flavor is more intense. Even the smell of it cooking was hungry-making, fire smoke and charred flesh.

I just wish we had some salt. And that I hadn't burned my tongue on the first bite.

"*La faim est la meilleure sauce,*" Col says.

More French, but it's an opportunity. Maybe if I tell the truth about myself slowly, it won't be so hard.

"I don't know what you just said, Col."

Halfway through a bite, he looks up at me. His fingers shine with grease, and there's blood on his shirt from skinning the rabbit.

"'Hunger is the best sauce'? You've never heard that before?"

"Not the proverb—I don't know French. I've been faking it."

He laughs. "Stop it, Rafi. I've watched your appearances in Montré. You're practically fluent."

"Not really," I say. "You see, studying French takes time away from learning to kill people."

Col chews thoughtfully. "I don't know why you're saying this, but I've seen you. No cyrano is that good. *Tu parle français.*"

Maybe this is a bad idea, revealing my lies to get him to trust me. But they're all I've got. My deceptions are only things that are really mine.

Just tell him.

Was that Rafi's voice inside me? Or my own?

And what if telling Col the truth dooms him, like it did Sensei Noriko?

Tell him everything.

"There are two of me," I whisper.

The world tips sideways, but somehow doesn't break apart.

Col just nods. "No kidding. There's you in the feeds, and the real you."

I swallow. "Right. But I mean literally."

He gives me a sympathetic look. "I think I know what you mean."

"I don't think you do, Col." Anger is building in me now. This is hard enough without him being a bubblehead. "There are *two* of me. I have a twin sister."

He still doesn't understand.

"She's real," I say. "A separate person."

Col looks away again, thoughtful. He tears a last piece of flesh from the rabbit's leg. Swallows it. Drops the bone into the fire.

Finally, he holds his hands out for calm. "Okay."

"That's it? 'Okay'?"

"I get it."

I stare at him. "Get *what*?"

"What it must be like, being you. Your mother dead before you were conceived. Tutors instead of school. A bubble of drones and bodyguards around you. And at the center of it all, a father like *him*."

My anger sputters. I have no idea what Col's babbling about.

"And that's only the start," he continues. "My mother told me about the body scans, Rafi, what your trainers must have done to you. And being taught to use that *abomination*."

He gestures at the pulse knife lying next to me.

I speak through clenched teeth. "What does that have to do with my sister?"

Col looks away, like he's embarrassed again.

"Growing up under threat, unable to walk around in your own city. That dust watching you. No privacy—but always alone. It must play tricks on your mind."

"Holy crap," I say. "You think Rafi's some kind of *delusion*?"

"Let me point out that *you* said that word, not . . ." He stares at me, frowning. "Wait. Her name's Rafi too?"

"*Yes*. I mean, no—mine *isn't*!"

166

I look up at the sky and let out a scream, which probably doesn't help my case. But there's no going back now.

"My name is Frey! We are two *different* people and thus have different names! She's the one you saw on the feeds. The one who speaks French and knows how to design dresses. The one who's smart and witty and knows which fork to use!"

I throw my rabbit leg into the fire, where it sputters hot grease.

"*I'm* the barbarian! The one who doesn't know anything except killing with ancient weapons. The one who's stupid enough to fall for a spoiled, smug bubblehead like *you*!"

My rant comes to a ragged halt. My throat hurts from yelling. And there's a shrieking in my head.

"Rafi," Col says softly. "It's okay."

"I'm not Rafi. And it's never okay."

He gently takes my hand, and the need to yell at him lifts a little.

But the shrieking is still there in my head.

Because it's not in my brain. It's out in the real world.

A shadow flickers over us, and at last I recognize the sound.

"Hovercar," I say. "Run for the trees."

FRIENDLY FIRE

I can't see the car overhead, just the smoke from our fire.

Carried by the wind from the coast, the telltale column stretches away to the west, a massive sign saying *Come get us.*

Hunger made me foolish.

I dash for the cover of the forest, calling the pulse knife to my hand.

Col's running back toward where we left the hoverboard to recharge. But its solar panels are open—it'll take him thirty seconds before he can make it flyable.

As I reach the trees, the hovercar roars into view. Its lifting fans churn leaves, dirt, and embers from our fire into a maelstrom. For a moment I can't see or breathe.

When the whirlwind passes, I look up. The hovercar is banking into a hard turn—it's spotted me. The camo skin is set to Shreve combat livery, gray and black.

A saucer-shaped scout craft, it's much smaller than the machines that brought me to Victoria. Only three crew, but armed with a pair of heavy kinetic guns. Its armor will stop my pulse knife cold.

One gun is training on me. The other turret swings along the forest, tracking Col.

I drop my pulse knife and raise my hands up high.

"Wait!" I scream into the roar of the lifting fans. "It's me!"

They can't open fire—Col and I are dressed in civilian clothes. My father's forces must still be searching for Rafi.

The barrel of the gun aligns with my eyes, until I'm staring into blackness. I know the stats—solid tungsten rounds, fifteen centimeters across, delivered at Mach 4.

The trees behind me will be sawdust. I'll be water vapor tinged with DNA.

The machine hovers a moment longer, dust wreathing around me, and my mind feels like it's a thousand klicks away. Like I'm looking down on a dream.

Then a voice crackles through loudspeakers.

"Miss Rafia. Please take cover."

They want me to get down so they can open fire on the forest. They think Col ran because he was keeping me prisoner.

"No!" I yell, moving sideways, putting myself in front of the gun tracking him. "Hold your fire!"

The machine wobbles a little, uncertain. The crew can't hear me in there, not over the engine roar.

A hatch irises open on the bottom, and two soldiers drop to the grass. They roll to absorb the shock of landing and come up with rifles leveled.

But not at me.

I get in the way again, try to yell over the roar of lifting fans. "Stop! He's a friend!"

One of them frowns at me, lowering her weapon, but the other's still sighting into the forest. His rifle's airscreen glimmers with a target.

I run straight into the whirlwind beneath the hovercar, and the man hesitates just long enough . . .

My fist catches his jaw. I yank the rifle from his hands, spinning around to jab its stock into the other soldier's face. She falls while he's still stumbling. I kick at his knee from the side, something snaps, and he goes down screaming.

I swing the rifle again, connecting solidly with his head. A few seconds later, neither of them are moving.

The hovercar is right over us. The big guns are still pointed into the trees.

At my gesture, the pulse knife rises up from the ground. It zooms past me into the hatch, set to a corkscrew pattern. Maybe it won't hit the pilot at full pulse.

The craft starts to shudder, wobbling above me like a top at the end of its spin. About to fall on me.

This was not my best plan.

I drop flat between the fallen soldiers, hands over my head, eyes shut. The tempest stages around me, then reels away—I look up.

The hovercar is slewing off into the trees. Whole branches disappear into the lifting fans, spewing out as wood chips and shredded leaves. The car cracks into a thick, old trunk. One fan comes down on a young tree, and its engine jams with a metal squeal.

The other three fans keep spinning, flipping the craft over and driving it top-first into the ground. Leaves and dust geyser up from the forest.

With a final grinding rattle, the machine goes silent.

I stand up, blinking, my ears ringing with the silence.

The soldier lying beside me groans. I pull the zip ties off her belt and bind their wrists, steal their medpacks, then shoulder one of the rifles.

I'm headed for the downed hovercar when a call comes from the air.

"Rafi!"

I turn to face Col, gliding up on the hoverboard. His eyes are wide at the destruction all around me.

"You couldn't just *run*?" he asks.

"Had to stop them from shooting you. You're welcome." I glance back at the bound soldiers and drop my voice. "And it's Frey."

"Okay, sure," he says, in his new Rafi-has-delusions voice. "But we should get out of here."

I point at the downed hovercar. "We should check on the pilot first."

Also, my pulse knife is in there somewhere.

TRANSMISSION

The hovercar sits among the trees, upside down and slantwise against an uprooted trunk. The lifting fans are motionless, ticking as they cool.

The hatch is on top of the machine now. I climb onto Col's hoverboard so he can fly me up. Leaves are still fluttering to the ground around us. At least a dozen trees are damaged.

So is the hovercar's camo skin. It keeps changing patterns randomly, from dappled forest to sky blue to parade colors.

I jump down onto the slanted armored hull, crawl to the hatch, and stick my head in.

"Hello?"

No answer.

"It's me, First Daughter Rafia. Don't shoot!"

"So that *is* your name," Col says.

"I'll explain later." I hand him the rifle and crawl inside.

The cabin lights are off, and all I can see is a jumble of wires, equipment, and fire-suppression foam. In a few spots, the pulse knife has stripped away everything down to the armored hull.

Most of the cabin is in darkness. My eyes adjust slowly.

"Anyone in here?"

Still nothing. But I hear a *drip, drip, drip.*

I've never been inside this tiny a scout car. It's about half the size of one of Rafi's closets. As I crawl, something jabs my knee—a sharp little rectangle of plastic.

A handscreen. Ruggedized for military use, with a satellite antenna to get signal out here in the wild.

I switch it on—a newsfeed from home. War footage that I don't want to see, but the screen's glow illuminates the tiny cabin.

The pilot's in front, still strapped into his seat. He's hanging upside down, unconscious.

Then I realize what the dripping sound is—blood trickling from his forehead. It could be a minor cut . . . or a concussion, his brain swelling in his skull. The iron smell fills my head.

I reach up to the control panel and switch on the cabin lights. He doesn't wake up.

If I unstrap him, he'll fall and crack his head against the hull armor. But I can't just leave him hanging here.

First things first. My pulse knife is somewhere in this wreckage. I splay my fingers, hoping it can see me in the glow of the handscreen.

There's a scrabbling sound, like a rat in the wires, and hot metal jumps into my hand.

The knife's blade is scored from bouncing around the inside of the hull, but it can still fly. I'm more worried about its battery light blinking yellow.

I crawl back out of the hatch, give the handscreen to Col.

"The pilot's hurt, maybe bad. How much juice does that hoverboard have?"

"Not a lot. About a hundred klicks before we have to recharge."

"That's far enough. I'm going to turn on the ship's distress beacon. Be ready to *move*."

"Why?" Col asks.

"Because once the beacon goes off, their backup will be on its way!"

He takes a slow breath. "I meant, why call for help? That pilot is part of an army that just murdered my family."

I stare back at Col, and for a moment I understand what he sees when he looks at me, trained to kill since the age of seven. That darkness in his eyes must also be in mine.

But soldiers wearing the uniform of Shreve have protected me and my sister our whole lives.

"Col. Have you ever heard of *just following orders?*"

"Yes. It's an old Rusty phrase, meaning *a crappy excuse for war crimes.*"

"So we just leave him here to die?" I gesture at the other two. "You want to shoot them too? They recognized me. That messes up your plan to stay hidden, doesn't it?"

"Good point." Col looks down at the rifle in his hands. It's still in fire mode, the airscreen glowing.

He raises it, aiming straight at the bound soldiers sixty meters away.

"Col," I say.

Maybe I could stop him. But my reflexes won't engage. All that exquisite battle calculus in my head refuses to add up.

Col is a problem I can't solve with my fists.

So I say, "That's exactly what my father would do."

He hesitates, then swears under his breath, lowers the rifle. "Hit the switch. I'll be ready."

"You'll thank me." I can still see the assassin some nights. Those legs just standing there after my knife burned away the rest of him.

I climb back down into the hovercar, trying not to smell the pilot's blood.

Now that the cabin lights are on, I see a medpack stuck to the bottom of his seat. A quick spurt of medspray to his forehead makes me feel better.

The emergency beacon is a rocker switch on the control panel. It starts blinking red when I give it a flick.

Scrambling back out of the hatch, I yell, "Let's move!"

"Wait." Col is staring at something in his hands.

The screen. The tinny sounds of newsfeed. Triumphant music, an exuberant announcer.

"What the hell, Col?" I jump up onto the hoverboard behind him. "We have to *go!*"

"But they just said . . ." He looks up, stares, like he doesn't recognize me.

Then his eyes drop back to the screen.

"Holy crap," he says. "There's two of you."

REVEALED

There's no time to talk, not with the rescue beacon blaring.

We ride hard and fast, keeping beneath the treetops, weaving through trunks and branches. Heading inland toward the mountains and the rebels.

I wonder what happens when we reach them. Col was right before—the rebels wouldn't let First Daughter Rafia join up, not in a hundred years.

But Frey? Maybe she has something to offer.

I don't know anymore.

Col is just as confused as me. When we stop to rest, he doesn't say much, or meet my eye. And I remember what Rafi always told me growing up . . . *This isn't normal.*

She meant that my father was wrong to hide me. That I didn't deserve to have my existence erased. But my sister's words also taught me what a freak I was.

That must be how Col sees me now—as some kind of aberration. Like a littlie lost in the forest and raised by wolves. Weird and tragic. Probably dangerous.

Of course, the whole world is dangerous now.

When hovercars glimmer in the distance, forcing us to hide, they're always in Shreve colors, not Victorian. My father has won. The only signs of resistance are wisps of smoke on the horizon.

It doesn't help that all the food in my escape kit is gone. Rabbits dot the forest floor, but we can't risk another fire. So we're hungry, exhausted, and Col keeps backtracking. He's looking for something, but he won't say what.

He doesn't trust me anymore.

I thought when he learned my secret, he would understand the ally I could be. But instead, he doesn't even know who I am.

The hoverboard is almost out of charge when he finally finds the perfect spot to land in, a long stretch of clearing with plenty of sun.

We unfold the solar panels and sit under a tree. We'll be stuck here for a while. Nothing to do but talk about what comes next.

But instead Col picks up the handscreen.

"Don't bother checking," I say. "What you saw was real. There's another version of me back in Shreve. The genuine Rafi."

He turns the screen on anyway, stares at it for a moment.

"Here's what I don't get," he says. "Why isn't the whole Shreve army out here looking for us? The soldiers back there saw your face."

I shrug. "Maybe nobody believed them? The army doesn't know there's two of me."

"Two of you," Col mutters at the screen, then looks up. "How did they hide you all this time?"

It takes a moment to answer. Telling these secrets feels like pulling my own teeth. But I need Col to understand the truth of me.

"There are special hallways in my father's house, just for me. Limos with hidden sections, private suites in all the clubs and hotels. Only about a dozen people ever saw me and Rafi together."

"But *why*?"

"To keep her safe. She only appears in places where we trust everyone. Anytime she had to go out into a crowd of randoms—public speeches, ceremonies, dancing at nightclubs—it was always me instead."

"All that trouble . . ." Col looks down at the screen again. "So he really does love her, doesn't he?"

"It's more than that. He lost our brother to kidnappers, and he hates to lose."

For a moment, Col looks ill. "And we thought we were safe with you under our roof."

"You weren't."

Col doesn't answer.

"You can blame me for all of it." I need to say this out loud, so it doesn't keep echoing in my head. "Losing your home. Your family. It happened because of *me*."

Maybe I'm expecting Col to argue. But he doesn't say a word.

So I keep talking into the silence.

"I didn't know how to warn you. I've never had to tell anyone about this before. Back home, there was never anyone I *could* tell, without them . . ." My voice falters. This isn't the right time to explain about Sensei Noriko, how knowing my secret can kill someone. "I really didn't think he'd sacrifice me."

"Your sister looks so happy." His eyes are glued to the screen.

My stomach clenches. "Rafi plays her role well. Always."

"But she must think you're dead. And she's *smiling*."

He holds up the screen for me to see.

I turn away. I don't want to see Rafi act the part of the triumphant, resourceful daughter. Or think about what she's feeling now.

I'd rather imagine her tantrum when my father told her I was dead. I hope she hit him, even if she can't throw a punch to save her life.

Col turns on the volume, and the tinny sound of crowds and martial music fills the air. His eyes narrow, and he glances from me to the screen, like he's comparing our faces.

I get up and walk away.

The world is spinning under me. I've escaped my father but lost everything else—my home, my sister, my city. My only ally doesn't know what to think of me.

What am I supposed to do now? Start my own army?

It was much easier being a secret. I only had to worry about half a life.

A rush of sound fills the air, and I almost dive for cover. But it's just wind in the leaves.

Col chose this forest clearing well. It lets sunlight down for the board's panels, but any aircraft would have to pass straight overhead to spot us.

But it's odd how long and narrow the clearing is. Too straight to be natural.

I kneel to take a closer look, and find an ancient layer of perma-crete below the shallow topsoil. So that's why trees don't grow here. This was some kind of Rusty construction.

I remember my warfare tutor explaining that most ancient aircraft couldn't hover—they needed "runways" to take off and land. The clearing is at least a kilometer long, a typical Rusty waste of space.

But if aircraft landed here, some kind of ruin must be close.

I walk back to Col.

"Do you know about any—"

"I need to ping my brother." He holds up the handscreen. "To tell him I'm alive. Can I use this?"

I take a slow breath, reminded that Col has bigger things to worry about than me. I'd love to let my own sister know I'm okay.

"Sorry, Col. But that's Shreve military issue. If you send a message with it, they'll find us."

He swears, his grip tightening on the screen. "It's locked on your city's propaganda feeds. Which are brain-missing! They're saying my mother threatened to hurt you. Like destroying my home was some kind of *rescue mission*."

"It's not about logic, Col. It's just how things work there."

He sighs. "I know. We spent months studying your city. The newsfeeds do whatever they're told."

"It's more than that. People in Shreve fear my father, but they *love* Rafi. For a whole night, everyone thought she was dead— that they were left with just *him*. They're so happy she's alive, they'll believe anything."

"That's what our psych team said." Col looks up from the screen. "Everyone in Shreve knows he's a murderer. But when

Rafi stands next to him, he's also a *father*. She's what makes him human."

I have to turn away. The truth of that lives in my bones, but I've never heard anyone say it out loud before.

"So what if everyone finds out there's *another* Rafi?" Col goes on. "A daughter he threw away? With a dozen glued-together bones from training to be killer?"

I remember the pity on Aribella's face when she told me about the body scans.

Not normal.

But Col's face is lighting up.

"Then he's not a father anymore. We could hurt him. Show everyone that he's . . ." He pauses. "Are you okay?"

I shake my head. It's hard to breathe.

When Rafi goes to a party, thousands of people watch and comment on what she wears, who she talks to. How many eyes would land on me if I told the freakish truth about us?

Millions.

I'd melt away. Erased at last.

"It's just I've never told anyone this secret before, Col. And you're talking about telling the whole world."

"Oh. I didn't think . . ." His voice fades. He stands up, takes my shoulders.

The world steadies a little.

"It's your secret to tell," he says. "Not mine."

The words replay in my head—once, twice—until I understand them.

It's a promise not to throw me away.

I take a slow breath. "Why would you care, Col? After all my lies? After what my father did to you?"

"That's complicated," he says.

I look up at him. Does he mean there's still something between us? Even after everything?

"If you go public with the truth, it will hurt your father."

"I *want* to hurt him."

As I say the words, the old, familiar ecstasy twinges in me— the thrill of combat coming on. A trickle of hum in my veins, but this isn't about fighting.

For the first time in my life, I have something to wield beyond my fists.

The truth of me has power.

"When you're ready, I'll help you tell everyone," Col says. "I couldn't be sure about Rafi. But you and I still have an alliance, Frey."

I meet his eyes. This is the first time he's used my real name. The first time *anyone* has who I've given it to myself.

Which makes me ask—

"An alliance? Is that all this is?"

He looks away. "That's also complicated."

A sudden anger rushes through me.

"Of *course*, it's complicated, Col! You're the son of a cultured first family, and I'm a freak who's been hidden in secret passages her whole life. A killing machine! The daughter of—"

"It's not that, Frey. There's something I have to tell you, about that kiss."

I take a step back. "What do you mean?"

He hesitates a moment, shakes his head.

"First, let me show you why we're here."

BUNKER

He leads me toward the near end of the clearing.

"This used to be a Rusty airport," he says.

I remember his long, winding search for the perfect spot to recharge. "So you were looking for this place?"

Col nods, gestures down the runway. "We chose it because you don't need navigation equipment to find it. The missing strip of forest is obvious from the air."

"Chose it for what?" I ask.

Col doesn't answer, just leads me under the canopy of trees at the end of the clearing.

It's cool in here, despite the noon sun. When I flick on my heat vision for a moment, scurrying animals appear around us. Nothing big enough to be dangerous, but when I switch back to normal vision, my hand stays on the knife.

"Watch your step," he says. A steep decline has opened up before us.

We descend into what looks like a crater. Except the four sides are oddly straight, and craters aren't square.

"More ruins?"

"The foundation of a tower, part of the airport." Col wobbles on a loose piece of stone, steadies himself. "All the metal was stripped a century ago."

"But there's still something valuable down here?"

He looks back to give me another smile, then keeps going.

The walls of the crater are old and crumbling—not the safest climb. But it gives me time to think.

What does all this have to do with our kiss?

What did he mean, *That's complicated?*

At the bottom of the crater is a rectangular stretch of level ground, about the size of the Palafoxes' ballroom. The trees down in this darkness are spindly, as if trying to reach up for sunlight.

Col is looking for something.

"They only brought me here once, two years ago. So this might take a—"

He halts, stomps on the ground.

A hollow sound echoes.

It takes us five minutes to clear the door of fallen branches and leaves. It's made of some kind of camo-plastic.

"No metal at all." Col spreads his right hand on the lock. The plastic comes alive, lighting up. "We made sure this place was worthless to salvagers."

The door sighs open, revealing an empty square of blackness. A stale smell rises up, desiccant and anti-mold nanos.

"Lights," Col calls down.

He smiles again as they flicker on.

"Watch out," he says. "The ladder can be wobbly."

The bunker, as Col calls it, is about as big as my father's private swimming pool.

It has a low ceiling, made of the same plastic as the door. A dozen columns bear the weight of the forest overhead. They're made of real wood, still no metal.

This place is hidden well.

Shelves line the walls, stacked with plastic cases. Each one has a palm-print lock like the outer door.

"Let me guess—only Palafoxes can open these."

"And a few people we trust," Col says. He's scanning the labels on the cases, which are in some kind of code.

"So this is what your mother meant?" I ask. "When she said you had some surprises for my father."

"Part of it, yes."

I frown. "But you heard that from Yandre, who overheard your mom at the party. And you knew about this place two years ago."

Col shrugs. "Yes, *Frey*. I may have lied to you a few times."

I raise my hands in surrender. "Fair enough."

He pulls one of the cases from a shelf. It reads his palm and opens, revealing a disassembled weapon in packing foam.

"Tell me about this," he says.

I kneel beside the case, lift up the barrel. It's made of spacecraft ceramics. Light as cardboard, strong as hull armor.

"It's a spheromak plasma gun. Twenty megabars, one-shot hydrogen battery. Organic manganese magnets, so it won't show up on a metal detector."

"It says all that on the case, Frey. But what does it *mean*?"

"It spits out plasma rings. Knocks down hovercars." I look around the room—all those shelves. "Or buildings, if you had enough of them."

"Trust me, we do." Col looks up. "You think the rebels would be interested?"

"They'd be thrilled. Their problem's always been no hovercars, no heavy weapons." I shrug. "That's what you get for living in the wild."

Col leans back with a smile of satisfaction.

"You had all this stuff," I say. "So why didn't you fight the rebels on your own? Why bring my father into it?"

"Because when you hit the rebels, they just fade back into the wild." Col takes the barrel of the plasma gun from my hand. "Knocking them out for good means doing things that we didn't want to do. Like using these on human beings."

"Which my father was happy to do."

Col nods. "My family worries a lot about appearances. But the dirty work still gets done."

He's not showing me all this just to prove that the rebels will welcome him. This room has something to do with the two of us.

I sit cross-legged beside him on the cool cement floor.

"Why are we here, Col?"

"I want you to understand my family." He gestures at the row of cases. "*This* is who we are."

Each of these guns could take out one hoverstrut, a dozen of them sending a skyscraper crashing to the ground. Col might be disgusted by my pulse knife, but his family is hoarding enough firepower to wreck a city.

"You Palafoxes," I say. "You're like Rafi on the outside. But on the inside you're . . . *me.*"

Col speaks softly, clearly. "You have to understand, Frey. Victoria's a small city. To protect ourselves, we do things we don't want to do. I never wanted to deceive you."

I stare at him. "When, exactly?"

"Every second since you met me, Frey." He takes a slow

breath. "I always knew you were a hostage in my home. My mother and I had a plan for you, and pretending I was innocent was part of it."

"What?" My hands are shaking.

"Our kiss was part of it too."

COUNTERPUNCH

I can hear the words that Col just said. There's a recording of them playing over and over in my brain.

But they don't make sense.

He's staring at me, waiting for a response.

"You *knew* I was a hostage?"

He nods. "It was my idea."

My gaze drifts past him. The rows of weapons stretch into infinity.

I can't breathe.

"Your father's a monster," Col says. "He would always be a danger to our city. But we wondered if you, his heir, might be different."

"I'm not the heir," I manage. "She is."

"Of course. But we thought we were getting the real Rafi. So we decided to learn all about her." He leans back as he continues, and I realize something awful—he's using his tour guide voice. "When we started negotiations with your father, we sent newsfeed cams to cover your city. But they were really remote polygraphs, there to spy on Rafia. Whenever either of you appeared in public, they measured your pulse, blood pressure, galvanic response."

I stare at him, feeling like my skin is being stripped away.

"At the same time," he says, "we did a psych analysis of every recording we could find—back to when you were a littlie. Studied your eye movements, micro-gestures, vocal intonations."

I shake my head. "What did all that tell you?"

"That you started to break when you were seven."

"Seven?" My voice fades. "When I started training?"

"Exactly."

"What do you mean by *break*?"

"Sometimes you were confident, certain of yourself. Other times, you acted like someone overwhelmed by ongoing trauma. Our psych team assumed a split was forming in your personality. It never occurred to them that you were actually *two people*."

"A sane one and a crazy one." I close my fists to keep my hands from shaking.

"That's not a useful way to talk, Frey."

"Really?" I can't look at him. "What would *you* call it?"

"What they did to you was brutal. The broken bones. Having to hide all those years. Having no friends, and *him* as a father."

"So it's not just the bones—*I'm* broken too."

Col takes my hand, soothes it open.

"Frey. You're the healthy one."

I stare at him. "What?"

"When our team explained the psychic break, they focused on something called foreign language anxiety. People who speak a second tongue, even fluently, have hitches in their grammar when they're anxious—or when they're falling apart inside. When Rafia speaks French, she gives herself away."

I start to say that it's impossible. Rafi's the confident one. Brash and imperious. But then I hear her voice in my head.

This isn't normal.

What if she didn't mean me?

"This is what I think," Col says. "She had to watch it all happen—you being brutalized, hidden away. She couldn't protect you, her own sister."

"No. It's my job to protect *her*."

"Exactly. *You* had a purpose, Frey. When the assassin tried to kill Rafia, you could save her." He looks away. "But she could never save you."

My mind rushes back to that day. What Rafi said to me later . . .

I just sat there screaming.

The whole time. Just not out loud.

I turn to Col, a rush of anger coming over me.

"So you knew Rafi was sick? And you thought it was okay to *keep her as a hostage?*"

"To get her away from him! To show her what it's like to live with a real family, in a normal city!" Col spreads his hands. "Your father can't live forever, and she's his heir. We thought if I could make an alliance with Rafia, we could change Shreve someday, without a war."

An alliance. My heart beats sideways once.

"Your grandmother," I say. "That first day, when she told you to give me a tour . . ."

He looks down at the ground. "Abuela was never particularly subtle."

"And the story about your hunting bow?"

"A way to get you down to the monastery, where you'd feel safe talking to me. Where I could make friends with you."

Something hard is pulsing in my throat. I can't breathe.

He's the first person I've ever kissed.

And he was faking it.

Col takes both my hands now. "But you really were different from what I expected, Frey. I just didn't know *why.*"

I pull away and stand up too fast. My head spins, and I reach out to steady myself—my hand brushes one of the plastic cases full of death.

He's still talking. "When I kissed you, it was real."

It doesn't matter what he says now.

His mother, his grandmother—they were conspiring with Col the whole time. Laughing behind my back when I thought he was really my friend.

I'm a freak, from a family of freaks. I have only one purpose in this world.

"I have to go home. My sister is hurting, and I need to save her."

My head is still spinning as I weave down the aisle, shelves full of weaponry on either side. Col's calling after me, but I don't care and I can't trust him.

My feet hit the ladder. It wobbles under my weight as I haul myself up toward the smells of forest and life.

I have to get back to Shreve—now. My sister has no one but me and she thinks I'm dead.

"Frey!" Col calls from below.

Telling him my name was a mistake. Giving up my sister, my home, for him was madness.

I pull myself up and out through the door, sucking in fresh air. Dark branches crisscross the sky.

"Don't move!" comes a voice from the trees. "We don't want to hurt you, but we will if we have to."

CAPTURE

There are four of them.

Kneeling at the edges of the crater, rifles raised, they have me surrounded. Their sneak suits are invisible against the forest, but shimmers of body heat escape.

All I can see is anger and betrayal. I hurl my knife, sending it in a sweeping arc that will burn them to the ground. It roars to full pulse for a millisecond—

Then sputters and falls into the leaves, lifeless.

The battery is dead.

So am I.

But the soldiers don't open fire. They must think I was throwing the knife away in surrender.

"Hands in the air," one of them calls down.

I obey, looking for some kind of weapon on the forest floor.

There are only branches, leaves, rocks. Nothing to equal four rifles aimed at me from above.

"We know you have Col Palafox," the leader shouts. "Surrender him to us—*now*."

I look up at her. How do they know Col is here?

Then I hear a clambering on the ladder behind me.

"Stay down!" I hiss.

"Zura?" he calls up.

"Col!" she cries. "*¡Estás vivo!*"

She comes racing down the crater wall. When her suit flickers from forest camo to combat livery, I realize two things.

One: She's a Special, surgically modified beyond any normal soldier. No other kind of human could make that descent look so effortless. Specials were the lethal endpoint of pretty-regime surgery. Their muscles enhanced, their reflexes speeded up, their bones reinforced with duralloy. Their minds were made cold and hard, and their faces fashioned with a fearsome angelic beauty.

At the start of the mind-rain, Special surgery was illegal. But it seems everything is permitted now.

Two: She's not wearing Shreve colors, but the light blue of the Victorian army.

Behind me, Col hauls himself up the ladder.

As the Special runs across the broken ground, she pulls down her sneak suit hood. She has dark hair and surgery that makes her almost frighteningly beautiful. Col runs to meet her and they embrace, smiling and laughing. Spanish spills from their lips, too fast for me to grasp any meaning.

I look up at the other three soldiers. They're making their graceful way down, all of them with the uncanny, inhuman grace of Specials. Only one keeps his rifle pointed at me. They look a little tired, like they've been on the run since the attack began.

I figure they won't shoot me if I lower my hands.

Part of me doesn't care. Too much is tangled in my head—my sister's illness, Col knowing I was a hostage, his false kiss.

Suddenly every old break in my bones burns, as if all my damage is on fire. I can feel the scar over my eye and the dirt on my face. Nothing seems solid or real, not even the forest floor beneath me.

I want my knife, but it's fallen somewhere in the leaves.

My feet shuffle toward it, and I drop to my knees, sweeping the undergrowth with my hands. Searching for the only thing I still trust.

There it is, hard metal in my hand.

When I raise it up into the air, one of the soldiers is standing there, ready to shoot.

"*No!*" comes Col's shout through the spindly trees.

The man hesitates, and seconds later Col is there, putting himself between me and the leveled rifle.

"*¡Esta es mi amiga!*"

My brain churns through the half-understood words.

My friend.

More Spanish flows around me, explanations and confusions.

I sit there, staring at my knife. What would the soldiers do if I just walked away? I could take Col's hoverboard and fly home to save my sister.

Or would he let them shoot me?

"Frey." Col kneels before me. "It's okay. They're Victorian."

"I can see that."

He's beaming. "But they're getting orders from the codebook!"

I shake my head. He might as well be speaking French.

Col gathers himself, grasps my shoulders. He leans close, his words slow and careful.

"They think my mother is still alive."

Zura, it turns out, is the woman who taught Col how to shoot a bow and arrow.

She and the others are Victorian House Guard, elite commandos who were on patrol with my father's forces when his treachery began.

"One minute, we're hunting rebels together," Zura explains in accented English. "The next, they start shooting at us. We got away, but we couldn't find any other friendly units. And then . . ."

She pauses to give me a wary look. I may be dirty and disheveled, but I'm still wearing my sister's face.

Col has ordered them not to ask why I look so much like *la princesa Rafia*. They must think I'm a commando surged for some undercover mission.

"You can talk in front of Frey," he says. "I trust her."

"Frey," Zura repeats carefully. "Yes, sir. A few hours ago, we got a message from the book."

Col turns to me. "The codebook is the keys to the Victorian army. It drops hidden messages in the global feeds, which only our forces can read. There's only one book, and my mother keeps it with her—*always*. She must have gotten out that night!"

"Col," I say softly. "That's wonderful."

The anger in my veins has sputtered out, but nothing has replaced it. Like there's a battery in my heart, and it's spent from all this fear and fury and betrayal. I don't feel anything.

I just want to go home and save my sister.

"The orders gave us a code to transmit," Zura continues. "It turned on the tracker on your hoverboard. We couldn't believe it when we got a signal!"

"Jefa put a tracker on my board?" Col shakes his head, laughing. "She always said she'd never do that."

"Thank the saints she did," Zura says. "And she must've

202

been the only one who knew about it. Which means she *has* to be alive."

Col takes a slow breath. For a moment he looks almost anguished, as if this new hope is too much to bear.

I reach for his hand. "Never underestimate your mother, Col. You can take that from me."

There's bitterness in my voice, but a weight is starting to lift. Maybe a loss I've been blaming myself for never really happened.

"Do you know where the book is?" Col asks Zura.

She shakes her head. "All we have is a location, deep in the mountains, to take you to. Your mother must be there."

Col turns to me, his eyes alight.

"Frey, she's alive."

He's waiting for me to be happy, to see that our alliance is back on track. As if he hadn't just told me that he played with my emotions from the moment I set foot in his home.

I was deceiving them too. But I never lied to Col about how I felt.

Then something hitches in my brain, and I turn to Zura. "How much of the Victorian army is left?"

"You'd need the codebook to know that. But we've been prepared for a guerrilla war, in case Shreve got the jump on us. There must be dozens of units still out there."

"Then why isn't someone here already?" I ask.

The two of them stare at me.

I gesture at the hidden doorway. "There's enough firepower in that bunker to level a city. Why hasn't Aribella sent someone to collect those guns?"

Col looks stricken for a moment. As if I've told him his mother is dead again.

"My guess is," Zura says, "they simply aren't here yet. It's only been hours since we got our orders. But Frey's right—we should take what we can carry."

"Of course." Col stands, brushing aside my doubts. "We're wasting daylight. Let's load the car and go."

The Specials spring into motion, two of them heading down into the bunker. Zura turns back toward their hovercar, which is waiting up in the clearing.

When I don't follow, Col hesitates. "Frey, are you coming?"

I take a breath.

Ten minutes ago I wanted to fly back home and save my sister. To leave the Palafoxes and their sophistication, their hypocrisy, behind forever.

But I have no plan, no food or water, no chance of winning against the whole Shreve army.

And here I have allies. I have Col.

Or at least I thought I did.

"You can't lie to me anymore," I say. "You can't use psych profiles, or polygraphs, or scans. Don't treat me like someone you're trying to trick, or fix, or control. Okay?"

"I promise. And let me ask you something too." He takes a moment to choose his words. "From now on, Frey, show me who you really are."

"Of course," I say.

But an impostor is exactly what I am.

NEWSFEED

The commandos' car is a light attack craft, its skin set to jungle camo. It's swift and loaded with firepower, but the hull is pitted and scarred. I'm not sure how long it can keep flying without repairs and a battery charge.

The Palafoxes better have a hidden factory somewhere, with solar panels the size of soccer fields.

It's cramped here inside the car. Six people in a machine designed for four, along with a hoverboard and eight plasma guns—as many as we could fit. Two of the Specials squat in the back, giving up their seats for me and Col.

The pair of us are eating spagbol, self-heating survival food that my father wouldn't allow anywhere near his hunting lodge. But hunger really is the best sauce, and it's delicious. Even better is the clean water from the hovercar's taps.

The mountains are an hour's flying time away, but it's taking forever. Every few minutes we dip down into the trees, cowering whenever the radar shows a blip.

Creeping along like this was tedious on Col's hoverboard. Squished inside this tiny, damaged car, it's downright sickmaking. One of the lifting fans is damaged, so the car rides at an odd, wobbly angle.

But Col looks more hopeful than he has since we watched his home turn into a column of smoke.

His mother might be alive. He has a bunker full of weapons, an army prepared for a guerrilla war. Maybe the Palafoxes still have a chance in this fight.

Maybe they can still hurt my father. Maybe together we can save Rafi.

I wonder what she's doing now. Is she on some balcony, smiling and waving at the crowds? Screaming at my father? Crying in our room, thinking I'm dead?

Is she really falling apart?

It seems like nonsense, diagnosing someone from readouts captured by hovercams. Psychological warfare teams aren't doctors, after all. Rafi sounded so happy when she called and told me how to make my dress. Like she was smiling the whole time.

Of course, she was also smiling on that balcony half an hour ago, thinking I was dead.

Maybe I'm not the only impostor in the family.

We're heading west, and the hot sun fills the hovercar as the afternoon drags on.

The Specials have given Col a set of Victorian battle fatigues. The forest camo makes him look older, harder. I'm still in my sweats and bloody nightshirt.

He's staring at an airscreen in front of him, drinking in every word about the war.

"Looks like a soft takeover so far," he says to me. "No troops in Victoria. But the feeds and city interface are under Shreve's control."

"They'll spread spy dust soon," I say. "Then they won't need soldiers."

"The other cities have cut off trade, at least," Col says. "They've promised never to buy the metal from your father's stolen ruins."

"Doesn't matter," I say. "He can always use it himself. He wants Shreve to be the biggest city in the world."

Col lets out a curse in Spanish, and the soldiers all glance at him, then at me. They've all had old-style Special surgery—a cold beauty that makes me shudder.

They still don't trust me. Of course, I look exactly like their enemy's daughter. It wasn't until Col let out a burst of angry Spanish that they let me charge my pulse knife.

"No one's talking about a war to free us," Col says. "All those treaties . . ."

His voice breaks off. The soldiers all sit up straighter.

On the airscreen is a row of three young faces. The hovering text gives their names.

In the middle is Teo Palafox.

He looks like his older brother, but with darker skin and pale gray eyes. He wears a bored look, like a littlie forced to sit for a school picture.

Col waves a hand, and the volume comes up.

—sometime last night. The School of Genève is conducting an investigation, in cooperation with the Warden Consortium. Authorities are concerned that the unexplained disappearances are related to the attack on the city of—

Col waves away the sound, and his head falls back into the crash cushions of his seat. No one says anything. The soldiers are motionless except for Zura's hand on the flight stick.

"They took him," Col murmurs. "And two of his friends. I *know* those kids."

I reach out from the backseat, wanting to put a hand on his shoulder. But I don't know who I am right now.

His fellow warrior? The girl he kissed?

Or am I the impostor again, my father's agent in his house?

I wait until Teo's face is gone from the screen, then gently take Col's arm.

"I'm sorry."

"You said he was *safe*." His voice breaks. "That the other cities wouldn't let this happen, not at a school."

I want to argue that it doesn't make sense. That no fourteen-year-old boy is such a threat to my father that he'd risk allying the whole world against him.

But Teo Palafox is missing.

"I was wrong," I say.

My father makes his own reality. Sometimes with nightmares.

APPROACH

"Almost at the rendezvous point."

Zura's voice startles me awake, and it takes a moment to remember where I am.

Late-afternoon sunlight slants into the cramped hovercar. The air is scented with spagbol and self-brewing coffee. My shoulder aches where I've leaned against the straps of my seat.

Col looks unslept, exhausted. "Put us down ten klicks away. I want to approach on foot."

Zura frowns but doesn't question the order.

"You think this is a trap?" I ask.

"Your father's been a step ahead of us since the beginning," Col says. "Until we know who's got the codebook, I'm not trusting anything I can't see with my own eyes."

"Fair enough."

He turns away from me, his expression hard.

Col wept when he thought that Aribella was dead. But he hasn't shed a single tear about his missing brother. Maybe he can't cry in front of his soldiers.

Zura brings the hovercar down in a narrow gorge, where a stream has nurtured a clump of trees. For long seconds, we slew back and forth, hacking away the branches with our lifting fans.

I'm already motion-sick, and we don't need the room to land. This last bit of rocking makes me want to either throw up or punch someone.

After another sick-making minute, we're on the ground at last. When my hatch pops open, I jump down gratefully onto the hard earth.

Rocks scrabble under my feet. Scrubby grass climbs the walls of the gorge, and the sunset turns the distant mountains pink and orange.

I suck in gulps of fresh air.

While Col and Zura confer, the commandos hide the car under the broken branches—hence our slashing descent. I join in the work, happy for anything that stretches my cramped muscles.

It's hard not to stare at the commandos, they move with such uncanny grace and speed.

After a long day's training, I used to ache for surgery to make me faster, stronger. But I can see why my father never let me have it. These commandos look almost inhuman, as swift and twitchy as insects.

"So down this gorge, then north?" Col is saying. An airscreen map hovers between him and Zura, mountain passes marked in red.

"Right." Zura points at a ridge on the screen. "We'll need cover. A sniper rifle or two up here."

"A plasma gun," Col says.

She pauses to look at him. The cruel beauty of her surged face makes it clear she's unhappy.

"In case a hovercar comes at us," Col adds.

Still no response.

That's when I realize—they've been trained not to question the orders of the Palafox heir.

"Col," I say. "A plasma gun can take down a cliff. You don't want one pointed in your direction, even by someone on your side."

He gives this a moment's thought, as if there's any question, then nods.

"Rifles, then. But you'll be next to me, Frey. You can carry a plasma gun, just in case."

"Sir, I doubt she has the necessary—" Zura begins.

"We can trust her judgment," Col says.

And that's that.

We start off as night falls.

Col and I are in borrowed sneak suits. Mine's the wrong size, too tight, and hot even as the desert cool comes down. Ten seconds after putting it on, the suit feels sticky inside.

I wonder if Specials sweat.

I stare down at myself as the camo adjusts, taking on the mottled browns of the desert.

Zura puts two of her commandos on overwatch duty. They scuttle up the mountainside, disappearing into the darkness of the cliffs. The last commando stays with the hovercar.

It's quiet as we walk, our suits fading into blackness as gradually as the sky. Col's carrying his hoverboard and bow, Zura a rifle, and I've got the plasma gun and my knife.

"Strange mix of firepower," I say. "Can't tell whether we're hunting dinosaurs or rabbits."

Col manages a smile at this. "I've still got a few explosive arrows, in case we spot a T. rex."

"We have extra rifles, sir." Zura sighs. "When I taught you how to use a bow, I never thought you'd bring one to a war."

Col shrugs. "We might have to kill someone silently."

Those words end the conversation—a reminder that this is not a hunting trip.

A moment later, Zura comes to a halt.

"Just so you two won't be startled, there's a small animal ahead. Probably a rabbit."

Specials must have night vision. Better than mine, it seems, since I can't see a thing out there.

"Check it out," Col says. "We'll wait."

"But it's just a—"

"Check it out."

Zura salutes and heads off into the darkness.

"I hope it's a volcano rabbit," I say. "Still want to see one of those."

Col smiles again, leaning his board on the ground. "They aren't as exciting as the name implies."

I want him to keep smiling, but jokes don't seem right. This is the first time we've been alone since finding out his brother is missing.

"Col, I'm sure Teo is—"

"That's not why I sent Zura away." He turns to me. "You have to prepare yourself. It's probably my mother with the codebook— I hope it is, anyway."

"Of course. I hope so too."

"Just know that I've got your back, no matter what she says or does."

I stare at him a moment, the gears in my tired brain meshing slowly. But finally I understand.

The rebels would welcome me, with my combat training and my store of family secrets. But when Aribella learns the truth of me, how I set her family up, she might have a different opinion.

And ultimately she commands these soldiers, not Col.

Then I realize something amazing. His little brother's missing, and Col's worried about . . . me.

"I'll be fine," I say.

"Don't be so sure." He looks ahead into the darkness. "You've never seen my mother angry."

"Trust me, I don't want to."

"Just stay calm when she gets going," he says. "I'll make her see who you really are."

"Col." For a second I can't say more.

The words are too much. *Who you really are.*

"You okay?" he asks.

"It's just . . . no one sees who I really am. It's not allowed. My whole life, it's been my job to make sure they don't."

"Not anymore." He puts a hand on my shoulder. "From now on, you're Frey. You don't have to lie."

The desert prisms with tears around me. It makes no sense. Col's the one with a missing brother, a wounded city, a home of smoke and ash . . .

And I'm the one crying.

He's too busy thinking about how to defend me from Aribella's wrath.

Before today, only one person in the world has ever spoken up for me. I've only ever had one ally, one friend. Two seems like more than I deserve.

"Did you mean it, back there in the bunker?" I ask. "That our kiss was real?"

He sets the board on the ground and pulls me toward him, our bodies pressing tight. The sneak suits feel as thin as a film of liquid between us.

"I'm not faking anything now," he says.

"But if it wasn't for me, you'd be—"

"In a smoking crater. Or caught by that scout car."

I press my ear against his chest, listening to his voice.

"And even if I'd survived all that, Frey, I'd be alone right now."

When he swallows, I can feel the pulse of his throat.

"You aren't alone, Col. I'm here."

"I know." He pulls away a little. "And I'll make sure Jefa understands what you mean to me."

He takes a breath to say more, but a scrabbling sound is coming from the darkness. It's Zura coming back.

She's running.

"Move!" she cries. "It wasn't a rabbit!"

JUMP MINES

In my night vision, I can see something following her.

Lots of somethings.

They're the size of rabbits, but their leaps carry them farther than any living creature. And I don't think rabbits come in packs of a hundred—

—or hunt humans.

Col steps onto the hoverboard. "Let's go!"

I jump on as it lifts into the air. We lean into motion, skimming downhill, loose stones skittering under the wash of our lifting fans.

With two people aboard, our top speed isn't much. Zura is running almost even with us, her surged legs taking inhumanly long strides.

When I glance back, the things are getting closer.

They look more like one-legged frogs than rabbits, their heads wrapped in camo skin, set to blend into the rocks. Their single feet are gleaming jackknives of metal that fling them high into the air.

I have no idea what happens if they catch us.

A stream of cracks comes from above—the Specials firing down from the cliffs.

One of the jumping machines is hit and goes careening sideways. It crashes into the side of the gorge and bursts with a blinding pulse of light.

The shock wave hits a second later, swatting us off the hoverboard. We go tumbling down the sandy slope.

When I bounce back to my feet, the taste of blood is in my mouth.

The blast lingers in my night vision—I can barely make out Col, who's been knocked to his hands and knees.

Zura skids to a halt to pull him to his feet. The board is just ahead of us, swerving to a riderless stop.

I jump on the board and look back at our pursuers. My pulse knife might take out two or three of them, but not dozens.

"What *are* they?" I yell.

Zura lifts Col back onto the board. "Jump mines."

My tutors have never mentioned those.

We lift off again. If there was only one of us on this board, maybe we could climb higher than the mines can jump. But I'm not volunteering to step off.

Covering fire streams down from the cliffs. Two waves of the mines break off and head up the slopes, hunting the Specials protecting us.

The Special back at the hovercar must have heard that explosion. I hope she can fly and shoot at the same time—the car's firepower would come in handy about now.

I've got the plasma gun, but I don't know how big its blast is. Or if the recoil will knock me off the board. Or if plasma rings are bright enough to see from orbit, bringing the entire Shreve army down on us.

Col's confidence in my judgment may have been misplaced.

I hit the priming trigger.

The gun begins to whine, its hydrogen battery growing hot. I glance back—maybe twenty of the mines are still after us. The rest are climbing up after the commandos.

The sooner I fire, the safer all of us will be.

"Brace for a weight shift!" I shout in Col's ear.

"What are you—?"

I leap from the board, skidding to a halt in the dirt. The gun's ready light turns green.

I shoulder the stock, aiming at the cluster of jump mines closing in on me.

And fire . . .

A spheromak of plasma spills from the rifle, like a smoke ring made of lightning and flame.

It streaks across the desert, lighting up the hills around us, bright as daylight. The jump mines bounding across its path flash into nothing.

The plasma ring keeps going. Mines crash together in its wake, drawn into the sudden column of turbulence.

I've aimed high enough that the plasma ring doesn't take down a cliff. It just streaks away into the atmosphere, a wrathful angel of flame.

There are still a dozen mines leaping toward me. More rifle fire comes from the Specials above, taking out one, two—

I drop the hot, expended plasma gun. Draw my knife.

"*Frey!*"

Col has come around on the board, ready to pick me up. But Zura leaps on with him and tilts them into motion.

"Wait!" Col yells. But he's the heir to House Palafox, and Zura is stronger and determined to save him. The board makes a wobbly turn and flies away.

Just a bodyguard doing her job, I guess.

I turn to face the jump mines.

Only eight are left coming at me. But on the cliffs above, a dozen more have reached one of the commandos. A mine soars over him, explodes in midair.

He falls.

The other commando is still shooting. More mines fall to the ground and twitch.

How many can my pulse knife take out?

Two? Three?

Racing away ahead, Col is invisible in his sneak suit, but Zura's arm shows a bright smear of body heat. She's been hit, her suit ripped open.

Another explosion sounds from the cliffs above. The covering fire goes silent.

I'm alone now. All I can do is run.

Then from the darkness ahead comes a sound—lifting fans.

The hovercar rises into view, its engines a bright constellation against the black sky.

I switch off my night vision just in time—the guns open up with a blinding salvo, fléchettes tearing up the desert behind me. As the car swoops a meter over my head, the rotor wash sends me sprawling.

A moment later, the mines chasing me have been cut to pieces. The car slews to a halt in the narrow gorge.

"No!" I stand up, waving. "Keep moving!"

The jump mines up on the cliffs are leaping back down.

They fall on the hovercar like exploding hail, pounding its armor. An engine fractures, and white-hot pieces fly in all directions.

I drop down and cover my head.

The hovercar tips over, hits the ground, cracks open. Two of the fans are still spinning, sending what's left of the machine skidding sideways toward a deep gorge. The car tumbles in and down, racks of burning ammunition crackling as it falls.

I stand up, stunned and deafened.

There are exactly two jump mines left.

And they've spotted me.

They leap through smoke and burning wreckage, twenty meters away and closing.

I let my pulse knife fly.

It sweeps through the first one, which explodes, knocking the knife off course. It catches the second with a glancing blow.

The mine crashes and rolls across the ground, landing at my feet.

I stare down, waiting for it to detonate.

GESTURES

One breath. Two.

Nothing happens.

One of the jump mine's feet jabs at the ground, trying to get it moving again. But the device only manages to roll back and forth a little, like an upended turtle.

It's too damaged to realize that it's right next to a target.

I stand there, motionless, counting another ten breaths.

Then, very slowly, I seal up my sneak suit till it covers everything but my eyes.

Nothing to see here.

Except—what happens when the mine decides it's broken? Does it self-destruct?

The lurching foot finally connects with dirt, and the mine rolls against my ankle. I pretend to be a tree.

Every little clank makes me twitch.

Then I hear something worse—footsteps.

"Frey?"

"Stop," I hiss. "Don't move."

"What are you . . ." A pause. "Oh."

Zura's a few meters behind me.

Two of us. Great.

"Stay back," I whisper.

There's no way out of this situation but to creep away and hope the mine is too damaged to spot us moving.

I slide a foot back through the dirt.

"Frey," Zura says softly. "Wait."

I freeze again. Give her a tiny, questioning shrug.

"Don't move. You could set it off."

No kidding. But is her plan for us to stand here until we starve to death?

The mine clanks once more, bumping against my ankle again. I don't dare whisper my question aloud.

Then something flies through the dark, strikes the dirt ten meters away.

An arrow.

The broken-sounding clank comes from my feet again, the mine pushing itself off across the ground. It struggles toward the arrow for a few meters, then comes to a halt again.

Another arrow whizzes past, buries itself in the dirt farther away.

The mine clanks into motion again, moving with painful

slowness, a wounded animal. But with every meter, it's less likely to kill me.

A third arrow lures it farther away.

I spot my knife hovering in the distance. Pull off a glove and signal to Col that he can stop using up his arrows.

I send my knife closer to the mine, then straight up at full pulse.

The mine hears the roar and explodes. The blast knocks me back on my heels and into Zura's arms.

"You okay?" she asks.

"Fine." I blink away the spots in my eyes, call the hot knife back into my hand. "But you should check on your commandos."

"I have," Zura says.

I turn to face her. She's wounded, one leg bloody, staring grimly at an airscreen in her palm.

"Two suits sending null vitals. No heartbeats, no EKG." She looks down into the gorge, where flames still flicker. "And no signal at all from Samon."

It hits me in a slow wave—there are only the three of us left.

Col glides up on his board, staring at the airscreen blankly. At every step of this battle, the soldiers endangered themselves to protect him.

I begin to see how that constant bubble of security weighs on Rafi. How watching me injure myself again and again to protect her must have hurt.

"You were right, Col," I say. "It was a trap."

"No, just bad luck." Zura closes her fist on the airscreen, snuffing it out. "Nobody sets up an ambush eight klicks out. They couldn't have known which direction we'd come from."

"Then what *were* those things?" I ask.

"The latest rebel trick," Zura says. "Mine fields that move at random, setting up in a new place every day."

"Rebels," Col breathes. "How long before they show up?"

"No telling. We might get Shreve units sniffing around too, after all those fireworks. We have to move."

I stare at them both. "Fine. But where are we *going*?"

For a moment, we look at one another, wreathed in dust and lit by the flames of the burning hovercar.

"Where the orders told us to go?" Zura suggests.

I shake my head. "We're going to hide eight klicks away from this *bonfire*?"

Col gathers himself, sets a determined face.

"There's nowhere else to go."

RENDEZVOUS POINT

We move fast—Zura running, me and Col on the hoverboard.

There's no point being stealthy now. Whoever's waiting for us at the rendezvous point heard that firefight. Either they've slipped away or gone to ground.

I just hope they don't start shooting when they see us charging in.

I also try not to think about the direction we're running—away from the rebellion that Col wanted to join yesterday, toward a woman who'll likely want to bury me.

At our frantic speed, eight kilometers doesn't take much time, or seem very far away from the wreckage behind us. But soon a breathless Zura calls us to a halt.

"Just over that ridge."

Col steps from the board. "We'll walk in slowly. Weapons down."

"Weapons?" I mutter. Our collective firepower is down to a rifle, a few grenades, a pulse knife, and a bow and arrow.

As we climb the ridge, I glance back the way we've come. No vehicles in the sky, no body heat. Just columns of smoke blotting out a stretch of stars.

Maybe when people see plasma guns blazing away, they investigate with caution.

We creep onto the ridge top with only the eye slits of our sneak suits open. Our destination doesn't look like much from up here. Just a flat expanse of rock, the perfect size for a hovercar to land.

"Anything?" Col asks.

Zura shakes her head. "I'll do a circuit."

"We don't have time," Col says. "We have to make contact before someone starts poking around back there."

He pulls his sneak suit down to reveal his face. Then stands up in plain view.

"*¡Hola!*" he calls down.

No answer.

"*Soy Col Palafox. ¿Hay alguien ahí?*"

Nothing but echoes.

He waits a moment, then sighs.

"Might as well go down."

We're in the right spot, at least.

There are footprints in the dirt, a few discarded food containers. A pile of rocks to one side suggests that someone has cleared the space.

But there's no fancy tech, nothing to detect our arrival and ping whoever's got the codebook.

No jump mines, at least.

Col is pacing. "They ran when the shooting started. They probably thought an army was coming down on them!"

"Plasma guns have that effect," Zura says, looking at me. "Not my first choice for dealing with mines."

"My first choice was *running away*," I point out. "But then someone flew off with our only hoverboard!"

"My job is to protect the heir, not—"

"Enough," Col says. "We're here now. What exactly did your orders say, Zura?"

"Search for the signal from your board. Find you, then report here." She shrugs. "There wasn't a backup plan for if nobody was around."

"Okay. So they'll pick another spot to meet. How long till they send that out?"

"It doesn't matter, sir. Our codebook receiver is at the bottom of a ravine."

For a moment, Col looks like a lost child. Then he gathers himself. "We need to find another Victorian unit. How do we do that?"

Zura shakes her head. "What's left of our forces are running silent, which means trying *not* to be found. They'll only listen to orders from the codebook. That's how our system was designed."

"Then we go back to the bunker," Col says. "Sooner or later, someone's bound to show up for those weapons."

"On foot? Through enemy territory?" Zura asks. "We can't fit three on that hoverboard. And we've already run into one bunch of jump mines!"

Col lets out a sigh. He's scratched up from our fall off the hoverboard. His face is dirty and streaked with sweat.

"We don't have a choice."

"Col," I say gently. "Let's get some sleep. Whoever wanted us here could show up tomorrow."

For once, Zura agrees with me. "We're too tired to walk into another firefight, sir."

"Of course," Col says, then frowns. "I don't suppose there's anything to eat."

That's when it occurs to me that we're back to nothing. No food, no water, and no wood to burn.

It's like the wild is always trying to starve me.

Zura has some good news—we don't have to sleep in our sweaty sneak suits. Thanks to clever Victorian military tech, they can be fused together into a stealth tent.

The only problem is, all I'm wearing under mine is a ripped nightshirt and undershorts. My sweatpants are back in that ravine, on fire, along with our food and our receiver.

And mountains get cold at night.

While Zura works, I huddle half-naked on a rock, hugging my legs to stay warm. The wild feels infinite around me, a boundless dark.

The whole world seems boundless now. No more combat training in the morning, ever. No more breakfasts with the Palafoxes, pretending to be Rafi. No pretending at all.

Just me and my allies—and the things in the dark that want to kill us.

Freedom has a way of being terrifying.

I wonder what Rafi's doing now. Is she being a good daughter, making speeches to support the war effort? Or fighting our father every step of the way?

Maybe some part of her feels this freedom too, with no little sister to take her place every time things get interesting. She used to envy me out there on the dance floor, in front of the cheering crowds. Solving problems with my fists.

Maybe she's happier now, being both edges of the knife.

Does she miss me as much as I miss her?

A red dot bobs out of the darkness, Col using the laser sight of his hunting bow like a flashlight.

As if he knows the dark thoughts in my head, he sits next to me and puts an arm around my shoulders. Out here, the simplest things make all the difference. Food. Safety. Warmth.

His body against mine makes everything dividing us—our warring families, our lies—seem less important.

"You promised me an army," I say. "And I don't even have pants."

He pulls me tighter, and the low shudder in my bones finally stills.

"Uniforms will be easy," he says. "I'm more worried about the army part. When this all started, we had three thousand soldiers, two hundred hovercars. We'll be lucky if a quarter of them are still out there."

I don't answer. Fifty warships against my father is nothing.

Col puts his arm around me again. "When Zura jumped on the board, left you to face those mines alone, I couldn't stop her."

"I get it, Col. Her job is to protect you. Just like me and my sister."

"Well, except she volunteered."

Right. Normal people choose their work.

It seems like that would only make life harder, having to decide. Being born to protect my sister always felt like destiny.

"You didn't choose to be first son," I say.

"No. But I could always run away and become a big-game hunter. Jefa would love that."

I pull away to look at his face.

"I hope she's okay, Col. Even if she hates me."

He shakes his head. "Fighting beside someone, it's hard to hate them."

I close my eyes, and see this war against my father stretching out before us. Running, fighting, maybe for years. Sleeping in the wild, hungry and uncertain.

But we also have this, Col's body next to mine.

I kiss him.

He kisses me.

All those explosions an hour ago deadened my senses, but now I can feel everything. The hard stone beneath us. The weight of his hands on my shoulders. A hint of rain chilling the desert air.

Col's lips are dry, edged with thirst and cold. Our breaths quicken, shallow and unsteady in each other's mouths. His fists knot in my borrowed shirt, our gentleness sharpening in the dark.

Then, between kisses—the soft dance of his tongue like he's saying my name—I murmur a stray thought.

"My sister."

Col pulls back, confused at first.

"Sorry," I say. "But the thought of her alone, with him. While I'm here with you, safe."

Col holds me closer. "I'm worried about Rafi too."

"We have to get a message to her. She needs to know I'm alive. That I'm coming for her."

"We'll take you to a city. You can tell the feeds everything."

A shudder goes through me. "That would just warn my father. I'm not ready for everyone to know."

"Then we'll figure something out." He kisses me again. "We'll save your sister."

"And your brother too," I say.

We're going to fight beside each other, maybe for a long time. This war seems endless, and we're only at the start.

We kiss again, the sounds of our lips as faint as whispers in the night.

STONE

Zura finishes and calls to us to get some sleep.

She's fused the smart fibers of our suits, making a tent just big enough for three. Its camo skin is pitch black in the darkness.

Some part of my brain registers that it's awkward, sharing a tent with Col and one of his soldiers. But most of me is too exhausted, too battered, to care. And I need to pee.

"Back in a minute," I say.

Zura sighs. "You should've done that in the suit."

I stare at her. "What?"

"Here in the wild, nothing's more important than water. The suits collect our sweat and urine, and filter it back into drinking water. It tastes funny, but the purifiers work almost perfectly."

"Almost? No thanks." I turn away and head into the darkness.

"Watch out for snakes!" Zura calls.

Right. Deserts are full of snakes, aren't they?

Hopefully in this cold, they'll be asleep, or hibernating, or whatever snakes do. But as always, cold-blooded creatures are invisible in heat vision, so I can't be sure.

The wild sucks sometimes.

I'm not gone very long, but Col and Zura are already asleep when I come back. They've left me the middle.

Great.

But at least it's warm inside the tent. The suits are opaque to infrared, the insulation almost perfect. Zura warned us that the heat of three bodies will make things downright hot by morning. I'm fine with that.

When I lie down, there's a rock in the middle of my back. It's under the floor of the tent, big as an apple, embedded in the ground. Trying to shift it aside through the tent fabric is useless.

I lie there, trying to sleep, but the stone is too big to ignore.

Did Zura not see it? Or did she leave it there on purpose?

I wonder if the rest of the Victorian army will feel the same way about me. If all they'll see is Rafia, the first daughter of the enemy, even after I explain who I really am.

Maybe alliances are bogus. Maybe I should have stayed an army of one. I could go back to Shreve, sneak into my father's house, and get my sister out . . .

Or maybe it's just this brain-wrecking *rock* in my back.

I sit up and unseal the tent. The desert air reaches in, icy fingers along my flesh.

Col stirs, a plaintive murmur pushing from his lips.

The cold outside is brutal after the warmth of the tent. The freezing sand sticks to my bare knees and palms like ice crystals.

I slide one arm under the tent.

With my fingers stretched out, I can just reach the stone. But it's half-buried, and it takes a solid minute of scrabbling before it pops out.

There's something in the hole—

A folded piece of paper.

I pull it out and stare in the starlight.

The paper is covered with coded markings, like on the weapons cases back in the Palafoxes' bunker. But this is handwritten, hasty and clumsy.

I stick my head back into the tent and whisper, "Col."

He doesn't respond. I grasp his bare ankle with my freezing hand.

He sputters awake, staring at me with confusion and annoyance.

I wave the paper. "Someone left us a note."

He blinks a few more times, then finally sits up.

A gust of wind rushes past me into the tent, and Zura jolts awake, reaching for her rifle.

"Relax," I say.

Col crawls halfway out into the starlight. When I hand him the paper, his eyes go wide.

"It's Victorian battle code," he says.

"Can you read it?"

"It says, 'Stay here. We'll check back soon.'" Col squints closer. "And then, 'Leave me the sign, so I'll know it's you. And watch out—this place is plagued by scorpions.'"

I sit up straight. "Scorpions? Fantastic."

"Better than fantastic." Col looks up from the paper. "This is my little brother's handwriting."

RAIN

The next morning it rains.

It's cold and miserable, and we hunker in the tent together. All we can do is wait.

After finding the note last night, we made a spiral of stones on the landing pad. It's the symbol of a fictional hero Col and Teo pretended to be when they were little—the "sign" Teo was asking for. Somehow, he's okay.

While we wait, Zura recounts battles from when she was fighting the rebels instead of my father. When she runs out of stories, Col tells us about his little brother, who was kicked out of his first boarding school for breaking curfew, and his second for bribing other students to take his tests.

When the time comes for me to entertain them, Zura gives me an expectant look. She's still wondering about the story behind my face.

"You can trust Zura with anything," Col says. "But it's up to you."

I hesitate. My story is something I should get used to telling, if we're going to spill it to the whole world one day. And I'll have to explain everything to Aribella, if she's going to understand my value to her struggle.

I like being bound to Col by the secrets we've shared. Once somebody else knows the truth of me, it won't be the same between us.

I'm selfish with him, and with my secrets.

"Not yet. Is that okay?"

Col takes my hand. "Of course."

"Can't wait," Zura says.

The day warms up slowly, but the rain doesn't relent.

"We should take the tent down," Zura says around noon. "The suits will collect more water if they're stretched out."

"Better than drinking our sweat," I say.

Col agrees.

We crawl out into the cold downpour, and we're muddy and soaked in seconds. But once I stop shivering, the feel of clean water against my skin is glorious.

Col and I stand side by side, drinking from our palms, rubbing two days' travel off our skin. Showering together in the rain feels almost normal, like this is a camping trip and not a war.

"Wish we had some soap," he says.

Zura looks up from taking apart the tent, pulls a blue wafer from a pocket of her fatigues. She tosses it to Col, who rubs it between his hands. A blue lather builds.

When he gives it to me, it smells exactly like the stuff they clean our kitchens with back at my father's house. It reminds me of playing hide-and-seek with my sister after the staff had all gone home. It also reminds me of having a whole kitchen full of food.

"Anything edible in those pockets?" I ask Zura.

"Just this." She pulls out a small bottle of powder. "Rub it into raw meat and it kills the parasites. Safer than food cooked on a fire."

"Sounds yummy." I turn to Col. "Your military tech creeps me out."

"Your military tech blew up my house."

"Oh, I didn't mean—" I begin, but Col breaks into a smile.

"My little brother's safe, Frey. I get to make jokes again."

"Sure. Just warn me it's a joke next time." I hand him the soap.

Col's smile fades. "I wonder if Abuela . . ."

He doesn't say more, but I can see him sink into the layers of everything he's lost. Even if Teo's okay, his home is still gone. His city conquered.

I gently change the subject. "How do you think Teo got back from Europe? His face is on all the feeds. It's not like he can buy a suborbital ticket."

"My mother must've sent someone to grab him."

"Why would they grab two of his friends?"

"For propaganda value?" he says. "You've seen the feeds. The cities are tightening the embargo."

"Yeah, I guess that does sound like Aribella."

Col shrugs. "I'm sure she told their parents."

I'm not. Once more, I remind myself to get back on her good side as soon as possible.

"I bet that note was her idea too," Col adds. "She knew I'd recognize Teo's handwriting."

"Messages within messages," I say softly.

But it seems risky to me, leaving so much to chance. If Zura had set up the tent in a different spot, we'd have missed the note completely.

My stomach rumbles.

"That parasite powder is starting to sound good," I say. "Do rabbits come out in the rain?"

Col shrugs. "Never thought about it."

"Wait," I say. "There's something about nature you *don't know*?"

"I don't hunt in the rain. My feathers get wet."

For a moment, I imagine Col as a large predatory bird. Then I realize—"Oh, the ones on your arrows."

He laughs, like this was a joke and not my brain gone briefly missing. After everything that's happened, Col still thinks I'm funny.

"Aren't deserts supposed to be dry?" I ask.

"Desert rains are infrequent. But when they happen, they can be torrential."

"Torrential," I say. "Such a tour guide word."

He comes closer. "We tour guides know all the good words."

A fresh wind is whipping through the camp. Water flows across my bare feet, and the rain slants and coils around us.

We're going to kiss again.

"Sir?" Zura's voice comes. "Incoming!"

I look up into the sky, blinking water from my eyes. That sound—it isn't wind.

It's lifting fans beating the air.

"Quick, Col. We have to . . ." But I'm not sure what there is to do.

There's no cover to hide behind. Col and I are half-naked, our sneak suits fused together into a tarp.

The hovercar looms into sight, descending in a fury. Its six lifting fans drive the rain like a sudden gale.

Zura is scrambling for her rifle, Col for his bow. But they're not going to take down an armored hovercar.

I gesture for my knife, but it must not be able to see me in the tempest. And I can't remember where I left it. Too much kissing, not enough paranoia.

We're helpless.

But as the car settles on the landing area, I realize that it's not a warcraft. It's a luxury limo, black and shiny.

The same kind my father rides around in.

I fall to my knees in the mud.

"No."

The doors butterfly open, like great wings spreading out to shield the occupants from the rain.

And they step out, like conquerors in a new world.

Teo Palafox and his two friends.

TEO PALAFOX

"Can you *not* get the seats muddy? This is a rental."

I stare at Srin. She looks about twelve years old, but she's in the same year as Teo at his fancy school. So she's either a teenager or some kind of prodigy.

I sit down with a wet squelch. Srin's gray eyes glare at me from beneath her short bobbed hair. Everything about her is neat and precise, from her school uniform to her arched eyebrows. But, like a quiet warning, her left little finger is surged to look like a tiny snake.

The leather seat shifts beneath my weight, adapting to my body. After two nights' sleep on hard ground, it feels like a feather bed.

"You rented a limo and brought it into a war zone?" Col asks.

"We're not brain-missing," Srin says. "We got insurance."

The three of them are arranged across the backseat—Teo, Srin, and Heron. They're all still wearing their school's uniform, dark blue sweaters and matching trousers, lilac shirts. Heron wears a dazed expression and a rumpled look, like he's been sleeping in his clothes.

The limo's soft pink lighting glints from the champagne glasses lined up on racks. There's a silver ice bucket next to my elbow.

Col sinks into his own luxurious seat. "But why are you in a limo at all? Why aren't there *soldiers* with you?"

A minute ago, when Teo tumbled out to hug his older brother in the rain, he looked like a little kid. He's skinnier than Col, his face softer and more open.

But now he crosses his arms, all business.

"I wanted to test the system first. Make sure the codebook wasn't compromised before meeting anyone face-to-face."

Col just stares at him.

"I knew you were out here somewhere," Teo explains. "So we had to find you first. Because you could *prove* who you really were, using the sign."

"We didn't want to walk into a trap," Srin chimes in.

"Wait," Col says. "*You* have the codebook? Why isn't Jefa running things?"

Teo stares back across the car.

"Mamá?" he says in a small voice. "She's dead."

"But . . . she always has the book!"

Teo shakes his head. "She gave it to me when I was here at winter break. To take back to school."

Col crumples into his seat.

I take his hand, my brain spinning. This is why no one's secured the family weapons back at the bunker. Why our only welcome here was a note left under a rock. Why we're sitting in this ridiculous hovercar.

Because a fourteen-year-old boy is commanding the Victorian army.

Aribella Palafox is dead.

"I'm sorry, Col." Teo looks like a little kid again. "I figured she told you about giving me the book—that you'd *know* it was me."

Col's hand is limp in mine, his eyes glassy.

His words come slowly. "That means she was worried about what might happen. She had a bigger plan. Maybe she got out somehow!"

"Col," Teo says. "I was talking to her when the missile hit."

There's no sound except the rain. I want to say something, but there isn't enough air in my lungs. The limo seems like it's shrinking, pressing in on us.

It takes Teo a moment to speak again.

"When she gave me the codebook, I thought it was just Jefa being Jefa. Giving me a lesson in responsibility. I kept it under my bed."

He stares at the rain-streaked window.

"Then everything went brain-missing. It was early morning, still dark. And suddenly this noise wakes us up."

"We thought it was a fire alarm," Heron says.

"I'd forgotten all about the book," Teo says. "But it was there, under my bed, screaming and blinking. So I ping Jefa and she answers right away, even though it's midnight here at home. She says we're under attack in the ruins, but it's under control. Except Col's being an idiot."

Col's hand flinches in mine. "What?"

"She said you were supposed to keep Rafia in line. But you'd gone off the rails. The tracker on your board said you were at the edge of the city. You were helping her escape." Teo gives me a sideways look.

I hold his gaze. He's one more person I have to explain myself to. One more who'll blame me for everything that's gone wrong.

"And you're *sure* she was still there at the end?" Col pleads.

Teo's voice goes soft. "Suddenly there was this alarm in the background, and she went quiet. Wouldn't answer when I asked what was going on. Then she said, 'I love you,' and there was a buzzing sound."

He slumps back in his seat.

Heron puts an arm around Teo. "We figured she'd hung up, or lost the connection. But then we turned on the feeds—they kept showing it, again and again."

I close my eyes for a moment, and see the missile hit. That column of black smoke rising, scattering ashes on the wind.

"That's why we decided to disappear," Srin says. "It was the only way to hit back."

Everyone looks at her.

"Wait," Col says. "You mean Jefa didn't send someone for you?"

"No. It was my idea." Srin's grim smile looks demented in the limo's soft lighting. "Maximum reputational damage for the enemy. We trashed our rooms to make it look like we fought the kidnappers. Even left some blood."

She holds up a hand. In the limo's pink lighting, I can see tiny scars on her fingertips.

Col stares at her, wide-eyed. "Do your families *know* you're okay?"

"Only my sister," Srin says. "She rented this limo, the leather of which your pants-missing friend is currently ruining. Byanca also chartered our cargo jet. Took a whole night to get across the ocean, but no one expects rich kids to travel in a cargo hold."

"But your parents—"

"We're dealing with a monster," Srin says. "Sacrifices have to be made."

Teo leans forward. "She's right, Col. This will hurt him. You've seen the feeds."

"But everyone thinks you've been kidnapped," Col says to Heron and Srin. "Maybe killed!"

"*That's the point!*" Teo cries. "Why should we care about their feelings, Col? The other first families watched our home destroyed, our mother murdered, our city taken, and none of them did anything! Let them all be afraid!"

There's a moment of shocked silence in the car, ringing with the muffled rain and the echoes of Teo's anger.

Then Heron raises a hand. "Actually, I only came along to make sure Teo doesn't do anything stupid. And can I point out that no one said *anything* about war zones?"

"It didn't say 'war zone' on the map," Teo mutters.

Col swears.

"Speaking of wars, sir," Zura says from the open limo door. "Now that we have transport, we might want to get out of rebel territory."

For a moment, Col looks lost. He's had his world turned inside out twice in the last few days. Maybe three times—I've lost count. But he understands now that we've been fooling ourselves.

His mother is gone.

I take a steadying breath. "Col, maybe we should get these kids somewhere safe."

"*Kids?*" Srin says.

"Right. Pack up the camp," Col orders Zura, then turns to his little brother. "We can get a Victorian warcraft to escort us. Give me the codebook."

Teo stares at his older brother defiantly, his face still red from yelling.

Then he looks at me.

"Not till you tell me what *she's* doing here."

TRUST ME

Everyone's looking at me.

Even Zura hesitates at the door, like she's waited too long for this story to walk away now.

"You're her, aren't you?" Teo says. "Rafia."

"Except muddy and without pants," Srin adds.

Heron leans forward. "Which is why that other Rafia—the one on the feeds—hasn't done any interviews yet. She's an impostor!"

It still feels too soon. Too huge. Too dangerous.

But there's no escaping the truth.

"It's the other way around. I'm the impostor."

The three of them are silent for a moment.

I let it soak in, for them and for me.

It's uncanny, having people I don't know staring at me, stunned, seeing what I really am. Like the ground is tilting under us all. Like they're all going to disappear tomorrow.

I wish I had more clothes on.

"Weird," Zura says. "I'll go pack up."

She turns away and disappears into the rain.

"No way." Srin looks at Col. "If this girl was an impostor, your security would've spotted her surgery. I mean, it's pretty good, but a quick DNA check—"

"We checked her DNA," Col says, then falls silent.

He wants me to tell it myself.

So I start talking.

"I'm Rafia's sister, born twenty-six minutes later." I listen to the rain for a moment. "Her body double. Her protector. Her identical twin."

Her only friend.

The only one who can save her.

"I was a trick to play on your family, Teo. Because unlike the real Rafia, I was something my father could throw away."

He stares at me. I'm expecting hatred in his eyes, or another scream from the bottom of his soul as he realizes everything I've cost him.

But all he says is—

"What's your name?"

"Frey." It comes out of my mouth in a whisper.

His expression changes then, and I see how much he looks like Aribella.

Because he pities me. Like she did.

Pity isn't something I'm ready for at all.

He says, "My brother would've been there when the missile hit, except for you. Right?"

"I guess so."

"Thank you, Frey," he says softly.

A layer of guilt slips from my shoulders.

Col leans forward. "Heron, Srin, you two have to keep this secret after you get home. Which will be as soon as possible."

Srin stares at him a moment, then starts laughing.

"Are you brain-missing, Col? You can't keep her a secret. Imagine the reputational damage!"

Heron turns to her. "Seriously, girl? Is it *that* much worse than kidnapping me and you?"

"*Way* worse. You're just a roommate who got in the way. I'm some kid from Teo's propaganda class." Srin points at me. "But Frey is her father's own flesh and blood, sacrificed to start a war!"

"Stop," Col says. "This isn't your propaganda class, Srin. It's not your story to tell."

"But you *can't* send us home!" Srin turns to me, pleading. "Once people see us back with our families, the outrage fades. We lose momentum. Everything goes back to normal!"

Normal—I hear it in my sister's voice.

"That's what everyone wants," Srin says. "To pretend that things are okay. But, Frey, you can *make* them pay attention."

I try to answer, but I can't.

Me and Col using my story against my father was one thing.

But hearing a stranger plot and strategize and calculate how damaging it will be—it feels like being an impostor again.

Col puts a hand on my shoulder, and the world steadies a little.

"You two are going home," he says.

"Really?" Srin smiles sweetly at him. "Limo, who holds your proxy ownership?"

"You do, General Srin," the limo says.

"And you won't go anywhere unless I tell you to?"

"That's correct, General."

There's a moment of impasse, but then Teo speaks up.

"Srin, my brother's right. You guys can do more for us from home. Tell everyone what it was like that night, how we ran away, fearing for my safety. Don't let them forget Victoria. Be the face of the resistance!"

"I *guess* that sounds bubbly," Srin mutters. "A shower might also be nice."

"Same," Heron says.

He looks like he's willing to go back to school, but Srin gave up too easily. I wonder if she's got another trick up her sleeve.

Teo turns his eyes to me, then to his brother.

"Col, do you really trust her?"

"Frey saved my life more than once. She fought beside our soldiers. And she's the only person in the world who hates her father as much as we do."

"Except Rafi," I murmur.

"All right, Frey." Teo holds out his hand. "If Col trusts you, I do too. Welcome to Victorian High Command."

"Also known as *my* limo," Srin grumbles.

We shake.

"Now," Col says, "will you please give me the codebook?"

Teo sighs, reaching under his seat to pull out a valise. It looks a lot like Rafi's favorite—alligator skin, brass fittings, retina locks.

He balances it on his lap, blinks it open.

"Don't let power go to our head, big brother." Teo pulls out a metal slate the size of a handscreen. "And be careful. This thing is noisy—it broadcasts all the way to the satellites. So if you don't want to get spotted, send your orders on the move, or someplace with a lot of random signals. Like a city."

"Got it." Col takes the codebook solemnly.

When he holds it up, light flashes across his face. He flinches as it takes a nip of skin for DNA matching.

A moment later, the device says, "You have command, Col Palafox."

His expression changes then—the exhaustion, the grief and sorrow fading a little. He looks like someone ready to take revenge.

Teo only looks relieved to give up the responsibility. He turns his open valise around to face me.

"Want some clothes, Frey? They might fit you."

I look at the three runaways in their school uniforms, their lilac shirts glowing in the soft limo lighting, and shake my head.

"I'll just wear my sneak suit."

Heron raises an eyebrow. "Those things don't look very comfortable."

"They aren't." I give him a tired smile. "But you never know when a battle's going to break out."

FAKING IT

The limo takes off in a roar, the windows blurring as it lifts up through the rain. But a minute later we break through the clouds and into sunlight. Shadows gyre across the floor as we veer west, out of the mountains, away from Victoria and Shreve.

I'd almost forgotten that flying could be luxurious. The seat is comfortable even in my damp sneak suit, and the limo rides as smoothly as any in my father's fleet.

It also has food. Yucca and truffled cheese croquettes. Crispy dumplings filled with duck and black mole. All of it cooked with real heat, popping out steaming from the panels in the walls.

"Want some bubbly with that?" Srin asks.

She's probably being sarcastic, but I don't care. "Is there any water?"

"Not since last night. Heron used it all for a bath."

"I'd hardly call that a bath," Heron says. "More like a sponging."

"This thing doesn't collect rain?" Zura glares at the flight controls, which are locked on autopilot. "There's water in your suit bladders, Frey."

"Great. But do you have to call them *bladders*?"

I find the drinking tube on my shoulder, wrest it free from its clasp, and put it to my lips. The water tastes normal enough.

"Mmmm, body temperature."

At least it's not my own purified sweat—or worse. But after a couple of days being thirsty, I can see why commandos wear these things. The deadliest part of the wild isn't snakes or scorpions. It's thirst and hunger.

Also jump mines.

Col must be starving too, but he's not eating. His eyes are locked on the codebook airscreen.

Maybe planning a war is easier than thinking about his mother in that house when the missile hit. Or his brother watching it happen over and over on the feeds, unable to change a thing.

I should say something comforting, but I don't have the words. My own mother was murdered before I was born. She's only ever been a figment on a screen, a face in which Rafi and I found pieces of our own. Her smile, always wide like ours, her thin hands as we got older.

So, in a way, I could never lose her.

All I can think to ask Col is, "Have you decided where to take them?"

"We can make it to Paz before dark. Spy dust is illegal there, and the council hates Shreve. It's the perfect place to send out orders." Col turns to his brother. "How much of our army's left? The codebook isn't telling me."

Teo looks up from eating. "I don't know. Anytime a unit transmits, there's a chance they could get spotted. I never asked for a head count."

Col frowns. "So what've they been doing all this time?"

"We sent out a general order to hide," Srin says. "I told Teo we should coordinate a few attacks, but he was too chicken."

"No, that was smart." Col turns to Zura. "But now we need to find out how much of an army we have. What's the safest way to do that?"

"Pick a rally point and assemble everyone. See for ourselves what we've got to work with."

Col's eyes light up. "I know just the place."

He turns back to the codebook. Its airscreen is about the size of a soccer ball. In the swirling cloud of data I can make out a map of the mountains, a few glowing cities, and a moving dot that must be us.

"By the way, Supreme Commander," Srin says, "didn't we send a light attack car to find you? It is conspicuously missing."

Col doesn't look up. "Destroyed in combat. We ran into jump mines."

"Mines? Were you taking a *walk*?"

"Yes. And you brought a rented limo into rebel territory."

"But we didn't *lose* it," Srin says.

Col doesn't answer, but I can see Zura holding her tongue, weighing whether Teo's friend from propaganda class is someone she's allowed to punch.

So I speak up, softly and clearly.

"Srin, the soldiers who served on that car fought valiantly, but they were killed. That's how wars work—people die. Which is why we're taking you home."

Her eyes spark, like she's about to argue, until Heron puts a hand on her arm. She settles back into her seat and mutters, "*Still* my limo."

The car falls silent, and Zura gives me the barest nod of thanks.

Col stays focused on the airscreen, waving his fingers. He looks uncertain, like a littlie learning how to use interface gestures for the first time.

Suddenly it's hard to believe that he's really in charge of an army, or even what's left of one. How can a guerrilla war be waged by a seventeen-year-old boy, from something that looks like a game screen?

My whole life, I always thought that I was the only impostor. That everyone else was certain they were real in some way that I could never understand. But what if they're all just faking too?

Maybe none of us know who we really are.

PROXY

The sun is setting when we spot the Pacific Ocean.

We're tired and bored after long hours in the limo. The feeds aren't telling us anything new, just rehashing the outrage about Teo and his two friends being missing. There's no real news out of Victoria. Reporters from other cities have been expelled, the locals silenced.

The whole city has gone dark. Tens of thousands of feeds—arguing politics, gossiping, sharing music and makeup tips—all of it has been wiped from the global interface.

Srin was right—Rafi hasn't appeared in public since that first day of the war. Everyone's noticed she's not being a good daughter. And saying that this time our father has gone so far that it's turned even his own blood against him.

I love that Rafi's fighting him, because she thinks he killed me with that missile. But I hate it that she thinks I'm dead.

I have to get word to her somehow, even if it gives our father warning that I'm still out here.

Col finally switches from the newsfeeds, turning to a nature doc about the white weed. We all watch in sullen fascination.

The weed is an artificial orchid that the Rusties unleashed three centuries ago. It almost crowded out all other plant life on earth, taking over farms and fields and prairies. Slashing, burning, and poisoning the weed failed. Only the old-growth forests were strong enough to resist.

"Rusty scientists engineered birds to eat it," Col adds to the grim commentary. "But they just spread the seeds in their droppings."

I wonder why he's obsessing about the weed. Maybe because people thought it couldn't be defeated, until a global effort got it under control.

Or maybe he's begun to admire things that can't be killed, no matter how hard everyone tries.

On the western plains below us, the weed is strewn like fresh snow. But the city of Paz sits on Baja Island, protected by a barrier of salt water.

As night falls, we cross the still blue straits and land outside the city, next to a train line. The quiet passenger station sits among a row of simple houses with gardens and low stone walls.

I remember my father joking about Paz, the city with no first family, where everyone's happy. Like that's such a bad thing.

We tumble out onto the station platform to stretch our legs.

"You want us to take a *train*?" Srin says. "Not a very dramatic entrance."

"Maybe quiet is better," Heron says. "Faking our own kidnapping seems kind of illegal."

"Just tell them you ran away," Col says. "You feared for your safety. Tell the Paz wardens that you want sanctuary . . . for all three of you."

"Wait," Teo says. "*Three* of us?"

"Yes." Col crosses his arms. "You're safer here than out fighting a guerrilla war. And you'll get more news coverage than your friends. You were right before—someone needs to be the face of Victoria. But it should be *you*, Teo."

"Forget that." Teo clenches his fists. "I'm not going to be the mascot for your war, Col."

"You don't understand how dangerous this is. I'd already be dead if it weren't for Frey and Zura."

"Which is why you need my help too!" Teo cries. He looks at me. "*You* don't think I should hide, do you, Frey?"

For a moment, I'm not sure what to say. I don't want to argue against Col, but I can't imagine being pushed aside either. The only meaning my life has ever had is in training, fighting, and protecting those I love.

That's what kept me whole when all my bones were being broken. How can I take that away from Teo?

"You might be safer with us," I tell him.

Col stares at me. "What do you mean?"

It takes me a second to understand it myself, but then I turn and take his hands.

"My sister hasn't given any interviews yet. Why do you think that is?"

He shrugs. "Because she's angry at your father? Because she thinks you're dead?"

"No, Col." I lean closer, speak softer. "It's what you told me in the bunker—Rafi's been falling apart since she was seven, because all she had was speeches and handshakes, and not someone she could protect. When the assassin came, I could save her. But she could never save *me*."

Col stares at me. "But Teo's only fourteen. I have to protect him."

"Exactly. Which means letting *him* protect *you*."

He shakes his head. "I don't under—"

"You don't have a choice," Srin cuts in.

Col wheels on her. "Would you please stay *out* of this!"

"Limo," she says calmly, "secure doors."

Beside us, the vast wings of the limo's doors fold up. Then the blue light of a security perimeter shines down on the station platform.

"Here's the deal." Srin adjusts her school sweater, as if she's about to give a speech. "You can take Teo back to the war, along with my limo. Or you can sit here with no transport, waiting for the Paz wardens to pick you up."

"Wardens? We're not breaking any laws."

Srin smiles. "You're registered combatants in a neutral city, equipped with sniper rifles, grenades, sneak suits."

"Um, sir?" Zura says. "That's all technically true."

"But Paz is on our side!" Col cries.

"Unofficially, yes," Srin says. "But once a complaint's on the record, they'll go by the rules of neutrality—and impound you all for the rest of the war. Paz isn't going to risk getting dragged into a fight with a missile-flinging maniac!"

Col sighs. "And who's making this complaint?"

"Limo. Transmit in thirty seconds."

"Yes, General Srin," the limo says.

Heron shakes his head. "Trust me. Don't call her bluff."

"Just ignore her," I say. "But let your brother stay in the fight."

"I just lost my mother . . . *again*." Col's voice is breaking. "I can't lose him too."

"He can't lose you either. You need each other right now."

"Twenty seconds," Srin says.

Col takes a slow breath, his eyes closed.

Tears are coming down his face. I can guess what he's seeing in his head—that missile coming down on his home, over and over in an endless loop.

"Fight together," I say.

"Ten seconds."

"Okay!" Col's cry echoes through the empty station. "Just do it."

"Cancel that order, Limo," Srin says calmly. "Transfer control of your rental proxy to Teo Palafox. And buy me and Heron tickets on the next train into town."

"Of course, General Srin. It's been a pleasure serving you."

DAWN

We spend the night on the southern tip of Baja Island, in a sea of solar panels the size of playing cards.

Our limo's almost out of charge, and the main batteries for Paz are in the ground below us, so we jack in overnight before heading to the rally point Col has chosen for what remains of the Victorian army.

I sleep with him out under the stars. The breezes blow cool off the ocean, and we hold each other for warmth. In the middle of the night I feel him crying. Silent shudders rack his body, his last hope for his mother dying in the contractions of his heart.

I try to comfort him with whispers, uncertain if they're lost in the roar from the surf. It's better than thinking about Rafi alone in her room—alone in her grief, with no friends who even knew she had a sister.

When dawn breaks at last, the field of solar panels stirs around us. Each has six legs, to move and angle themselves as needed as the day goes on. Now they're all tilting together toward the red glimmers in the east, like flowers waiting for the sun.

One of the panels has crawled onto my wadded-up sneak suit, questing for more light. I place it gently on the ground.

Pulling on my suit, I realize that it fits me better now. It's learning the shape of my body. Or maybe it's because I've gotten rid of my nightshirt underneath. The liquid weight of the dew collected overnight feels reassuring.

With water and my knife, I can survive the wild.

I kneel beside Col. "You awake?"

A murmur comes from his lips, and I lean closer to kiss them. His eyes spring open.

"Frey?"

"Expecting someone else?"

He smiles, sits up. The tiny machines around us skitter out of his shadow. The sun is igniting the horizon now, turning the host of solar panels into a dark ruby sea.

We pause to watch the dawn—the sun pulling itself up, light rippling across the panels as they drink in energy, the world shifting from crimson to orange.

"Look," Col says. "You're beautiful."

"What do you . . . ?" I look down.

My suit's in camo mode, matching the solar panels around us. I shimmer like stained glass, a hundred reflections of the dawn mapped onto my body.

Col kisses me, and we stay there until the sugary smells of pastries and sweet coffee spill from the open limo doors.

Teo and Zura are eating breakfast inside.

Teo's school uniform looks more rumpled than ever, but Zura's fatigues are still immaculate.

She doesn't waste time. "Morning, sir. Units should be arriving at the rally point by now. We're fully recharged."

"Then let's head south," Col says, taking a cup of coffee. "Care to do the honors, little brother?"

"Limo, head to programmed destination," Teo orders, beaming at us as the lifting fans begin to spin.

I smile back at him. Srin only gave him the limo's proxy to make sure Col keeps his word, but it gives Teo a role in the fight against my father.

As we lift into the air, I look out the window.

From this height, the solar panels glint like bright, rippling water. The sun is fully risen now, the reds and oranges fading into reflected blue sky.

"Something's happening," Col says from the next window. "Over the city."

I squint through the sunlight.

A fleet of hovercars is rising from the center of Teo. They spiral into the air, flinging out in all directions like a wheel of fireworks.

Zura joins us at the windows. "That looks like a search pattern."

"Anything to do with us?" Col asks.

"Limo," Teo says. "Local newsfeed."

An airscreen fills the center of the cabin.

At first it's just images of warden hovercars, and the Spanish is too rapid for me. But then the screen fills with the smiling, triumphant face of Srin. Heron stands beside her, looking faintly embarrassed.

"Uh-oh," I say. "Anyone care to translate?"

Col sighs. "She says they were kidnapped by your father. That they made a daring escape."

"I *knew* she wouldn't stick with the truth," Teo says. "It's not dramatic enough!"

I shake my head. "So those wardens are looking for kidnappers. Can this thing go any faster?"

"Limo?" Teo says. "Maximum speed, please."

"We are traveling at the maximum safe speed, sir."

"Yeah, but we want to go at an *unsafe* speed. It's, um, a medical emergency?"

"Correcting course," the limo says. "The nearest hospital is—"

"Don't turn back!" Teo cries. "I need my . . . pills. Which are only available at the destination. Please go there at top speed!"

The limo considers this a moment. "You will require liability—"

"Put it on the account!"

The pitch of the lifting fans increases.

"Rentals," mutters Zura.

I raise my hands for calm. "What can the Paz wardens do to us? We didn't really kidnap Srin and Heron."

"They'll find our weapons," Zura says. "And when the limo spills its records, they'll know we spent last night jacking the city power grid. They'll have to impound us."

Teo leans back. "Yes, this would be a bad situation, *if* we were in some armored hovercar. But they won't be looking for kidnappers in a rented—"

"Apologies, sir," the limo says. "We are stopping under official orders from the Paz constabulary."

The lifting fans shift in pitch again.

Col sighs. "You were saying?"

WARDENS

"Override that?" Teo tries. "Keep going toward . . . my very important pills?"

"I cannot override local wardens," the limo says.

"Who comes to a war in a rented limousine?" Col shouts into the air.

"Col," I say. "We need a real hovercar. This is our chance."

He shakes his head. "If we attack Paz, that's one less ally."

"They'll never know it was us, sir." Zura turns from the window. She makes a few gestures, and her sneak suit camo shifts to black-and-gray Shreve combat livery.

My brain starts to spin. *This* I understand.

Being an impostor is what I was born to do.

And suddenly I know how to catch the wardens off guard, how to hurt my father, and how to get what I want more than anything else.

"I'll steal you that car," I say. "Just let me do the talking."

The limo lands when we reach the edge of the mainland.

When the doors open, a cool ocean breeze fills the cabin. This clifftop overlooks the Baja Sea, which is ashine with morning light. Screeching gulls surround us for a moment, but soon they're scattered by the roar of lifting fans.

The warden car comes down ten meters away. It's half the size of the limo, not much armor or weaponry, built for speed and quick turns.

Three wardens get out, looking bored at first, like they don't expect to find anything nefarious in this fancy car. But then they notice the mud on the limo's skids, the streaks from yesterday's rain. One of them puts a hand on the stunner in her holster.

When I step out into the sunlight, they're all stunned.

I've set my sneak suit to replay its camo from half an hour ago—the brilliant dawn captured in a million solar panels. It looks like something Rafi would design, a formfitting bodysuit for the most avant-garde of parties.

All my years of pretending flow back into the muscles of my body, my face.

"Good morning, officers," I say in my best Rafi voice. "Or is it afternoon? I hope you've come to arrest my hangover. I've just been to the *most* battery-draining party in your *lovely* city."

None of them speaks.

Rafi's never been to Paz, which my father hates for its happiness-loving, elected government. She doesn't travel without bodyguards, or talk to commoners.

"Ma'am," one of them finally sputters. "We're authorized to search all—"

"Be my guest." I gesture toward the limo. "But please don't impound my coffeemaker. I need it desperately."

"Uh, thank you." As he walks past, his eyes lock onto mine in disbelief. My smile is perfect Rafi.

Then Teo sticks his head out, surprising the warden. At the same moment, Zura comes bounding over the top of the limo, her sneak suit set to Shreve combat livery.

Her leap carries her to the warden midway between me and their car, crumpling her with a kick to her stomach.

I kidney-strike the man beside me. He staggers, and I take him in a sleeper hold until he crumples to the ground.

Spinning around, I see the last warden falling to Zura's blows.

She turns to us, smiling. "Well, that was easier than—"

An arc of lightning shoots from the warden car, and Zura shudders and falls. There's a stun cannon on the car's roof.

My knife leaps into my hand, and I hurl it at the warden car. The stun cannon explodes into a shower of metal pieces and discharged electricity.

The knife weaves its way home to my hand, hot and sparking.

Col and Teo are out of the limo now, running toward the warden car. Teo's carrying his suitcases and Col has the sniper rifle and his bow.

I stand ready with my knife. I can't see any more weapons mounted on the car. But if the hovercar's AI is allowed to stun people, it must be smart enough to fly itself away.

Maybe it's transmitting home for orders . . .

I spot an antenna dish on the car's rear hatch and send my knife to turn it into a shower of metal flakes.

Teo kneels next to Zura. Col jumps into the car. A moment later, sparks fly from the cockpit doors. So much for the car's AI.

Teo's running back toward me, a grenade from Zura's belt in his hand.

"What's that for?"

"Limo!" he orders, twisting the grenade to its longest setting. "Turn off fire suppression for safety check. Secure doors, please."

"Yes, sir," the car says.

As the doors begin to fold closed, Teo tosses the grenade inside.

"What are you—"

"It knows I'm the proxy, here of my own free will. And the

rally point's in the destination log." Teo swallows. "Limo, go for a spin over the water. Head for the middle of the Baja Sea."

"With no one aboard, sir?"

"Just go!"

Teo and I watch as the machine rises into the air. As it banks over the ocean, he takes my hand.

"Five, four, three . . ."

The limo jerks in midair, jets of fire gushing from its windows. It veers into a spin, falling like a leaf, trailing a spiral of smoke and flame.

I barely hear the splash over the roar of waves against the cliff.

"Poor limo," Teo says sadly.

"Come on!" Col yells.

We turn and run.

He's dragged Zura into the back of the warden car. She's unconscious, and her sneak suit's camo is blinking random colors.

"Is she breathing?" I ask, jumping into the back.

"Paz wardens are strictly nonlethal," Col says. "But check the vitals on the wrist of her suit!"

"All green," Teo says. "But is there a medkit, just in case?"

"Let her sleep," I say. "That's the safest way to get over a stun-blast."

I look back toward Paz to see if anything's coming our way. Nothing yet.

Col pulls himself forward into the cockpit, where the remains of the AI module are still smoking. He starts throwing switches, and the lifting fans begin to whine.

"You better strap in back there," Col says. "I don't really know how to fly without an AI, and this car's going to take off like a volcano rabbit."

FLIGHT

The warden car jumps into the air, pressing me down into my seat.

After the smooth ride of the limo, it's like being on a hoverboard. We lurch into a sickening turn, veering southward down the coast.

"My radar's out!" Col yells.

"That's what that was?" I look back at the smoking antenna on the rear hatch. "My mistake."

"Anyone following us?" Col asks.

"Not yet," Teo says from the back, strapping Zura into her seat. "Since when can you fly a hovercar, Col?"

"I've been practicing." Col's voice drops a little. "On a simulator."

"*On a what?*" Teo cries.

"I can take off and fly pretty well. Landing's the tricky

part. As long as Zura wakes up before we run out of juice, we'll be fine."

The car jolts to the left, slewing inland for long seconds before Col gets it under control.

"We're going to die!" Teo yells.

"Just a wind sheer off the ocean," Col says grimly. His right hand is white-knuckled on the flight stick.

I reach out, brushing my fingertips across the clenched muscles on his arm. "You're doing great."

"This feels just like the simulator . . ." He spares me a glance and a smile. "Except more dizzy-making."

The car bucks again beneath us, then dives for an awful moment toward the cliffs. Col wrestles with the flight stick until we're straight and level again.

"Maybe get out of this ocean wind?" I say.

"I have to stay on the coast. I don't know how else to navigate."

"So we don't know where we're going?" Teo yells.

"The codebook's got a map," I say. "I'll navigate."

"Right," Col says, and pushes the stick left. "Thanks."

We slip across the coastal cliffs, over rain forest, and finally onto a desert spotted with encroachments of white weed. The air steadies around us.

I pull my hand from Col's arm, take a deep breath.

At last I can think about what I did back there.

I've shown my face—Rafi's face—to wardens looking for

kidnappers. And right before we attacked, they saw Teo emerging from my limo. There's no way this doesn't make the feeds, even in Shreve.

I've told my sister I'm alive.

Tonight, she won't go to sleep thinking that she'll always be alone. She'll know I'm okay. She'll know I'm coming for her.

My father will also figure out it was me, of course. And that I'm working with the Palafoxes. But that's fine with me.

I'm coming for him too.

The other Paz wardens don't follow us.

It's hard to blame them. We overwhelmed three of their officers, using a pulse knife and a Special—a military-grade attack.

And maybe Paz doesn't want to shoot down a car carrying the first daughter of Shreve. They remember what happened to the last city that made my father angry.

An hour into the flight, Teo says, "I miss the limo. There was food and way better coffee. And we could watch the feeds when flying got boring."

"You call this *boring*?" Col mutters. His fist is still tight around the flight stick.

My eyes are glued to the codebook. Our glowing blue dot is making its way south toward the rally point. By now, what's left of the Victorian army is there waiting for us.

Instead of running, being hunted, soon we'll do some hunting of our own.

"The scenery's okay," Teo says. "But I'd rather watch the feeds going after Frey's dad. He's gone from war criminal to kidnapper to car thief!"

"Paz doesn't have a real army," I say. "He doesn't care about them. But this is the first time Rafi's been part of anything like a kidnapping. It'll look like he's turning her into a war criminal. That's bad for him at home."

Col glances over at me. "Won't it be bad for her too?"

"In the long run. But at least she knows I'm alive."

Our underbelly brushes the canopy of the jungle, making us all jump. We're trying to stay low and out of sight. Warden cars don't have camo skin.

I wonder if the Shreve army is searching for us. My father knows I'm a danger to him. But does he want his entire military learning his oldest secret?

A groan comes from the backseat.

"Zura!" Teo says. "Good to have you back."

I turn to look. Her head is in her hands, and her beautiful face is pale.

"What happened?"

"Stun cannon," I say. "The car shot you after you took out the wardens."

"I'm sick of cars with brains." She looks out the window at the trees flashing past. "We got away, I see."

"We're not *completely* helpless without you," Col says.

"I guess not, sir." A wan smile crosses Zura's face. "How far are we from the rally point?"

"Eight hours, plus recharging time." Col turns back to face her. "Do you suppose you could, um, take over? I haven't learned how to land yet."

Zura takes a slow breath.

"Lucky I woke up, then."

CRATER

It's early evening when we finally approach the rally point.

We're deep in the south of the continent by now, flying through cloud-wreathed mountaintops. The unpressurized cabin is cold, and Zura gives us pills for altitude sickness.

Col and his brother are in the backseat. I'm up front with Zura, bored and butt-numb from sitting all day.

The clouds part, revealing a huge mountain in our path. Its peak rises another thousand meters over us, flat-topped and girdled with shining snow.

"The White Mountain," Zura says.

Col leans forward. "You never saw a volcano rabbit, Frey. So I got you a volcano."

"Thanks. It's . . . impressive."

As we approach, the sunset glints across the peak. I've never seen snow this far south. Or a mountain this tall.

The hovercar keeps climbing.

"Wait, are we going *inside* that thing?" I ask.

"Into the caldera, yes," Col says. "It's too high for recon drones to fly. We can use the codebook without getting traced—the sides of the crater will dampen the signal spill. And there's a whole glacier full of fresh water!"

"It's super cold and hard to get to." Teo snorts. "Face it. You just wanted a secret base inside a volcano."

"Since I was a littlie," Col says. "But it's warm in the caldera, and half a klick across. We could fit a hundred hovercars inside!"

"Hopefully that's what we'll find," Zura says.

Col reaches forward and takes my hand. His gaze is sharp with excitement.

Then I see the mist rising up out of the caldera, like a pot of water about to boil.

"Wait. It's *hot* in there? This volcano's dead, right?"

"Not extinct," Col says. "But it hasn't blown in ninety years."

"Well, that makes me feel better."

We crest the lip of the caldera, and a huge crater opens up below us. Roiling steam hides everything inside. The inner cliffs are bare stone, too warm for snow to stick.

The rising air hits us as we descend, and the car shudders a little. I can see signs of an encampment through the mist—hovercars, tents, solar panels on a high shelf of rock. Soldiers scurry into position at our approach.

Col really has an army.

Seeing those faces gazing up at us, fingers seem to close around my chest. Soon everyone in that army will know my secret.

It recalls an old nightmare of mine—walking out onstage to give a speech for Rafi, certain that the whole audience will see through me.

"Frey," Zura says gently. "You might want to wear that."

She gestures down at the compartment in front of my seat. It's full of warden stuff—wrist ties, safety flares, a medkit . . . and a breather mask for fire rescues. Just big enough to cover my mouth and chin, so Col's army won't be gawking at me from the moment we land.

"Thanks."

She shrugs. "I don't want to get shot for driving around a kidnapper."

That's right—my encounter with the Paz wardens has probably been on the feeds all day. The world thinks that Rafi kidnapped the Palafoxes' second son.

Fantastic.

I set my sneak suit to Victorian livery, just so it's clear whose side I'm on.

In the turbulent winds of the caldera, the landing is tricky, our skids scraping the stone. Mist boils around our lifting fans, and I can feel the heat of the volcano even here inside the car.

But that's not why I'm sweating.

A squad of soldiers in Victorian uniforms approaches, rifles leveled. They look more confused than hostile—maybe because we're in a warden car from a city two thousand klicks away.

But when Col emerges from the back door, they break into cheers.

"Sir!" A soldier steps forward, saluting sharply. He looks barely older than Col. "Good to see you!"

"You too." Col claps him on the shoulder.

The shouts of astonishment redouble as Teo steps from the car.

While they're distracted, I swing down onto the stone, my face covered by the mask. More soldiers are gathering around us, maybe thirty altogether.

A few give me curious looks, but most of them are crowding around the brothers Palafox.

Then one of the soldiers looks straight at me.

"You're her, aren't you?" she asks.

"Um . . ." It's hard to answer, when half the time I don't know who I am. "Depends?"

She nods slowly. "Secret ops, I get it. But just so you know, there've been rumors since I got here. About one of our units. They responded to an emergency beacon, first day of the war."

I frown. "A beacon?"

"Turned out to be a crashed Shreve scout car. Weird thing was, there were two troopers tied up outside."

"I heard this one too," says another soldier, crowding closer to me. "Hostiles were incoming, so they had to run. But they grabbed the tied-up soldiers for transport to a neutral city. That's when it got brain-missing. The whole way there, these two prisoners wouldn't shut up about who knocked out their car. Someone with a knife, who looked just like . . . well, kind of like *you*, ma'am."

"And that story from Paz today," the first soldier says. "Teo getting kidnapped by a certain first daughter. But here he is, safe and sound, with you."

She smiles at me, takes my hand, and pumps it once. "So whatever it is you do, thanks for doing it."

The other soldier winks. "Making that bubblehead look like a kidnapper? Legendary!"

Others have overheard them, and the crowd is turning its attention to me. I see Col watching.

Waiting for me to say something.

This is my chance to get it over with. I grab the seal of the mask and tear it off, all at once.

The soldiers' eyes light up, and one lets out a low whistle.

"Spitting image," he says.

Others are gathering around me now, and I hear the story repeated—the scout car, Teo, my sister. This small army has been here most of the day, with nothing to do but swap war stories. By now they've all heard versions of this outlandish tale.

Col hoists himself up on the warden car's landing skid.

He waves for silence.

"Everyone! Just so you know, this is Frey. She might look like one of them, but she's on our side. She saved my life!"

All those eyes turn to me, and for a moment it's like stepping into blinding sun. I'm certain they can see all my secrets, everything I've ever thought or felt.

Of course, these soldiers have no idea what I really am. They must think I'm some kind of spy surged to look like Rafi. They're all in need of a good story about their side winning, and that's what I mean to them.

Then the strangest thing happens—they start clapping.

I've had a lifetime of applause. People clapping for my father when I stand dutifully next to him onstage. For Rafi when I deliver her speeches in front of crowds of randoms.

But this is for me, Frey.

Suddenly dozens of people know my name. And somehow all that attention isn't a pulse knife shredding me to mist.

I stand there, real and solid.

Seen.

There must have been a part of me that was always hungry for this. Because now I want everyone to know my name, my story. At last I'm not afraid they'll all disappear tomorrow for knowing too much.

Because they're an army, not one unlucky tutor.

Col steps down from the landing skid. He pulls me into a hug.

"Thanks for the introduction," I whisper.

"Didn't want anyone starting trouble." He pulls back, shrugs. "And they need a hero right now."

That word sends a mad giggle through me. Just being able to say my own name is enough.

"Flattery. You're going to be a good leader, Col."

"I have to be." His smile stays firm on his face. "Just talked to the ranking officer here. Three troopships, two scout cars, and six light attack craft."

I stare at him. "That's everything?"

He nods. "Eleven surviving hovercars. Counting you, me, and my little brother, the Victorian army is sixty-seven people."

HIGH
COMMAND

"The good news is, we have a glacier," Dr. Leyva says. "My math: It contains enough water to last us three million years."

A grim laugh travels around the table.

The Victorian High Command is meeting in a warm, steamy tent the size of my sister's dressing room. Our table is made from a jump deck borrowed from one of the troopships. It's big enough for the seven of us, but we've got nothing to put on it except an airscreen projector and a coffeemaker.

Col and I have been here at the White Mountain for two days, and we're still trying to figure out how to fight my father with next to no army.

"Food is another matter," Leyva says. "We have six days' worth, if we ration. Which *some* of us would prefer not to do."

He gestures to his own belly, and smiles go around the table.

Everyone here adores Dr. Leyva. He was a top scientist in Victoria, and the host of a science-and-cooking feed that the whole city followed. He wasn't in the military, but in the chaotic hours after the war began, he grabbed his medkit, flagged down a Victorian unit, and came here ready to serve his city.

Col shares an unhappy glance with his little brother. Teo has been anti-volcano from the start.

"One of the neutral cities will help," Col says. "Six days is long enough to figure out something."

"Also long enough for the dust to take hold in our city," Dr. Leyva says. "Our fellow citizens can already see it in the air. That means they're starting to watch what they say, what they read, even what they think. A change is coming over our citizens."

"What can we do to stop it?" Col asks.

Leyva shrugs. "Show me a room and I can clear the dust from it—for an hour or so. But once it's in the air, it replicates itself. It comes back, like mold."

"We can't defend every breath of air in Victoria," Zura says. "We're a guerrilla force—we have to *attack*. Disrupt Shreve's power grid. Hit their factories. Make the war so painful that it's not worth occupying us."

Zura is at this meeting as the commander of the House Guard. Because all the other Guard officers are dead, captured, or missing. She's been in a grim mood since her promotion.

But she's wrong about my father.

"Shreve doesn't use much power," Dr. Leyva says. "Their buildings don't hover. And their factories are deep underground— even a plasma gun can't get through five hundred meters of dirt."

"We'll hit their transport, then," Zura says.

"Their trade's already embargoed, and their citizens can't travel without permits." Dr. Leyva leans back, smiling to himself. "It's almost as if Shreve was expecting to fight this kind of war."

"Is there *anything* we can do to hurt them?" Zura asks.

More suggestions come, and I glance at Col. He gives me an encouraging nod. But it's hard, speaking up in front of people who know my real name. Part of me always has to pretend that I'm giving a speech for Rafi.

Finally there's a lull in the conversation.

"Sabotage won't work," I say. "No amount of pain will make my father walk away from a conquest."

The table is silent for a moment. Hearing the words *my father* from my lips still makes them uneasy. In all of Victoria's ragtag army, only the people in this room know what I really am.

"What about the citizens of Shreve?" Major Sarcos asks me. "Don't they have a breaking point?"

"Of course," I say. "But if they're broken, how do they stand up against my father?"

Sarcos doesn't answer the question. He's the highest-ranking officer to make it here to the White Mountain. But he seems too cautious and uncertain to command an army.

"We can't hurt him by force alone," I say.

"Exactly," comes a voice from the end of the table, and my spine contracts a little.

It's Artura Vigil, the head of the Palafoxes' psych warfare team. She's the one who recommended taking me as a hostage, who analyzed me and Rafi from afar, who scanned me while I slept.

She's like a grown-up version of Srin.

"We have to cut his support off at the root," she says. "Prove to his people that he's a monster."

"They know that already!" Teo cries. "He killed my mother, our grandmother. Everyone thinks he raised his own daughter to be a kidnapper—and they don't care!"

"They care about Rafia," I say.

The table goes quiet. I have their attention again.

But then Vigil starts talking. "That means they'll care about you too, Frey. So we tell your story. Show the scans of your body. Let you explain what it was like, watching your sister—"

"We've been over this," Col interrupts. "Reputational damage doesn't win wars."

Vigil just stares at him, uncomprehending.

"We can only make this revelation once," I say. "And what if it doesn't work? What if the whole world hears my tragic story, and the next day my father's still in charge?"

No one has an answer to that.

This was all much simpler when all I wanted was to hurt

him. To make him see me for once. To know that I existed beyond his schemes.

But hurting my father isn't enough anymore. We have a city to save.

I have to destroy him.

"Well, you all know what I think," Zura says.

Col nods, to show he's not ignoring her, but he doesn't reply.

Zura wants to kill my father.

The problem is, he hasn't appeared in public since the start of the war. His house, already a fortress, is now protected by the elite of the Shreve military.

We could raze it to the ground, I suppose. Get close enough to hit it with a hundred plasma guns at once.

But my sister lives there too.

If only there was a way to separate them.

"Rafi's the key to this," I say. "She can change things."

Teo sighs. "But she's not in charge."

"Not yet." This idea has been growing clearer in my brain since we arrived at the White Mountain. "But she's always been more popular than my father. If Shreve had a choice, they'd pick *her*. That's different than asking them to surrender to Victoria."

Dr. Leyva laughs darkly. "Alas, Shreve isn't holding an election anytime soon."

"Not an election." It takes me a few seconds to say the rest. "A coup."

A scout car takes off outside, heading off to do some

recon. The sides of the tent flutter, and for a moment it's too loud to talk.

But it gives my words time to sink in—I'm suggesting a revolt against my own father. An end to his rule forever. The others look confused, but for me it's like a storm is clearing in my head.

This is the only way to really win. To be safe at last.

To fix my sister.

When the sound of the takeoff fades, I go on.

"Rafi hates my father as much as any of you. Since he shot a missile at me, even more."

"You said that in the limo," Teo says. "But does that mean she wants to replace him?"

I hear the promise Rafi made the night before I left.

When I'm in charge, I'll tell the whole city about you.

Back then, I thought she was talking about him dying of old age. But Rafi's virtues have never included patience.

"Even before this war began," I say, "she was making plans to take power."

"Wanting to overthrow him is one thing," Zura says. "But making it happen is another."

I remember the day of the assassination attempt. When Rafi wanted to keep her scar, and Dr. Orteg went quiet. Because if she played up her injury too much, her popularity might exceed our father's in a way that was . . . dangerous.

"Trust me," I say. "This is what he's always feared."

Zura shakes her head. "He has the best army in the world. Why should he be afraid of a sixteen-year-old girl?"

"He's afraid of everything," I tell them. "That's why he made me."

None of them knows how to answer that. But for me this is all becoming clearer, down to the right quote from the warrior Sun Tzu.

" 'When the enemy tries to rest, make them toil. When they want to eat, starve them. When they're settled, make them move,' " I recite. "We'll bleed his army in battle, and make sure the embargo keeps Shreve hungry. And when they're really starting to hurt, Rafi will promise to make it all stop. Our father's army will never surrender to Victoria, but they might give control to *her*."

Everyone looks at me, not quite believing that my sister can pull this off.

It's Artura Vigil who speaks up. "But Rafia hasn't appeared in public since the day the war started. There's no chance of getting her away from your father. She can't declare a coup against him from inside his own house!"

That's when I see it—

"She doesn't have to declare the revolt herself." I give them all my best Rafi smile. "That's what I was born to do."

PART III

COUP D'ETAT

It is twice the pleasure to deceive the deceiver.

—Jean de La Fontaine

SABOTAGE

Three weeks later, a power station splays out below us, a million tiny reflectors mirroring the night sky.

Zura and I are crawling back to the rest of our team, carrying a stolen solar panel. It's bigger, more rugged than the ones in Teo, the size and weight of a combat boot. Like everything in Shreve, it's designed to resist an attack. When I grabbed the panel, it rolled into its ceramic shell, hardy enough to survive a bomb blast.

Luckily, bombing this power station isn't our plan.

Col and Dr. Leyva are waiting for us in the dark, invisible in their own sneak suits.

"This looks easy enough," Leyva says, taking the solar panel from me.

He pulls a cutting tool from his kit and starts to work,

dismantling the panel. He connects it to his handscreen, which comes alight with schematics and code.

"I was right—these things pass system updates to each other, like rumors." Leyva smiles as he taps away.

"How long will this take?" Col asks. He's staring at the city.

Shreve sits on the horizon, its dark skyline dotted with hovercraft on patrol. Only twenty kilometers away, I can make out my father's tower at the city's edge. It rises high above the forest, a corona of guardian hovercraft glinting in the moonlight overhead.

The sight of it makes me twitchy, like a snake in the corner of my vision.

"A piece of Trojan code is like a good ragout," Dr. Leyva says. "You can't rush it."

Col lowers his field glasses and sighs. "This is why no one ever actually *makes* your recipes, Doctor. They're too complicated."

"Indeed," Leyva says. "They only watched for my good looks and charm."

Zura peels away the face of her sneak suit to glare at him. She wants this mission done quickly. Farther up the hill, two more Specials await, invisible in their sneak suits.

With the Victorian army so depleted, Col's soldiers have accepted him fighting alongside them. But this mission has taken us closer to my father's city than we've dared go before, and everyone is nervous.

Last night on our way here, our hovercar was hit with a spray of fléchettes from a hidden ground unit. It sounded like thunder and hail. No one was hurt, but it was a reminder that war can become deadly with no warning at all.

I move next to Col. "Is this the first time you've seen Shreve?"

He lowers the field glasses, still staring at the city. "Yeah. It's not as evil-looking as I expected. But you can't see spy dust, I guess."

"You can at sunset. It turns the horizon brown and red. Like in the history feeds—the death skies after the last Rusty wars."

A shiver goes through Col. "I wonder if the sunsets in Victoria have changed yet."

"Not yet," I say. "We still have time."

He turns to me. "Is it weird, being this close to home?"

It takes a moment to answer. I was the one who asked for our team to take this mission, a chance to be near Shreve again.

No, not the city—Rafi.

I miss her more every day. And now that I'm close, it only hurts to think how near she is.

My sister still hasn't appeared in public. She should be out visiting the troops, or giving speeches in conquered Victoria. But she hasn't been seen, not even to deny that it was her stealing that warden car in Paz.

That means she's not cooperating with my father. There must be open warfare between the two of them inside that tower.

Col's still waiting for an answer.

"I don't miss Shreve," I tell him. "I hardly ever went out into the city. And it's not like I had any friends."

He takes my hand, looking sorry for me. He had a real home, of course, even if it's blown to pieces now. And he still has a whole city that he loves and that loves him back.

He may have lost his mother, but I was born an orphan.

"I just want my sister," I say.

Once Rafi's safe, my father's city can burn to the ground for all I care.

We've been hitting Shreve hard these last weeks. When they collect metal from the conquered ruins, we attack their freighters. When they try to occupy Victoria, we knock their hovercraft down with plasma guns. This leaves the citizens free to fight the spy dust, clearing it house by house with nanos devised by scientists in neutral cities.

None of this will topple my father, of course. But all of it weakens him for the day when his own daughter declares herself the new leader of Shreve.

My last speech in Rafi's voice.

Leyva utters a soft cry of triumph. "Got it!"

He unplugs his screen from the solar panel, reaches for his tool kit again.

"How long to put it back together?" Col asks. "Or is that also a ragout?"

"More like a boiled egg—anything longer than three minutes is the work of a fool." Dr. Leyva's tools move swiftly as he speaks, their metal whispers blending with the night wind.

Now that we're about to leave, the seconds seem to drag. I just want to be out of here. Away from the sight of that baleful tower.

"Got it." Dr. Leyva sets the solar panel down in the grass. It crawls away, back toward the rest of the colony. "They'll all be infected by sunrise."

Col watches with grim satisfaction.

"Sir," Zaru says. "If you please."

"She means come *on*." I take his arm and pull him up the hill. Our hovercar is parked on the other side. Its damaged camo skin won't hide it once the sun comes up.

We meet the other two Specials on the hilltop. They're carrying plasma guns and have those wary, serious expressions that Victorian soldiers wear whenever Col is on a mission with them.

"Too bad we can't stay and watch," Dr. Leyva says as we descend toward the car. "All those solar panels crawling into Shreve and causing havoc!"

I laugh. "This is war, Doctor. Go for stealth, not spectacle."

"War *is* spectacle."

This hovercar is larger than the one we lost to the jump mines. It carries six, with heavier armor and firepower, larger batteries—only the best for the heir of Victoria. Its underside is peppered with scars from the fléchettes last night. But nothing got through.

I settle in the backseat between Col and Dr. Leyva. The three Specials sit in front.

The doors seal around us, vibrations building as the lifting fans spin up.

Something sounds funny to me.

I glance at Col, who's putting on his seat straps. He pauses, frowning, like he hears it too.

As we lift into the air, the car tips sideways. Zura starts swearing, flipping switches.

Dr. Leyva's weight slides into me, squashing us both against Col. The car is sliding down the hill now, our landing skids scraping against grass and rock.

We're crashing.

GYROSCOPE

The skids catch, and we start to roll.

Suddenly I'm hanging upside down, my straps cutting into my shoulders. Col slides up the wall toward the ceiling—he wasn't strapped in. He hits with a *thump*, arms up just in time to protect his head.

I grab onto him. The car is still rolling, and seconds later we're right-side up, then upside down again. The world wheels around me, and Col and I cling to each other.

My stomach lurches. My hair is in my eyes. A loose water bottle bounces around the cabin, along with Dr. Leyva's tool kit.

We crash down onto our skids again and start sliding, and Col's full weight tumbles down on me. We're wrapped around each other like two terrified littlies.

The car is still sliding down the hillside. The lifting fans are shrieking, Zura yelling as she tries to shut them down.

The car's skids catch on hard rock again, and we roll over once more. This time Col and I are ready, and he stays in my arms.

The fans spin down at last. As their whine fades, the car settles on a patch of level ground.

The only problem is, we're upside down . . .

And twenty kilometers from my father's house.

"It was the gyroscope," Zura says.

She and Dr. Leyva are kneeling on the belly of the upended hovercar, staring down into its guts.

The rest of us are on the ground, standing in the gouges left by the sliding car. Col has a medwipe shoved into his bloody nose. My left eye is darkening where his elbow hit, and I have the twitchy-making feeling that I will never leave my father's city behind.

Everyone else is okay. Even the hovercar is mostly undamaged—except for its delicate, crucial sense of balance.

"I missed it last night," Dr. Leyva says. "One of those fléchettes, lodged in the gyro case."

"But we flew level on the way here," Col says.

Leyva nods. "It wasn't a direct hit. But every klick we traveled, the flechette was in there vibrating, nudging the gyro out of whack."

"This is my fault," Zura says. "I knew the controls felt wrong."

"It's just bad luck," Col says, but she doesn't answer. She's still angry with herself for lifting off before the Palafox heir was safely strapped into his seat.

Leyva drops from the hovercar's belly onto the grass. "It's just lucky we're carrying a spare gyroscope. This is the only car in the fleet that has one."

I smile at Col. "It's nice to be the heir."

"We need an ally with a factory," he mutters.

This is our army's real problem—after long weeks in the wild, our ships need maintenance. Our hole in the wall can print clothing and equipment, but not serious military hardware.

This is why the rebels don't use hovercars. The wild is unkind to complicated machines.

"I can switch the new one in," Zura says. "But it'll take a few hours."

"You mean, we'll still be here after dawn," Dr. Leyva says.

Zura nods. "We can't let the sabotage go ahead, or they'll come looking for the people who planted that code. You'll have to save your recipe for another day, Doctor."

Leyva sighs, then picks up his tool kit and handscreen.

"It was too good to be true. Come on, Frey."

Dr. Leyva and I climb back to the other side of the hill, then creep down to the edge of the solar colony.

The sky is already changing color, the stars in the east fading into an inky blue. In the distance, Shreve is lighting up. The factory belt teems with drones and self-driving trucks.

I bring us to a halt thirty meters from the nearest panels.

"Wait here. I'll be back with one in a minute."

"It's too late," he says.

I stare at him. "What is?"

"It would take hours for new code to spread through the whole colony. Once the sun comes up, my sabotage program is going to activate. Shreve will notice something's wrong, no matter what we do."

I stare at him. "Why didn't you tell Zura that?"

"I didn't want her rushing the repair job, like she rushed our takeoff. I've already been in one hovercar crash today." He takes my shoulder. "And you and I will be more useful here. We have a weapon, when Shreve comes looking for who hijacked their power station."

He gestures out at the countless panels, their reflectors rippling into position as dawn spills across the sky.

I shake my head. "You're going to fight off half the Shreve army with a bunch of solar panels?"

"No, with the most powerful object in the solar system. Might I borrow your plasma gun?"

I sigh and hand the weapon over. "Are you being cryptic for dramatic effect, Doctor?"

"You're clever enough to figure it out." He pulls the hydrogen battery off the rifle's plasma chamber.

I stand there, watching him work.

I should warn Zura what's happening, but we're too close to the city to risk a ping. I could climb back, but I don't want to leave Leyva alone. And maybe he's right—a rushed repair job can only make things worse.

There's nothing to do but wait, and try to figure out what Dr. Leyva is up to.

As the sun rises, the colony of solar panels begins to stir.

Instead of jockeying for light, they're flowing away toward the outskirts of Shreve. Leyva's plan was for them to attack the city's infrastructure—clogging drains, getting in the way of loading drones, covering up the markings in the road that guide cargo trucks.

There was also something about starting fires. That must be what he has in mind now. I'm pretty sure the most powerful object in the solar system is the sun. But I'm not sure why he needs to take my weapon apart.

While Dr. Leyva works, I pace back and forth. My father's tower is too close for me to relax. It's all I can do not to stare at it.

I imagine him inside, plotting his next moves against us. Is he still angry that I've turned against him?

Or, now that I've served my purpose, does he even care?

A couple of hours after dawn, someone in Shreve notices the solar colony's strange behavior. A hovercar peels off from the formation over the city and heads toward us.

"Are we ready?" I ask.

"Maybe." Dr. Leyva hands me his improvised contraption. It looks like a demented littlie's science project—the laser torch from his tool kit mated with what's left of my plasma gun. "Have you figured it out yet?"

I look down at the horde of solar panels. They're set to high reflectivity, glittering like mirrors in the sun.

Hundreds of thousands of them.

"Archimedes," I say.

"Ah." The doctor looks impressed with me.

"It's a legend, about an ancient inventor. He burned ships with mirrors, like a pre-Rusty laser. My military tutor taught me that one when I was ten."

When I told Rafi, we spent the day incinerating ants.

I raise my altered plasma gun. "So this is a target indicator?"

"Exactly," Leyva says. "The sabotage code contains a swarming function. Light something up with that, and all the panels will focus on it. But don't fire till you have to. Not sure how many shots you'll get before it all burns out."

I sigh, checking the seals on my sneak suit.

In the sky, the scout ship has come to a halt directly above the colony of panels. It lingers there, drifting back and forth like a survey drone.

The crew probably thinks this is a malfunction, not an attack. Maybe they'll send out a team in a groundcar to investigate. That might buy Zura another hour for her repairs.

The scout car rises up, and for a moment I think it's headed home to Shreve. But then it starts a slow loop around the edges of the solar colony.

Searching.

Motionless in our suits, Leyva and I are invisible. But on the other side of the hill, the hovercar is belly up, its camo skin damaged by flechettes and the crash.

I see the exact moment when the scout spots our car. It drops a little in the sky, taking a closer look. Then the scream of its lifting fans changes in pitch.

It wheels into a tight turn—

—and a ring of plasma streaks up from behind the hill. Two lifting fans vaporized, the scout car spins earthward, out of control.

It crashes against our side of the hill, and begins to roll downward in a gyre of flame.

Headed straight toward us.

SOLAR POWER

Dr. Leyva's staring, transfixed.

"Run!" I grab his arm and pull him out of the scout car's path.

It's hurtling faster as it comes, flinging off hot metal parts. Its remaining lifting fans are still spinning, sending it careening from side to side, a crooked flaming wheel.

Dr. Leyva stumbles, and his tool kit spills.

"Leave it!" I shout.

"Well, obviously." He rises to his feet. "Hold on, Frey. It's going to miss us."

I turn in time to see the wreck thunder past, leaving a dark trail of burned grass behind.

Dr. Leyva looks ecstatic.

"The transcendent spectacle of objects in calamitous motion," he murmurs. "War is such beautiful collisions."

"That *was* pretty bubbly," I say.

The scout car rolls onward until it loses momentum on the flatter ground. It spirals to a stop like a spent coin.

Leyva looks up. "But nothing compared to what comes next."

Half a dozen hovercars are approaching us from Shreve. These aren't scouts—they're armored attack craft, heavier than anything in our fleet.

I let out a whistle. "A bunch of *mirrors* are going to take those down?"

"We'll see." He smiles. "Aim it as you would a gun."

I take another look at the contraption. The laser torch has been fitted with a new lens. I recognize the double-trigger mechanism from the plasma gun, from which the battery and other, more mysterious parts have been borrowed.

When I pull the priming trigger, a familiar whine fills the air. "How many shots?"

Leyva shrugs. "One or two—or maybe zero? Just keep pulling the trigger till it breaks."

I give him a tired look, aim the device at the center of the approaching squadron, and fire.

The laser torch lights up in my hands, hot and buzzing.

A bright spot appears on one of the distant hovercars, a ruby circle of light. My target is moving, and at first it's hard to keep the laser steady.

But as I hold my aim, the car grows brighter and brighter. Thousands of tiny lights join mine, then tens of thousands more, until my target is glowing like the sun.

It doesn't burst into flame—duralloy armor doesn't burn. But its six engines are already spinning a thousand times a second. It doesn't take much for one of them to overheat.

A plume of smoke erupts, then a second, coiling around the hovercar. It banks in the sky, spinning downward like a leaf.

"Wow," I breathe. "This thing really works."

"Solar power," Dr. Leyva says reverently.

I shift the laser to another car in the squadron, and seconds later its engines are smoking too.

The horde of mirrors seems to take on a life of its own. As each car falls, the collective focus shifts to the next brightest in the sky. One by one, the squadron is turned into tumbling motes of smoke and flame.

I release the trigger. Dr. Leyva's contraption is hot in my hands, and a whiff of burned plastic hits my nose. The lens looks darkened in the center.

"Nice work, Doctor. But I think your gun is fried."

"We should probably get back to the ship, then."

We turn and run.

At the top of the hill, Leyva comes to a panting halt. I turn and look back at Shreve.

More hovercraft have formed into attack squadrons. But they aren't hurtling toward us. They've come to a halt at the city's edge, hovering motionless.

"They're afraid," Leyva says, breathless.

Of course. They've seen the panels take down six of their

own, and Shreve is surrounded by solar stations. The crews must think they're all infected.

Until they can figure out what's going on, they're trapped inside the city limits.

I look down the far side of the hill.

Our hovercar is still upside down, but its fans are spinning. Col and the two Specials are waiting a safe distance away. Zura must be at the controls, taking all the risk herself.

Are her repairs really finished? Or is it simply that we have no choice?

The car rises slowly into the air, the engines screaming. It climbs until it's almost level with us, wobbling uncertainly.

"And now the tricky part," Leyva murmurs.

In one motion, two of the four lifting fans roll over in their frames. The car flips to right-side up, then back to upside down, then over again. For a moment it looks like it's going to careen away, end over end—

But it steadies in the air, all four fans pointing downward at last.

I let out an exhausted sigh. "She did it."

"Frey," Leyva says softly. "Your father's house."

I turn back to face the city.

The squadrons that threatened to come at us have pulled back from the edge of the solar colony. Instead of retaking their stations over the city, most of the Shreve fleet is now in a tight ring around my father's tower.

They're guarding him, leaving the rest of the city open to attack.

"Of course," I say. "They think this is just a diversion."

"Not completely incorrect," Dr. Leyva says. "In the long run, we're coming for him. Now we know how he'll react."

I could have told him that. No diversion is big enough for my father to leave himself vulnerable.

Nothing will come easy.

"We should go." Leyva gestures at a last scout car lingering at the city's outskirts.

It's drifting slowly over the infected solar colony, testing the waters, ready to retreat if the mirrors turn on it.

I raise Leyva's contraption. But when I pull the priming trigger, the gun sputters in my hands. The battery is dripping, the last of its hydrogen bound with oxygen in the air, turned to water.

"Bring that along," Leyva says. "If the enemy think it's my usual standard of work, we shall hardly strike terror in their hearts."

"Your secret is safe with me."

We race down the hill.

Zura is landing, and Col is waving for us to hurry.

FLIGHT

As we speed away from Shreve, Dr. Leyva isn't entirely truthful with the others.

". . . and when we couldn't reverse the sabotage code, Frey and I decided to cobble together a weapon."

"Two *hours* without a word from you," Zura grumbles from the pilot seat. "We thought you'd been captured."

Dr. Leyva shrugs. "But think of the results—all it cost us was a plasma gun. Shreve lost six hovercars!"

Col listens, gazing with admiration at the makeshift weapon in my hands. I'll have to tell him later that Leyva's plan was not quite as improvised as he's admitting.

But it got the job done. We're headed back to base. My father's army is bloodied and tentative. And, for the first time, we've brought the fight to the city of Shreve itself.

"Well, you scared them." Col turns to the airscreen in front of him. "There's no pursuit yet."

"Most of the fleet went straight to my father's tower," I say. "He's more concerned with his own safety than catching us."

"They're also guarding Rafia," Dr. Leyva says. "He may have an inkling of our plans for her."

I stare out the window at the forest flashing past. That's still the problem—how do I declare a war against my father with Rafi in his house?

We have to steal her away somehow. Or cut them both off from the feeds so my father can't reveal that I'm an impostor. But as long as she's in his tower, neither option seems likely.

The airscreen lights up.

"Three blips," Col says. "Not from the city—they're right in front of us!"

Zura turns from her controls. "Probably Shreve units coming back from night patrol. They'll be low on juice. Won't be able to chase us for long."

"Right," Col says. "Head for the water, then."

Zura banks us into a sharp turn—southeast, toward the gulf, a long detour on the way back to the White Mountain.

The Shreve hovercars stay on our tail. They aren't fast enough to catch us, but we can't seem to shake them either.

An hour passes. Two. By the time we reach the waters of the gulf, it's almost noon. The high sun sets the ocean sparkling around us.

As I squint in the light, I wonder what it was like for the crews of those doomed hovercars back in Shreve. All those stings of sunlight swarming them, like death from a million bees.

Dr. Leyva's brilliance has a cruel streak.

But maybe I shouldn't judge. I killed someone with a pulse knife when I was fifteen.

We fly farther into the gulf, until there's no land within a hundred klicks. A dangerous place for hovercars with low batteries to follow us.

But the blips on the radar stay in pursuit, like they've got all the juice in the world. Shreve must have hidden recharging bases out in the wild, just like we do.

I lean against Col, trying to get some sleep while I can. But the twitchiness I've felt since seeing the skyline of home lingers in my bones. I can feel those hovercars pursuing us, like fragments of my father's will.

Only the warmth of Col's body keeps me from jumping out of my skin.

"This isn't working," Zura finally says. "If we go any farther out of our way, we won't make it home without stopping to charge."

Col swears. "But we can't lead them back to the White Mountain."

I lean forward in my seat, my muscles coiled tight.

"Then let's fight them."

Zura looks back at me. "It's three to one."

"I didn't say fight *fair*."

"What do you mean?" Col asks.

I look around the cabin. It's full of mission gear—plasma guns, spare sneak suits, body armor, hoverboards, my pulse knife.

A plan starts to form.

"Just get us to an island," I say. "One with mountains, and plenty of cover."

Col's eyes light up. "I know just the place."

AMBUSH

"Five, four, three . . ."

Col and I push ourselves out the hovercar door.

We fall for long, dizzy-making seconds, the board shuddering under our feet in the wind of the drop.

A war cry—more like a scream—leaps from my mouth. My arms are out wide in the warm air, like a tightrope walker's. Col's hands are tight around my waist.

For a moment it feels like we'll fly apart—me, Col, and the board all scattered on the waves below. But the magnetics in our crash bracelets keep us together. And finally the lifting fans spin up, the hoverboard bringing us to a knee-bending halt in midair.

"Whoa," he says in my ear. "This is *not* your safest plan."

I don't answer—while my father is in power, I'll never be safe. We lean sideways and peel away, giving the Specials some room.

They're just overhead, already falling from the car on two hoverboards. Not bothering with midair halts, they execute elegant turns and zoom off toward the island a few kilometers away.

"Show-offs," I say. "Come on."

We lean together, Col's arms still tight around my waist. The board slides down the tropical air currents. The shallow sea below is bright azure, rippled with sunshine and dark stripes of coral beneath the waves.

We're in the Cubans, a string of islands two hundred klicks south of the mainland. The patch of land we've chosen is just a tidal plain with a craggy peak rising at either end.

Col and I head toward the island's highest point. Buffeted by a stiff ocean wind, the board jerks and hitches beneath us. But it's good to stretch my muscles, to feel him pressed against me in the unsettled air.

I try to notice every detail, to hang on to this moment of us alone together over the bright sea—endless, boundless, brief.

We arrive at the summit, step from the board onto a pile of rubble. The peak is crowned with the crumbling remains of an old fort, its view commanding the entire island.

"Looks like someone's had this idea before," Col says, unstrapping the plasma gun from his shoulder.

"Always take the high ground." My sneak suit shifts, taking on the colors of the ancient concrete and its rusted metal skeleton.

I check my plasma gun.

Zura's voice comes in my ear.

Last transmission before they're close enough to hear us—

Everybody in position?

Col taps his ear. "We're ready."

The two Specials answer that they're almost set. I see their board landing a few klicks away, on the island's other peak. A moment later, they've disappeared into the rocks.

Zura's voice comes again.

Don't wait for me to start this.

When you get a shot, take it.

"Will do." Col takes cover beside me. "Be careful, everyone."

Below us, our hovercar is landing on the tidal plain, midway between the two peaks. Its solar panels slowly unfurl, their dark mirrors catching the sun. Exactly like a car that's run out of juice in the worst possible spot.

Our pursuers should pass right between us and the Specials on the other peak.

There's nothing to do now but wait.

Waiting is nervous-making.

"Four plasma guns," I murmur. "And they've got three hover-cars. We've only got one shot to spare."

Col raises his field glasses. "Your math is solid."

I look at him. "Shouldn't you be lecturing me on the plant life?"

Col does not disappoint. "Before the seas rose, this whole archipelago was one long island. Mountains, rain forests, swamps—a biological superpower. A paradise."

"Huh." There are more old bunkers strewn below us, their metal skeletons rusting in the sun. "Looks more like a military base than a resort."

Col shrugs. "There was a conflict about economic systems."

"That's Rusties for you," I say.

The birds, at least, are making good use of the bunkers. Feathers and droppings litter the ground. Every cranny is stuffed with the spirals of old nests.

I feel this privacy again, tinged with the hum of an approaching battle.

It makes me want to touch him.

"I miss this, Col. The two of us, alone in the wild."

"Me too. Sorry about my war getting in the way."

I smile, but it's not really a joke. The war that connects us, divides us.

"You've got an army to command, Col. A whole world to convince that Victoria shouldn't be forgotten. That's a lot."

He lowers his field glasses. But he's still looking out over the ocean, not at me.

"Sometimes it's like we're fighting two different wars," he says.

I shrug. "You're trying to save your city. I'm just trying to save my sister. That must seem small to you."

He finally turns to me.

"Frey. Your whole life, you had to hide—private suites, secret compartments, hidden hallways, small spaces. But that doesn't mean *you're* small."

I wrap my arms around myself, wanting to disappear under this open sky. "What am I, then?"

"Angry, unyielding, fierce." He narrows his eyes, like he's looking for the truth of me. "Strange and dangerous."

"Like a pulse knife?"

"I guess. And loyal too. Maybe the best word is *steadfast*."

I look away. "That's a tour guide word."

"Yeah." He shrugs. "How about I make it yours?"

"Okay. Sure."

He drops his hands and bows, like he's asking me to dance. "I swear to you, Frey, I'll never call anyone else steadfast."

As I laugh at this, something crumbles inside me. Something that had turned to stone so gradually, I hadn't even realized.

"That's the nicest promise anyone's ever made me."

A smile breaks on his face.

"I can do better, once we . . ." He turns to the ocean, reaching for his weapon. "Hear that?"

I squint out across the water, switching to heat vision. In the distance, I can make out three bright constellations of lifting fans.

"It's them."

We sink into the rocks. Seal our sneak suits. Hit the priming triggers on our plasma guns.

The pulse of battle builds now. My tension, coiled inside me all day, is strung taut and shimmering.

Col's promise echoes in my ears, and I am steadfast. Ready to fight.

The three hovercars come skimming low across the waves. An iridescent spray plumes from their lifting fans.

They're slowing down. Spreading out, like big cats hunting. Cautious, now that we've stopped running.

Soon they're close enough that I can see their black-and-gray livery, the battle scars on their hulls. One hovers at a crooked angle, its left rear engine flame-blackened and silent.

My finger itches to squeeze the firing trigger.

But the formation glides to a halt, just out of range. I swear softly under my breath, wanting the fight to begin.

One of the three cars rises a little into the air. And something odd happens.

The belly hatch opens, and a long piece of metal is lowered down. At first it looks like an antenna or a signal jammer.

But tied to it is a white flag.

WHITE FLAG

"It's a lie," I say.

Col lowers his aim. "Why would they surrender?"

"They wouldn't. And if they wanted to parley, they'd use radio, not a flag."

I squint through the scope on my gun. The white flag is smudged and threadbare. Like someone's T-shirt pressed into a higher purpose.

It hangs limp in the still air.

"This has to be a trick," I say.

"It's three to one. They don't need to trick us." He reaches for the field glasses. "Or maybe they suspect an ambush?"

I look at our hovercar on the floodplain, its solar panels splayed out, defenseless. The two peaks looming over it with crisscrossing fields of fire.

I shrug. "As ambushes go, it's not what I'd call subtle."

"I'm going to ask Zura." Col reaches for his ear.

I grab his hand. "If we ping her, they'll know we're here. We might as well wave our own white flag!"

"Then what do we do?"

"Wait for them to get closer." I turn back to my rifle, peer through the scope. "Then shoot them."

Col lets out a sigh. In the end, of course, all these decisions are on him. He always feels the weight of keeping his soldiers safe.

But this is where I'm an expert. A false flag of surrender is exactly something my father would do.

A ping comes in my ear—Zura's voice.

Shreve craft. Please state your purpose.

I nod. She's broadcasting on a wide spectrum, so we can hear too.

There's radio silence for a long moment.

Shreve craft, do you read?

Still nothing.

Do you read?

"Maybe their radio's out," Col says.

"All *three* of them?" I shake my head. "This isn't even a particularly good trick. It makes no sense."

"But what if . . ."

Col falls silent—the hovercar with the white flag is easing into motion.

It glides slowly toward the island, headed straight for the tidal plain. Its course will carry it right between us and the Specials on the other peak.

"Well, that makes this easy," I say. "Those pilots are brave, I'll give them that."

"Frey. We can't just . . . *murder* them."

"Col, this is my father—that might be the point! If they trick us, we're dead or captured. If we shoot them, we'll doubt ourselves." I look straight into his eyes. "You can't win. There's *never* a clean victory. Get used to that!"

I turn away. Aim my weapon. The thwarted ecstasy of combat has soured into anger.

"Frey. Look at me."

I don't answer, my eye glued to my scope.

The white flag is fluttering now in the wind of the car's passage. It's not just smudges—someone's deliberately streaked the T-shirt with black.

They're trying to make it *look* improvised.

"That first day of the war," he says, "you didn't let me shoot those soldiers."

My scope lights up—the target is within range now. But I hesitate.

The other two cars are staying back. If I take down this one, they'll open fire on us.

"Col, step on the board and get away from here. I'll handle this." When the two remaining Shreve cars come after me, the Specials on the other peak will have a clean shot.

And Col will be safe.

"This is what your father would do," he says.

"One hit on Zura's car and we're stuck here, Col! What if he knows you were on this mission, and this is all a plan to capture you?"

"Frey, he's not all-knowing."

"If you're a fool, he doesn't have to be. So just—"

My voice chokes off.

The breeze has stiffened, the white flag stretching out to its full length.

It's a T-shirt, all right, but the black marks on it aren't smudges. They're symbols I've seen before—in the ruins.

And words in English . . .

I lower my rifle. "Give me the field glasses."

Col hands them over, and I raise them to my face, thumbing at the focus button.

She's not coming to save us.

I drop the field glasses and tap my ear.

"Everyone, hold your fire."

A sigh rushes out of Col as Zura's voice comes back to me.

State your reasons.

"These aren't Shreve hovercars. They're rebels."

REBELS

We stay hidden on the high ground, watching the black-and-gray hovercar land on the floodplain a hundred meters from our own.

The belly hatch opens, and half a dozen crew spill out.

I was right—instead of uniforms or sneak suits, they're wearing handmade clothes. Fleece jackets, hand-knitted sweaters, shoes made from animal skin. There's no way Shreve soldiers would go to all this trouble just to trick us.

I hand the field glasses back to Col. "You finally got your wish. Looks like we're joining the rebels."

"Or they're joining us," he says.

We ping the two Specials to keep their position, then take the hoverboard down.

Zura and Dr. Leyva are waiting on the wet sand. Most of the

rebels look like young runaways fighting to save the earth—wiry muscles, unsurged faces, threadbare clothes.

One of them looks familiar. From home? From Victoria?

Then it hits me—the last time I saw them, instead of hand-made forest camo they were wearing a feathered blue ball gown.

"Yandre?" Col asks as we step from the board.

"Chico! It's you!"

They embrace, and a torrent of Spanish follows. But when Yandre sees my face, their words break off.

"What the—"

I sigh—life will be easier once the whole world knows. But for now I have to give my little speech again.

"I'm Rafia's twin sister, born twenty-six minutes later. Hidden from birth. Raised as a body double. A decoy."

The rebels all stare at me, dumbfounded.

"And now a 'Fox," Yandre says with a smile, and gives Col a playful punch. "Aren't you the charmer?"

A woman dressed in stitched-together skins comes closer to me, inspecting my face. She's older than the other rebels, with the green armband of a unit boss.

The rebels don't have ranks. Each group elects their own boss, more like pirates than a real army.

"You were the hostage in Victoria, right?" she asks. "You got the 'Foxes to drop their guard—and then switched *sides*?"

I hold her gaze. "That's about right."

"Huh." She turns to Col. "And you're fine with that . . . because she's your *girlfriend* now?"

He looks a little unsteady for a moment. No one in his own forces would dare ask such a question.

But he answers in a firm voice. "Frey saved my life. She's fought beside us—and against her father."

The woman shrugs, turns to me.

"You're sixteen, right? Not a bad age to work out family issues." She turns back to Col. "Well, you 'Foxes might be stuck up, but I've never known you to be stupid. Guess I'll take your word she's on our side."

She waves a hand, and the other two hovercars head in.

"I'm Boss Charles, and we're Carson's Raiders. You 'Foxes got any food?"

We eat lunch with the Raiders on the beach, in the cool of the ocean breeze and the shade of unfurled solar panels.

There's not much hunting on the island, but Col manages to take down a few birds with his bow while the rebels watch and heckle. We roast those on an open fire and empty all our survival rations to feed our new allies.

Dr. Leyva and Zura are busy gathering information from the Raiders. The rebels have stepped up operations against my father, coming from as far away as Patagon to fight him.

Col sits beside his old friend Yandre, as happy as I've seen him since the war started.

"I should have known it was you, Chico." Yandre's gesture takes in the mountains, the beach, the sky. "Who else is fussy enough to run for four hours, just to find the perfect tropical island for an ambush?"

In our laughter, all the day's anxieties—being so close to my father's house, fighting the Shreve army, almost firing on a white flag—unravel in my chest.

The Palafoxes' bash seems like a thousand years ago, but seeing Yandre again brings back the wonder of that night.

"Since when are you a rebel?" Col asks.

"A confession," Yandre says. "Remember all those stories about my brother? His greenie friends? The playful acts of sabotage?"

Col blinks. "Wait. That was really *you*?"

"I've been a rebel since I was Teo's age." Yandre turns to me. "And just for the record, Frey, I only shoot at people who invade my city. I voted against attacking your convoy."

"Um, thanks?" I say, then shake my head. "It doesn't matter. I was a different person, traveling under a different name."

"Well put."

"But why were you chasing us in Shreve hovercars?" Col asks. "And why the radio silence? We almost shot you!"

Yandre chews slowly, basking in our attention for a moment before sharing the tale.

"Three days ago, we were on patrol in the mountains. We're a light unit—hoverboards and sniper rifles—so we don't usually mess with armored cars. But we stumbled on these three heavy Shreve cars recharging, and it was too good to pass up."

Boss Charles leans into the conversation. "We got the jump on the crews, but the commander managed to run some kind of anti-capture program. The autopilots, radios, codebooks—all of it was smoking when we got inside the cars. Took us a day to get them flying again."

"Okay," I say. "So you didn't have radios. But why were you coming after *us*?"

Yandre looks up at the Shreve cars looming over us.

"We rebels don't fight in tin cans. We can't keep these flying for long—we don't have the parts. But you 'Foxes have a fleet of your own. Now that you're fighting for the planet, we figured you should have them."

"It was Yandre's idea," Boss Charles says. "I voted against it but got out-talked."

Yandre spreads their hands. "My insubordination is matched only by my charm."

"At least we got lunch," the boss grumbles.

I look up at the three machines. They're heavy attack craft, with about as much firepower as the rest of Col's fleet put together.

But they're also hard to maintain. And thanks to that quick-thinking Shreve officer, they're missing most of their software.

"Not sure we can use them either," I say.

"Maybe chop them up for parts?" Col suggests.

I shake my head. "Anything my father builds is incompatible with the rest of the world. So you have to buy your parts from him."

"Told you, 'Dre," Boss Charles says. "Waste of a day. I'm going swimming."

She stands up and walks toward the water, dropping her clothing on the sand along the way.

Half the other rebels spring to their feet and follow her. Soon the beach is covered with handmade clothes, the water full of splashing, naked bodies.

Yandre sighs. "At least I got to see you, Chico."

"It's good to see you too," Col says. "But I'm sure there's something we can do with these ships. Deploy the weapons on the ground, or trade them for something we *can* use."

"Or take a page from my father's book," I say. "Attack Shreve with them, force them to fire on their own ships."

Yandre's eyes light up at that. "Maybe during the peace conference, when he's away."

Col and I both stare at them.

Yandre sees our expressions, and smiles.

"Ah. You mean you haven't heard?"

WAR COUNCIL

A few days later, the rebel delegation lands inside the White Mountain. They seem impressed.

We've got hot showers now—melted glacier water piped along the steaming crater walls—and enough solar panels to recharge a hovercar in just a few hours.

Instead of a tent, we hold the War Council in a real building. It's made from trees and smells like sap and fresh-cut wood. The table is the same recycled jump deck, but someone has burned the Palafox seal into the center.

I'm pretty sure the rebels only care about the showers.

They've sent three bosses—Boss Charles and two others she's fought beside—and Yandre. For us it's me, Col, and Teo at the table, along with Zura, Major Sarcos, Artura Vigil, and Dr. Leyva.

A tight group for keeping secrets.

The first thing Col asks is "How certain are you that this peace conference is real?"

"Our spies in the city governments all say the same thing," Boss Charles says. "Shreve wants to make a deal. But in secret, so they don't look like the pressure's getting to them. The conference location is completely off the grid. A small island in the Pacific. No feeds allowed."

"What's Shreve offering to get the embargo lifted?" Col asks.

"That's also secret."

"Of course," I say. "My father doesn't go into negotiations without a few surprises ready. He'll propose something unexpected, just tempting enough to divide the other cities."

The rebels are watching me closely, still a little perplexed by sitting at parley with their enemy's daughter. Even Yandre gives me a double take every now and then.

I'm starting to wonder if people will always look at me this way, once my secret's out. Maybe pretending to be Rafi was the normal part of my life, and it's all gawking and whispering from here on.

"It doesn't matter what he's offering," Zura says. "If we time our attack right, he'll be out of power before the conference even starts."

Everyone's eyes turn to me again, taking my measure as an impostor.

I'm ready to convince them. I've dressed like Rafi today, in the exact suit she wore for my father's birthday last year. (Or as close as our hole in the wall could come to it, at least.) Yandre did my hair and makeup earlier, and I'm sitting with Rafi's balletic posture. Prim and upright, shoulders back.

Imperious.

"It's time to bring freedom back to Shreve," I say in her voice. "My father's rule must end."

Charles gives a grumbly chuckle, like she always does when I imitate my sister.

Boss X leans forward, his strange eyes slicing through me. He's the most extreme of the rebels, radically surged into a cross between a wolf and a man. He gave up his "human name" when he joined them, and his voice has been surged to a low growl.

"So you're going to conquer him with oratory?"

"Every revolution starts with the right words," I say.

Boss X looks unconvinced. "He's going to make his own speech—threaten them to stay in line, remind them who's in charge. We should cut him off from the feeds."

"We don't have to," I say. "If he speaks up from some island in the middle of the ocean, he'll have to admit he snuck away to bargain for peace."

"And we can't attack the conference," Teo says. "We have allies there."

Boss X shrugs. "Your allies, not ours."

"We don't want to start a larger war," Col says. "We want to end this one."

"But the people in Shreve have breathed dust for ten years,"

Boss Charles says. "They've got no weapons. How do they over-throw an army?"

"They don't have to," I explain. "My father doesn't go any-where without his favorite officers, his most loyal units. Whatever's left in the city will be easy to sway to our side."

"Even if the revolt isn't total," Col says, "our forces will be there to tip the balance."

He waves a hand, and the airscreen projector sputters to life. A scale model of my home city appears on the table. The stolid skyline, the new defenses and the suborbital pads. The ragtag Victorian fleet appears in the surrounding farm belt.

I stand and point a ringed finger at my father's tower on the outskirts.

"This is our objective—the seat of his power."

Dr. Leyva stands beside me. "From there, we take control of the city feeds to broadcast Frey's speech. We'll also corrupt the dust with a virus. For the first time in a decade, the people of Shreve can say whatever they want about their dear leader. Freedom, all at once!"

The third boss starts to shake his head. He's the oldest of them, with an unsurged face and static tattoos. He has an accent I've never heard before. And a strange name—Andrew Simpson Smith.

According to Yandre, he once fought alongside Tally Youngblood herself.

"I have seen that tower," he says. "Many drones protect it."

"You're right," I say. "It's the best defended spot in the whole city. We'll have to take it by stealth, not force."

A low growl comes from Boss X. "So you're sneaking in? I was promised a stand-up fight."

"A fight is what you'll get." I fix his yellow, lupine eyes with my best Rafi stare. "We'll launch a full-on assault on the city. And once the sky is full of damaged Shreve hovercraft in retreat, my team will slip in alongside them."

With a wave of my hand, the cityscape is replaced with an image of one of our captured hovercars. Zura has skinned it to match the Shreve Home Guard. She's also added some bogus battle scars and smoke bombs on two of the engines.

"This is our Trojan horse—a damaged Shreve car fleeing from the front line. We'll crash-land near the tower, fight our way through any household guards, and grab my sister. Then we take control of the feeds, and I declare a new era for the city."

Yandre speaks up. "What if Rafia's with your father?"

I draw a slow breath, trying not to show any emotion.

"She won't be."

Yandre looks sympathetic, but says, "You can't know that, Frey."

"It won't matter," Col cuts in. "We'll have his tower, his dust, and our own Rafia, ready to make the speech that the people of Shreve have always wanted her to make. All he'll have is a reluctant daughter."

The three rebel bosses look at me.

"Reluctant?" Charles asks.

"My sister despises him." There's certainty in my voice again. "Even if he puts her on the feeds to show that I'm not real, I'll be the more convincing Rafia."

They look like they believe me, but then Artura Vigil speaks up.

"It seems like a gamble, putting everything we've got into one battle." She looks at Major Sarcos. "Isn't that the riskiest thing a guerrilla army can do?"

Sarcos looks uncomfortable. He's never liked the idea of shifting from sabotage to all-out battle.

Vigil turns to me. "And isn't this exactly the sort of dangerous venture your father would *want* us to try, Rafia?"

I give her a cold glare. "My name is Frey."

"So you keep telling us. And yet your plan seems designed to deliver us straight to your father."

Col sits up straighter. "What are you saying, Artura?"

"She tells us there's a real Rafia back in Shreve. But we've only seen that girl for a few moments on a balcony, waving and smiling. That other girl has given no interviews, no speeches on the feeds—as if she's trying to hide something." Artura's eyes sweep the room. "While here in front of us sits a much more convincing Rafia, telling us to send our army into danger. What if this whole story about twins is a lie?"

The world turns inside out for a moment. What if I'm the real Rafi, and the girl back in Shreve is the impostor?

I grip the edge of the table, reminding myself that I'm real.

Col places a hand on mine. "This is absurd. There's no way anyone could've planned all this from the beginning."

"She is no doubt improvising," Vigil says. "But Rafia's already admitted coming to Victoria to make us lower our guard. Why shouldn't she play the same trick twice, if we're foolish enough to fall for it?"

They're all looking at me, but I don't know what to say. I've spent my whole life convincing people that I *am* Rafi. How am I supposed to do the opposite?

Maybe dressing up like my sister today was a bad idea.

"Her name is Frey," Col says softly, and the world settles a little around me. "And we know she's on our side. She could've captured me on the way here!"

"Me too," Teo points out.

Vigil only smiles, her cool expression reminding me a little of Srin.

"Even with you two captured, there'd still be an army, Col."

"No, there wouldn't," I argue. "I could've told my father where this base is. He'd be here already!"

Vigil's smile doesn't fade. "Isn't it easier if we come to him? And better for his reputation he wins this war defending his own city instead of hunting down strays?"

"Frey is exactly who she says she is!" Col shouts. "I'm certain of it. That's the last we'll hear of this ridiculous *theory*."

Vigil bows her head, and the table falls silent.

But that glimmer of distrust stays on all their faces. It's an unlikely story that Vigil is telling, but no stranger than the truth of me.

I was born a lie. Why should any of them believe me now?

I want to speak for myself, to keep the argument going in spite of Col's orders. But the words don't come, because part of me is never really certain who I am.

It's Boss Charles who breaks the silence, letting out a huge laugh.

"What a mess!" She claps me on the shoulder. "Maybe you're Rafia, maybe you're Frey. Maybe your little coup works, maybe it fails. But my Raiders are in either way. It'll be the most chaos we've seen since Tally Youngblood disappeared!"

"She's not coming to save us," Boss Andrew says reverently. "Which is why we have to take chances. My people will join as well."

It's hardly a ringing endorsement, but at least they aren't running away.

We all turn to Boss X.

For a long moment, he doesn't look human at all. The corners of his mouth droop and his ears go back against his head. I don't know what the expression means, but it charges the air in the room.

"My pack will join on one condition," he says. "I'm coming along in your captured hovercar."

"Um, okay." Col gives him a frown. "But I thought you wanted a stand-up fight, not sneaking around."

"There'll be plenty of fighting." A ripple goes across Boss X's fur as he turns to me. "And a little sneaking is worth a visit to your father's house."

"For what purpose?" Col asks.

"It's personal," Boss X says. He leans back and doesn't say another word.

"Rebels," Zura mutters softly.

I give Col the slightest shrug. Boss X's personal business doesn't matter to me. Nor do I care if the rebels are more interested in causing chaos than in trusting me.

All that matters is that we have a plan to save my sister.

GOOD-BYE

As our hoverboards rise above the lip of the crater, the freezing wind sets my blood humming. It's almost sunset, a week after our meeting with the rebels.

At this altitude, the sky is upside down—a layer of red-tinged cloud spreads out beneath our mountaintop, with only cold blue overhead.

It's just me and the brothers Palafox. A last dinner before we leave Teo behind in safety. By this time tomorrow, Col and I will be headed into battle.

"Thank you both," I say. "For trusting me."

Col turns from the sunset. "You're not still worried about Artura, are you? Nobody believes her stupid theory."

I sigh into the cold wind. "She believes it. And I bet she's still whispering in your officers' ears."

"Then she's brain-missing," Teo says. "Srin says that's the

348

problem with psych warfare. You drive yourself mad along with the enemy."

Col smiles. "Frey and I know all about that. When we met, we were so busy lying to each other, we almost forgot who we were."

"Almost," I say, taking his hand.

A cloud of steam swirls up from the depths of the caldera, setting us wobbling on our boards. We descend to the solid rock of the crater's edge, where the warm volcanic air alternates with the mountain wind.

Teo pulls a few self-heating meals from his pack. He places them in a neat, ceremonious row. This could be our last dinner together here at the White Mountain. It could be Col's and my last dinner ever.

"I've got PadThai, SpagBol, and SwedeBalls," Teo says. "Three timeless classics of camping cuisine."

Col sighs. "Anything without rabbit."

"Same," I say. In the last month, I've seen plenty of volcano rabbits, and eaten most of them.

Teo passes out the meals, and we pull the heating tabs. I cup mine in my hands, grateful for the warmth as it boils the prefab noodles into something edible.

If we win tomorrow, I'll never have to eat camping food again.

And if we lose, it'll be my fault.

Artura Vigil was right about one thing—throwing the whole Victorian army into one battle is a dangerous plan. And now that she's doubted me in front of everyone, they won't ever forget that it was *my* plan.

Their enemy's daughter.

I look up from my food. "You think your soldiers still trust me?"

Teo shrugs. "You heard the rebels—they don't care whose side you're on. They just want to shake things up."

"And my officers will obey orders," Col says.

"Great," I say. "Nothing like comrades-in-arms who have to be *ordered* to trust me."

"Zura trusts you," he says. "That counts for something."

It does, because Zura is coming with me in the stolen hovercar. No other Victorian officer is willing to go on a crash-landing commando mission.

Col himself will stay with the main fleet.

"What if Artura's right about the rest?" I ask. "That it's a terrible plan to begin with?"

"It's the perfect plan," Col says, blowing on his food. "A coup will end the war quickly. And it means freedom not only for Victoria, but for Shreve too."

"But we're risking your whole army, Col."

"Better than risking the soul of my city."

I shake my head, not sure what he means.

"It'll take years to win a guerrilla war," Teo explains. "Long enough for the dust to choke everyone. No one daring to say what they think, or to keep a diary, in case some Shreve warden arrests them for having the wrong opinion."

"Everyone in Victoria has their own feed," Col says, "and tells their own story. That's the soul of our city."

"I grew up breathing spy dust," I say. "And I have a soul."

"Sure," Col says quickly. "I just meant, freedom's easy to lose and hard to get back."

I look away. From the moment I learned to talk, I've had to watch my words, my gestures, the way I stand and walk. I know the value of freedom more intimately than anyone. But I don't have time for philosophical discussions.

Not until my sister is safe.

"You're right," I say. "If we can end this tomorrow, it's worth the risk."

"Which is why you should take *me*," Teo grumbles.

Col just stares into his food. They've had this argument a dozen times in the last week.

"We have to leave someone in charge here, Teo," I say.

"In charge of *what*?" he cries. "You're taking everyone else with you!"

Col turns to his brother, and for a moment I think he's going to be angry.

But his words come softly. "Frey's plan will work, but something might happen to me in the fight. If I have bad luck, we need a Palafox to pull Victoria back together."

I wonder if that's really true. Certainly everyone in this army thinks so, or they wouldn't follow Col's orders just because of his last name. And maybe that's what matters—people believe that the first families bind their cities together, and that belief makes the magic work. At least, I hope so.

Because when Rafi declares war on our father tomorrow, it has to tear Shreve to pieces.

RAIDING PARTY

We take the captured hovercar down a riverbed. Beneath the treetops, out of radar coverage.

Yandre, Boss X, and I are up top, spotting for Zura as she pilots us through tight spots. We crouch behind the rail gun turrets, ducking branches, X's fur rippling in the wind.

There are ten of us in the raiding party—three more of Zura's Specials down below, along with Dr. Leyva and his two best techs. Their job is to take over Shreve's feeds and spy dust, once we have control of my father's tower.

Col's back with the main force, in the largest Victorian ship.

"Why so glum?" Yandre calls to me above the engine noise.

I shrug. "I've never been on a mission without Col before."

"Chica, how sweet."

Boss X is staring at me. "So what are you, exactly?"

I give him a confused look.

"He means, are you a 'Fox or a rebel?" Yandre says. "I've been wondering that myself."

"A Palafox?" I stare at them both. "Are you asking if Col and I got *married*?"

Yandre lets out a long laugh. "Frey, we know you like Col, but that's different from being a 'Fox. That army back there, they *need* a first family. It makes them feel complete, having someone in charge."

I remember how Aribella made me feel that first day. Like she deserved to command a whole city.

But I shake my head. "I'm not in Col's army. I'm not even a Victorian."

"*I'm* a Victorian," Yandre says. "It's my city too. But I'm not a 'Fox. You get it?"

"Sure—you're a rebel. That's bigger than any city."

"Exactly. I'm against anyone who messes with my planet." Yandre waves their hand at the sky, the river, the forest. "*This* is what we rebels are fighting for. So what about you?"

Both of them are watching me now, but I don't know how to answer.

Last night, Col was talking about saving our two cities. But cities don't mean anything to me. My whole life has been spent as a prisoner of my father's schemes, or running from him. Those are the only two realities I understand.

Before I can answer, the hovercar eases to a halt. The banks of the river are tightening, the trees bowing in to scrape our armor.

For the next few minutes, we talk Zura through the squeeze, meter by painstaking meter, pushing aside branches as we go. It's slow going, but we're too close to Shreve to rise above the treetops.

Finally the river widens, and the car can fly freely again.

It's Boss X who gets back to the conversation.

"Ask yourself a simple question," he says. "Who do you fight for? Col Palafox?"

I find myself shaking my head.

Boss X lets out a grumbly laugh. "Don't feel bad if it's true. When I first joined up, it was for a boy. Took me a while to see anything bigger."

"No. I'm fighting *beside* Col—not *for* him." I shrug. "We're allies. And I've never even thought about the whole planet."

Yandre shrugs. "Not everyone's a rebel."

"The truth is, I'm fighting for Rafia," I say. "I was only supposed to be an extension of her, but she saw me as a real person. That's why I exist."

I look away at the lifting fans, wreathed in spray from the river. The sunlight turns to arcs of color in that mist.

"And I'm also fighting *against* my father. There's something wrong with him, worse than his strip mines and his spy dust. Even if we all lived back in the old days, before humans had the power to wreck the planet, I'd still fight him."

Boss X makes a sound between a growl and a laugh. "Nothing

wrong with making it personal. What matters, Frey, is that you fight beside us—up here."

It takes me a moment to understand. The 'Foxes are all down inside the car. The three of us are up in the cold wind, getting whacked by tree branches.

Maybe that makes me an honorary rebel.

"I'm glad you trust me," I say.

"I like a girl who carries a knife," X says. "Blades make it personal. Muscle and metal, point and edge."

"It's higher-tech than it looks," I admit.

His yellow eyes narrow. "Too bad. A knife should be simple."

For a moment, I consider asking him what his personal business is in my father's house. But then the hovercar glides to a halt again.

The riverbanks aren't the issue this time. We're within sight of the valley where Col plans to lure the Shreve army into battle tonight.

This is our hiding spot.

Soon Zura's voice crackles in our ears.

Setting down in thirty seconds. Hold on to something.

And if you rebels don't object to hurting trees, we could use a little camouflage.

BATTLE

We spend the afternoon hidden there, moving our solar panels out of the shifting shadows, getting back to full charge before night comes.

The rest of the Victorian army, along with our rebel allies, will come in high and hard when the sun goes down. We want the added cover of darkness, and for the citizens of Shreve to be home from work and watching the feeds when I declare my coup d'etat.

The waiting gives me time to miss Col.

When his officers didn't let him join the tower raid, it was fine with me. I'd rather have just Rafi to worry about keeping safe tonight.

But I'd somehow forgotten—since my father attacked House Palafox, Col and I haven't been apart for longer than a few hours. It seems like years since then, a lifetime of running and fighting.

If this war ends tonight, what do he and I have left?

"We need to do your face," Yandre says as the sun goes down.

We both smile at the absurdity of this. But Rafi would never go on the feeds looking windblown and disheveled, especially not to declare herself the new leader of Shreve.

Adorning my hands are three rings made of recycled iron, my father's chosen symbol of wealth. My sneak suit has a stored image of Rafi's favorite dress from the waist up.

My hair will have to wait until after the battle. But we do my makeup atop the stolen hovercar in the dimming light, Yandre working with skilled hands to make me look my part.

The imperious first daughter of Shreve.

The battle starts on schedule.

The hoverboards come in first—rebels attacking cargo trucks and greenhouses on the outskirts of Shreve. Like any one of a dozen nuisance raids they've mounted these last weeks.

But this time when my father's light, nimble hovercars respond, the rebels don't scatter and retreat. They open up with Victorian plasma guns, sending a dozen burning wrecks to the ground.

A low growl comes from Boss X as we watch the fight. His fur is twitching, his hands flexing with a wolfish need to join.

"Soon," I say.

Slowly, like a giant waking up, the Shreve military responds.

Two squadrons of heavy attack craft rise over the city. Their massive searchlights wink on, and a blue-tinged daylight spills across the valley.

But instead of venturing out to take on the rebels, they open fire from a distance, safe from the plasma guns. A barrage of steel flechettes glitters across the valley, like sleet in the searchlights.

I wince, seeing distant figures falling from their boards.

"At least we know he's not home," Boss X murmurs, gazing at the edge of the city.

I raise my field glasses. No extra squadrons have moved to protect my father's tower.

Victorian hovercars come forward, and the rebels shelter under their armor. The Shreve response looks sluggish to me—as if they're pinging my father for guidance—but soon they take the bait.

The heavy craft move out to engage the Victorian fleet.

"Get ready," Zura says.

We clear the branches from the topside, stow our gear below, strap in for a crash landing. Beside me, Boss X looks uneasy, staring at his seat restraints like they're strangling him.

We wait, blind to the battle raging overhead—

Until a coded ping comes from our high command.

"Hold on," Zura says as the lifting fans spin up.

We fly low and hard toward my father's tower, our car tipped at a crooked, wounded angle. The metal deck shudders under my feet as our belly armor cracks against treetops. We slew randomly from side to side.

"Do we have to fly *this* badly?" Dr. Leyva asks Zura.

"Afraid so," she says, her hands tight on the flight stick. "The smoke pots malfunctioned. We don't look like we're on fire."

Boss X gives me a sidelong look. He points at his belt, studded with a selection of grenades and a spare pair of crash bracelets. "Topside?"

I'm already unstrapping myself from the seat.

I take the offered crash bracelets and slam them on my wrists. A smoke grenade goes into my pocket.

"Frey," Zura says. "Sit down."

I ignore her. Boss X is already climbing the ladder to the topside hatch.

"I'm *ordering* you to sit down and strap in," she says.

"I'm not in your army."

Dr. Leyva speaks up. "If you get yourself killed, Frey, this has all been pointless."

"Same if we get shot down! We have to look like the real thing, or my father's house defenses will—"

Boss X opens the hatch above us, and a screaming wind whips my words away. I grab a rung of the ladder and pull myself up into the booming, floodlit night.

I am steadfast.

CRASH LANDING

The wind is a cold gale across the topside.

I twist my crash bracelets on, and their magnetics pull me down. They drag like lead weights on my wrists, clanking against the metal hull as I pull myself toward the right rear engine.

Boss X is making his way forward, his eyes squinting against the wind, his fur pushed flat.

Around us, the night sky flashes and burns—explosions, searchlights, damaged hovercars. A stray fléchette glances off the armor to my right, leaving a dent the size of a fist.

The deck tips and shudders beneath me, Zura flying like a drunk woman.

We skim a stand of tall trees, and our lifting fans hack their tops into wood chips and eye-stinging pine scent.

When I can see again, Shreve sits in the distance. My father's tower is alight, its usual complement of drones swirling around its summit. Most are armed, but some will have sensors, radar, scanners.

This battle damage has to look real.

I haul myself the last few meters. The engine roar grows louder, the hull vibrating, the fan sucking the air down into its blades like a hurricane.

Trying to pull me in . . .

I'm close enough. I pull the smoke grenade out and realize there's nothing to attach it with.

Except my crash bracelets.

I pull one off, twist it to the highest setting. It clings to the vibrating engine casing, and the metal grenade clings to it in turn, immovable when I try to pry them loose.

I pull the pin and crawl back a few meters, counting under my breath.

The grenade flashes, its smoke pouring down into the lifting fan, then outward behind us in a spreading trail.

I turn to Boss X. The front right engine is already spilling smoke, and he's hauled himself to the rear of the car.

He rises into a crouch, unsteady in the wind.

"Ready to jump?" he calls.

"Jump?"

I stare wide-eyed at my father's tower, looming ever closer.

Zura is slowing us, readying to take the car skidding into the dirt. There isn't time to get back inside and strap in.

All we have is our crash bracelets—in fact, I've only got one.

Boss X is wearing both his. The belt is gone from his waist, wrapped around the grenade, I guess.

Then I remember the first time Naya let me take my pulse knife out of the training area.

I showed off for Rafi, making the knife fly around our bedroom. She asked if it was strong enough to pick me up.

Clinging with all the strength in my young hands, I let its magnetic lifters pull me to the ceiling of our bedroom while my sister laughed and threw pillows.

A pulse knife can carry me.

Of course, I probably weighed less then.

I crawl to the rear of the hovercar, find a spot next to Boss X, and look down at the trees whipping past below.

We're still flying very fast.

I pull my hood up over my head and face, switch the suit to light armor mode. It turns black, the nanos stiffening to hardened scales.

Smoke wreathes around us, and sounds of battle shake the air. At the edge of my father's estate, the treetops shooting past below turn to a blur of grass. The lifting fans switch over to silent magnetics.

"On three," X growls, his lips pulled back from his teeth in a beatific smile. "One, two . . ."

We jump straight up, caught in the wind, the car zooming away ahead.

Below us, my father's perfectly manicured gardens are a riot of color in the floodlights. For a moment I'm in free fall, both hands wrapped around my buzzing knife . . .

Then my left wrist snaps taut, the bracelet trying to slow me down. The knife roars to life, and it feels like my shoulders are being yanked from their sockets. My iron-ringed fingers twist painfully in the magnetic fields.

I fall, hit a row of hedges slantways, scraping across the tops of leaves and branches. The stiffened sneak suit is tougher than bare skin, but it still feels like being dragged across thorns and brambles.

The hedges bring me to a gradual, thrashing halt. It takes a painful moment to pull myself from the ruined plants.

Fifty meters farther on, Boss X is standing up, gingerly rubbing his wrists.

He's watching our Shreve hovercar.

It crashes just as planned.

The smoking right-side fans tip down into the gardens, sending up a spray of flowers and dirt. The car tries to slew sideways, but Zura holds it steady. The drag slows it until the fans snap off and career away across the gardens, still smoking.

The car goes into a spin, out of control now. But its magnetics keep it a few meters above the ground, a swirl of smoke and sparks.

Finally it rear-ends into the base of the tower, tearing out a gaping chunk of the cargo bay wall.

As the hatches pop open and Specials spill out, Boss X and I are already running toward the gap.

HOME
INVASION

This late, the loading bay is empty of workers. The cargo trucks and lifting drones sit silent, red in the running lights of our crashed hovercar.

The entries to the rest of the house are secured. But Rafi and I have played hide-and-seek a hundred times here—I know what's behind every door.

"This way!" My pulse knife roars to life, flies at the largest roller door. With a shriek of tearing metal, a jagged hole opens up.

We leap through, run across the carpeted lobby floor, and into the largest room in my father's house. The ballroom, full of bare tables and an empty stage.

This is where I saved my sister's life a year ago. When not in use, it's where the house security drones go to recharge.

We catch them sleeping, not expecting attackers pouring from a fallen Shreve ship. The drones try to sputter to life, their weapons crash-charging like the hum of bees. But the Specials' barrage guns open fire, cutting them to pieces.

Boss X extends his pulse lance—like my knife, but two meters long—and chops the supports out from under the balcony. It crashes down onto a dozen waking drones.

I pull the barrage gun from my belt and let my own fire spill wild, hitting the tables, the lights, the ornate ceiling. Some simple, angry part of me thrills to be laying waste to my childhood home.

In seconds, the wreckage of fifty drones litters the ballroom floor. Another twenty or so will be on station throughout the house. Sirens are ringing now.

I start for the stairs, but then I see him—Boss X, up on the stage.

Yandre takes my shoulder. "Five seconds."

X slashes at the stage with his pulse lance. Sparks and sawdust fly, then he kneels and pulls free a jagged triangle of wood. He brings it to his lips.

"The man X joined the rebels for," Yandre says. "He died here."

My mind can't grasp this.

"It wasn't an authorized mission," Yandre says. "And he wasn't trying to kill your sister."

I manage to nod. "My father was meant to give that speech."

I don't tell them the rest. That I made the kill that day—and that it was the best day of my life.

Boss X leaps down from the stage, the token piece of wood clutched in his hand.

We charge up the emergency stairway, up toward the control room, toward my sister. Dr. Leyva and his techs take the lead now, spraying anti-dust nanos and scanning for traps.

Boss X is behind us, sweeping his pulse lance across the landing below. It sends rubble crashing down on anyone who might be following. But it means there's no way back now.

I glance at Yandre.

They shrug. "It's a wolf thing. No retreats."

But it's more than that. This is as personal to Boss X as it is to me.

I bring the party to a halt on the stairwell, ten floors up. Just outside the control room and the medical center, and below my old bedroom.

"There'll be drones on this floor," I say. "Or soldiers."

The Specials push me out of the way, set blast caps on the stairway door.

The roar of the explosion echoes down the stairs.

We charge out the gaping hole. Metal shards of the door are everywhere—

But the med center is empty.

Nothing but shiny furniture and equipment, and that giant picture window showing the battle outside in all its glory. Missiles crisscrossing the night, rings of plasma aflame, hovercars veering, burning, falling. Rebel antiaircraft spider-webs stretch across the sky.

For a moment I can't breathe.

All this destruction—for Victoria, for the planet, for the rule of law and normalcy.

But also for me.

I helped plan this battle, nudging flickering soldiers and machine-like toys across an airscreen table. Quoting Sun Tzu and Niccolò Machiavelli. Pouring out every second of training that my father subjected me to.

His creature.

He made me, and I made this spectacle before us.

"Magnificent," Dr. Leyva says softly. "But we're losing."

It's true. The army of Shreve has left the city almost defense-less, surging out across the farm belt against the rebels and Victorians. So many hovercars, drones, jump troops . . .

Then I realize—the score of ships guarding this tower have joined the fray, tipping the balance. Once we invaded my father's home, it left them with no reason to stay here.

So they headed straight at Col.

"No," I murmur.

"Focus," Zura says. "Where's the control room?"

I point.

"Why is no one here?" Boss X says. His pulse lance buzzes in his hand.

One of the techs raises an instrument. "There's some kind of magnetic field building. Frey, is this room equipped with—"

Her voice cuts off, and she crumples to one knee. Blood spurts from her throat and down her chest, setting off camo reactions in her suit.

I flinch from a metal flash in the corner of my eye. Something shiny darts past, and a lock of my hair falls, cut clean off.

Boss X cries out in pain. A shiny bone pin juts from his shoulder.

Suddenly the air is full of metal—scissors, suturing needles, pins, every medical instrument in flight.

I shut my eyes, knowing this room from endless training injuries, and grab a cushion from the surge table, wrap it around my head.

Some deadly code in the walls is running pinpoint lifter magnets, sending every small piece of metal swirling through the air, thrusting at anything with body heat.

A Special falls, something shiny protruding from his eye. I hear the buzz of Boss X's pulse lance as he fends off flitting projectiles. Objects *thunk* into my cushion, stab at my hardened sneak suit, slice my hands.

Sooner or later, one of them will find a vein.

But then the barrage tapers off.

I peer out.

Yandre stands in the center of the room, their face bleeding, their jacket in ribbons of leather. They hold a crash bracelet high in the air, surrounded by a lacerating hurricane of metal.

Of course. The bracelet's magnet is much stronger than any pinpoint lifter, and has drawn all that flying metal toward itself. But the vortex around Yandre's hand is closing, spinning quicker as it tightens, like water in a drain.

Once it consumes the bracelet—and Yandre's hand—the metal storm will break free again.

I hurl my knife at the picture window. The reinforced glass resists for a moment, then webs, cracks, shatters. Glittering shards spill out into the night, letting in the roar of wind and battle thunder.

Yandre takes slow, steady steps to the window, then drops the bracelet out.

The storm of metal follows, spinning into the dark.

I look around—one tech and two Specials dead. Boss X's fur streaked with blood. Yandre's arm streaming. Zura emerges unscathed from beneath a massage table.

The cold, ten-story wind sets everything rustling around us.

Dr. Leyva goes to work, looking for medspray and bandages. When he turns to me, I wave him off. My hardened sneak suit saved me from the worst.

And the battle is still raging outside.

"The control room's through that door," I say to the surviving tech. "I'll be back in five minutes."

"Frey . . ." Zura warns me.

I shake my head, taking a pair of grenades from Boss X's belt. He only nods.

I make for the stairs. The eleventh floor, where I used to sleep.

Zura doesn't try to stop me.

The stairwell is dark, sirens echoing from all directions. But there's movement below me. In night vision, I can see the two security drones drifting up on silent lifters.

There's no point in stealth anymore.

My barrage gun fills the stairwell with sparks and smoke, leaving them in jittering pieces. I set a grenade on a slow timer and send it bouncing down.

The door to the eleventh floor is secured, but the barrage gun shreds it off its hinges.

I dive through the doorway, aiming and firing at a lone figure in the hall. But my gun sputters, its status light blinking red.

I'm out of ammo.

"Frey," comes a familiar voice. "It's good to see you."

I squint through the soft glow of emergency lights. She stands there, lean and poised and strong.

Unarmed. Unworried by the likes of me.

My trainer, Naya.

NAYA

I drop the empty barrage gun, raise my pulse knife.

"Out of my way. I don't want to hurt you."

"You've never hurt me, Frey."

"Trust me, it wasn't for lack of trying."

Naya wears a familiar expression. That perfect focus, probing for weaknesses, judging me. For a moment, I'm a defenseless seven-year-old again.

"Your stance has gotten sloppy," she says.

I glance down at my feet.

She's right. My weight's too far back.

"I'm out of practice. Not a lot of fistfights in real wars, turns out."

"We can remedy that." She raises her hands, and I remember how beautiful I used to think she was—that blend of elegance, strength, and menace.

Now all I can see is the sadness in her eyes.

"I'm not going to fight you fair, Naya. You'll win."

"Then at least I've taught you something."

"Get out of my way."

"No, Frey. I serve the heir, not you."

I can see past her to Rafi's door. My old bedroom.

A weight lifts from me. "She's here?"

"Yes, Frey. She misses you."

My pulse knife is set humming with a squeeze.

Gently, careful not to crush it.

Firmly, so it doesn't fly away.

"Don't make me hurt you."

Naya shakes her head. "There's no other way."

There are many other ways—the world has taught me that in the last month. But in this house, there is only one.

I throw my knife.

It roars into her. Broken fingers, broken ribs. Sprains and dislocations. Burning muscles, battered pride. All that pain, traded for slivers of praise.

Nothing is left of her but the smell of rust.

I knock on my bedroom door.

"Rafi. It's me."

An endless moment of silence, then softly, "Frey?"

My eyes sting, something rising in my throat. My first answer isn't even a word.

I grip my last grenade. "Stand back. I'm about to blow this—"

The door slides open.

Rafia stands there, her face alight.

She's in the dress she wore for our sixteenth birthday—a gradient of feathers shifting like sunrise from orange to red, rubies tracing her waist. Her eyes are set off by a new necklace of slim gray metal.

For a beautiful moment, I'm certain that the Palafox psych team was wrong. This is Rafi—my confident big sister, every strand of hair in place, every accessory curated.

Until her arms wrap around me, and I feel the shudders in her grip, the panic in her heartbeat.

Her door wasn't even locked. She's too beaten to run.

She pulls away, spins once around. "I dressed up in your favorite, little sister. When the sirens started, I *knew* you'd come."

I can hardly breathe. "You're beautiful."

"And you're . . . *real*." Her words come in a whisper. "He said you were dead. Half of me, gone."

The need in her gaze makes me ashamed. I didn't miss her with that intensity. The world was too busy hitting me. I had a war to fight, a boy to learn.

While she was stuck in this room.

I can see it behind her, the walls set to the same colors she picked when we were ten. The photos of us together, erased from the house servers, but taped to our wall. The velvet dog whose tiny artificial brain learned to tell us apart, even when our father couldn't.

The room looks to me smaller now. Not even half a life.

Rafi reaches out, runs a finger across the scar above my eye—our scar.

"Nice makeup," she says. "Who did it?"

"A friend."

"You have friends now," she murmurs, ecstatic and jealous and sad.

After this long apart, it's strange to see my face in hers. Like some pretty-era software showing what the surgeons will make of me. More elegant, more refined.

More fragile.

She looks at her fingertip—it's slick from touching my face. It's on my hands as well, and in my hair.

"Naya," I say.

"Oh, poor Frey. When the sirens started, I told her to run away. I'm sorry she didn't."

I take my sister's hand.

"It's not our fault. Come on."

We take the stairs down to the med center.

The commandos stare at our identical faces—that baffled expression I'm so used to, redoubled. As if no one ever really believed there were two of me.

Rafi greets them like visitors in our home. A haughty nod and a measuring glance for each. And through her gaze I realize how motley a company we are. The rebels in their skins, Yandre's arm in bandages, all of them are injured in some way.

Dr. Leyva finds his voice first.

"We've corrupted the spy dust, citywide. And the feeds are under our control." He looks out the broken window. "But there isn't much time to turn this fight around."

Against the dark sky, the battle seems muted now. Streaks of light and smoke, but no more burning rings—the Palafoxes' plasma guns must be expended.

"This speech better be good," Boss X says.

"A speech?" Rafi clasps her hands. "Lucky I dressed up."

"No, big sister. This one's mine."

She draws herself taller, imperious again. "And what exactly are you going to say?"

"That you're declaring a coup against him. That we've shut down the dust, so the army and citizens can side with you. That you'll be the leader now, and everything will change."

"You can handle all that?"

For a moment, I'm her little sister again. But I hold her gaze.

"I'm ready for this."

She smiles. "Here's what I think, Frey. If we really want to hit him hard, we should address our city together."

No one speaks.

It slowly ticks into place in my brain—this is all our plans combined. Tearing everything away from him at once. His power, his city, his home, his secrets.

"You're right," I say.

Boss X lets out a rumbling laugh.

SPEECH

We stand side by side.

The camera hovers in the middle of the room, framing me and Rafi in the broken picture window. With the battle blazing behind us, it will be obvious we're talking live from our father's tower.

Bitter cold wind flutters the jagged safety glass, and more Shreve soldiers are storming the stairs now. Others are flying up the tower walls on hoverboards. Shots ring out as our commandos fight them off.

None of it ruffles my sister in the least.

I'd almost forgotten that persuasion was her job, not mine.

When the hovercam winks on, Rafi greets the people of Shreve. She tells them that she is in control of the tower. Then she fulfills her promise from the night before I left, and tells them our secret.

"As you can see," my big sister says, "I am not alone. I have never been alone."

My mouth goes dry. Somehow I can feel the curious gaze of two million people shifting between us, comparing us. One in a damaged sneak suit, her hair wild, covered with a slick of blood. The other, perfect as always.

A knife with two edges.

"I want you all to meet my twin, Frey. Though in fact many of you have met her already, and all of you have cheered for her. She took my place in crowds, in receiving lines, whenever there was danger. She was my first protector." Rafi's voice turns cold. "Because your leader raised one of his daughters to take a bullet."

It's strange, this revelation unfolding here. There are no shocked faces in the crowd. No audience metrics in an eye-screen. Just my sister laying bare the truth of me before a hovering cam.

"Since we were seven years old, Frey has been trained to kill. Every brutal day, she was harmed by her teachers, and there was nothing I could do to help her." Rafi's voice breaks, both genuine and exquisitely artful. "And every time I left our bubble, I had to wipe her from my mind, to pretend to everyone that she didn't exist. Our father made me an accomplice in Frey's pain—in her erasure—every hour, every moment."

Her voice falters again, showing them what Col taught me to see—how hiding me twisted her inside. But she never loses her train of thought, never misses a beat. This speech is so perfect that I wonder if Rafi has been writing it all her life. Practicing it under her breath. Dreaming it in the bed next to mine.

Waiting for this moment.

It was worth risking everything to give her this chance.

"Frey fooled you all, because she is magnificent. But she didn't deserve this. This is not normal."

She looks at me, and I realize it's my turn.

Rafi's already made the speech I practiced. There's no more to say about my broken bones, or hidden passageways, or Sensei Noriko. All I have left to say is what matters to me now.

"When this war began, our father threw me away. I was nothing to him but a way to steal some metal, conquer a city, and murder a family in their own home."

My voice wavers. Not artfully, like Rafi's, but with a shudder in my chest.

"When he sent that missile to destroy House Palafox, he thought I would die with them. A sacrifice to make him look daring and strong. The only reason I'm alive is that one of our father's intended victims was helping me escape. I owe Col Palafox my life."

I wonder if Col is watching. By now the whole world must have tuned in, except for people with a battle to fight. But I hope he's seeing this somehow.

"Col and his army are here to free you. Stop fighting him, and start fighting your real enemy. We call on you, the citizens and army of Shreve, to join us. To reject our father. To make Shreve a normal city again."

It's strange. I expected to utter these words in Rafi's voice. But at long last, I'm using my own.

And suddenly I know how to end this.

"I'm free of my father's lies now, a freedom that you all deserve. It won't be easy, or steady, but it will be *yours*. Because the only sure path to freedom is to seize it for your—"

The lights go out. The hovercam falls to the floor.

Dr. Leyva appears at the door to the control room. "They cut the power! That's all we can do here!"

I turn to face the window.

In the night sky, the booms and streaks of flame are fading, the struggle ending in a whimper. Without the chaos of battle, how can Shreve soldiers declare themselves for Rafia?

There's no Victorian army left to tip the balance. Just a galaxy of lights wheeling in the air, away from the fight, toward us. The army of Shreve is headed home to retake our father's tower.

We were too late.

"Did they hear us?" I ask.

Dr. Leyva nods, staring at a handscreen. "It was on all the feeds. The whole city is talking, reacting. But they can't digest this right away. And we're out of time."

"Poor Frey," Rafi says softly. "Did you think one speech would change everything?"

"I just thought . . ." But I'm not sure of the rest.

"It *was* a good speech," she says. "We're perfect together."

Boss X claps my shoulder. "It was a start, but we need to get out of here."

It takes me a moment to realize that they're all looking at me, waiting for whatever's next.

My head is spinning. The next step was supposed to be victory. But we were too slow in taking the tower, Col's army too weak.

All there is to do is run. But there's shooting all around us.

"We have to get out through the trophy room," I say. "It's one place they can't blow up. Two floors down."

"We *can't* go down!" Zura calls from the broken stairway door. Gunfire lights up the stairwell behind her.

"Yes, we can." I squeeze my knife and let it fall.

It hits the floor screaming, billowing dust. When it leaps back into my hand a moment later, a jagged hole has opened, full of fire-suppression foam and sparking wires.

"Me first," Boss X rumbles.

His pulse lance buzzing, he leaps through. I follow, grabbing onto the edge to swing out of his way.

He's fighting drones, his lance slicing elegant arcs through the air. As I land, my knife takes one out—then sputters to the ground.

Its battery light goes red.

I'm unarmed, but Zura has dropped through, her barrage guns adding to the din. Moments later, the ninth floor is secure.

One more floor to go.

"Cut here," I tell Boss X.

He attacks the floor with his pulse lance. By the time the others are all down behind us, we're ready to descend again.

This room is quiet and dark. As I thought, Father's security wouldn't dare start a firefight here. Nothing is more precious to him than his trophies.

They're mostly portraits. Paintings of his former allies, his enemies, all the people who no longer appear in the Shreve propaganda feeds. Erased people, existing only in this abyss of memory.

Our father never forgets his victories.

There are normal hunting trophies too—the stuffed heads of stags and boars and lions. A hundred kills at least, and a rack of hunting rifles and hoverboards.

"Are these boards charged?" Zura asks.

"Always, in case of a fire. But the guns aren't loaded."

"Good enough." She pulls a hoverboard off the wall.

While the others climb down from the floor above, I orient myself. This room is our father's guilty pleasure, with no windows to let in prying eyes. But the outer wall should be right here, behind this portrait of—

Me.

Frey.

Definitely not Rafi. Not with that mussed hair, the workout clothes, the knife in my hand. A sheen of sweat, and that look of battle ecstasy in my eyes. Wilder than I ever pictured myself.

Our father already has a portrait of me in his trophy room.

But he only thought I was dead for a few days. How long does it take to paint someone?

Was this ready before I left for Victoria?

Then I see her, hanging right across from me—Aribella Palafox.

The painting captures her confidence, her certainty. Every stroke of the brush reminds me how formidable she was.

But she's gone, and I'm still here.

A voice rumbles in my ear. "One day, your father's picture will hang here too."

I look up at Boss X. His fur is blood-matted, one eye clouded by injury. But his expression is very human, very sad.

I wonder if the assassin—his lost love—is among these faces. But that's not for me to ask.

I'm not ready to tell X what I did.

His lance buzzes to life in his hand, and he raises it up, a look of wolfish glee on his face. For a moment I think he knows somehow, and he's going to burn me down.

But all he says is "Time to go. Which wall do I cut?"

COLLAR

I take the portrait of me off the wall, out of Boss X's way.

I don't want it sliced to pieces. I want my father to see my face every day, knowing that I'm still out there. Alive, fighting, looking for more ways to hurt him.

That girl in the painting looks so fierce, so strong. I want her to be the truth of me.

My sister joins me to stare at it.

"*You*, Frey? How sweet. That means he thought about you."

I look around the room, all those lost faces.

"Yeah, but I'm hanging here with his enemies."

"Silly Frey. Dad loves his enemies more than his friends." She waves a hand at the paintings. "For one thing, he knows what to *do* with enemies. You mount them on a wall with the other stuffed heads."

Her voice is trembling. I look into her eyes, and see a kind of panic there.

"I always hated this room." She wraps her arms around herself. "It's like being in his head, the only thing worse than being in his family. You lucked out on that, you know—not being a real daughter. I wish I could give you back those twenty-six minutes."

"I know."

I was only a throwaway, a tool. But she had to be his daughter all those years. I hated not being seen, but being seen was worse. I was never in a room alone with him.

What if all that time, she was protecting me too?

"Do you suppose there's a painting of me?" she asks. "In storage somewhere? Ready to hang?"

"It doesn't matter, Rafi. We're leaving." I take her hands. "It's going to be okay."

"It's not."

"It's different out there, Rafi. There's a whole world where he can't touch you. You never have to see him again!"

Her voice goes soft. "But I can't come."

"What do you mean?"

Rafi's fingers go to her throat, touching the new necklace. "If I leave the house, this goes off."

I stare at it. "He put a tracker on you?"

"No. A bomb."

387

The wall is almost open.

Boss X has carved away the insulation and wiring, but the outer wall of the tower is solid duralloy. Too strong for a pulse lance.

Zura is setting explosive charges.

Shreve forces have occupied most of the building. But the spy dust is corrupted. They don't know where we are, or that we're about to blast our way out of the tower. The floor above us is full of proximity grenades, and Yandre holds our last plasma gun in their good arm, for any hovercars in our path.

But my sister is wearing a bomb around her neck.

"Anything?" I ask Dr. Leyva.

He's staring at his handscreen. "I've pulled all the code from the necklace. It's nothing too head-scratching."

I nod. "He wouldn't bother with anything complicated. Rafi's not great at tech stuff."

She looks at me slantwise. "*Rafi* is standing right here."

"The problem is," Leyva says, "I don't have time to run a hardware schematic."

"What does that mean?" I ask.

Rafi groans. "It means that the bomb around my neck is being defused by *the host of a cooking feed!*"

"A *science* of cooking feed." Leyva stares at his screen. "I've been hacking Shreve code for a month now. It's mostly been easy. But when I see code this simple, I worry there's a trap—a trigger hidden in the hardware."

He looks up at her.

"This is you, after all—*la princessa Rafia*. You're more important than a bunch of solar panels."

Rafi swallows. "So I'm stuck here."

He holds out the screen. "My hack is ready to go. Just push that button. But—"

"But my head might blow up. What are the odds?"

Leyva lowers the screen. "You'd know better than I."

I shake my head, my anger building. "If you don't know, Doctor, how are *we* supposed to?"

Leyva spreads his hands. "It's not about the bomb—it's about your father. If he'd wanted to, he could've made this code too strong to break in a few minutes. But he made it easy."

"Which means?"

"Maybe it's a trick, to kill Rafi if she tries to escape. Or maybe he wanted it simple, so there wasn't any danger of a bogus line of code killing her."

"And you can't tell which?"

"If we had two more hours." Leyva looks back at Zura.

She's almost done setting the charges. Our surviving tech has the hoverboards ready to go. Yandre has the plasma gun shouldered.

"What do you think, little sister?" Rafi fingers the necklace. "Would he rather kill me than let me go?"

Everything I know about our father goes rushing through me. It's acid in my veins.

"He hates to lose, Rafi." My voice starts to shake. "If you get away from him, it's like losing Seanan again. He can't let that happen."

"He wouldn't kill me," she says.

I step closer to her.

"The whole time I was at House Palafox, I thought the same. But he tried to, because nothing matters to him except *winning*. I'm sorry, Rafi. I swear to you I'll come back and save—"

Rafi takes the handscreen from Leyva, pushes the button.

The necklace pops open.

I stare—relieved, astonished, a sliver of me shattered.

"Sorry, little sister." She gives me a gentle smile. "It sucks, I know. But it's not like he'd ever throw *me* away."

CLICK

We stand on our hoverboards, ready to fly.

The charges are set. Yandre has already pulled the priming trigger on their plasma gun. The whine of its battery fills the trophy room like a boiling tea kettle.

Above us, the proximity grenades are going off one by one. The enemy clearing that floor. But they're taking their time—

They think we're trapped here.

We're only waiting for an opening outside.

"We should have a clear path in five, four, three . . ." Dr. Leyva begins, then shakes his head. "No, wait. Heavy attack ship in the way."

I groan. "Stop *doing* that!"

Leyva shrugs, staring at his handscreen. "You think this is easy?"

He's watching the newly free and rampant feeds of the citizens of Shreve. Two million people, all broadcasting whatever they want for the first time since our father took over.

Most of them are covering the battle, of course. Thousands are standing on their roofs, pointing cams at the tower, where signs of combat still flash in the windows.

They all want to know if they're really free yet.

They aren't, because we failed.

But at least I've saved my sister.

She's waiting on her board with the rest of us, wearing a sneak suit stripped from a dead Special. The camo is set to midnight black, but on Rafi it looks like a fashion choice.

Her feathered dress is neatly folded in the corner. The open bomb collar sits on top, a good-bye note from a runaway.

Boss X shifts nervously on his motionless board. "You're sure blowing out that wall won't kill us?"

"The charges are ninety-eight percent directional," Zura says. "You can trust Victorian tech."

"Ninety-eight." Boss X spits on the floor.

"Let's go, Doctor," Zura says. "We're just giving them more time to surround us."

Leyva shakes his head. "Actually, they're moving away from the tower and back toward the city. There are demonstrations popping up—fireworks, crowds, like All Saints' Day in Victoria. The military's more worried about its own citizens than us!"

"*Told* you it was a good speech," Rafi says.

I share a smile with her, but I'm worried about what happens to all those protestors next week, when the spy dust is back in the air again.

Does one night of freedom really change anything?

"There's still the matter of soldiers coming for us." Zura glances up at the hole in the ceiling.

Searchlights are crawling the floor up there.

"Another heavy unit's peeling away," Leyva says, staring at his screen. "Heading back out to the battlefield. Something's happening out there!"

I stand straighter on my hoverboard, hopeful for a moment.

Maybe the Victorians held some units in reserve. Maybe they're still fighting, and there's time for the rebellion in Shreve to take hold . . .

But then Dr. Leyva's face crumples.

"No," he says softly.

"What *now?*" Zura yells.

Leyva looks straight at me. "I'm sorry, Frey. It's just coming on the feeds. Why the battle ended sooner than we thought—his car was shot down."

I shake my head. "What do you mean?"

He hands the screen to me. "That heavy unit just went out to take custody of him."

I stare at the image on the feeds.

Col Palafox.

He's dirty, bloody. His eyes glazed, his wrists tied with smart plastic. Surrounded by two Shreve soldiers.

My father's prisoner.

"Please, no." My voice breaks.

Rafi puts a hand softly on my shoulder. "Poor Frey. You looked so sweet in that red jacket."

I look up at the others, pleading for a plan, some way to rescue Col. Yandre turns away, swearing under their breath.

Only Zura meets my eyes, her expression one of utter hatred. She must be wondering if Artura Vigil was right.

"It's not your fault," Rafi whispers in my ear.

But it is. This was all my plan.

A *whomp* comes from the floor above us, a smoke canister exploding. The billowing edge of a thick cloud pushes through the hole in the ceiling.

"Doctor," Zura says. "We have to go *now*."

Leyva doesn't take the screen from me, just nods his assent. Everyone steps back onto their boards.

Zura hits the charges. The wall blows outward in a furious roar, shards of duralloy tearing through the hovercars and drones outside. The force of the blast sends me staggering backward.

And all I can think is: Col is being brought here to this tower, a captive. Because he listened to me, followed my plan. Threw his army away for my sister.

The hoverboards rise up, their lifting fans at maximum speed. The wind ripples the paintings around us, stirs the dust and smoke in the room.

My team shoots off into the night, Yandre sending a blazing spheromak of plasma bolting out ahead of them, shredding still more hovercars in their path.

All in camo black, they disappear against the dark sky.

They won't notice I'm missing until it's too late to turn around.

I step from my hoverboard. Strip my sneak suit off, my gloves, and earpiece.

Shivering in the cold wind coming through the jagged hole, I cross to the dress that Rafi wore for our sixteenth birthday. They never made a copy for me. The party was only for half a dozen friends—no need for a body double.

But Rafi never forgot that I liked this dress. She wore it for me tonight.

I slip it over my head. The smart fibers beneath the feathers stretch; our bodies have parted ways over the last month, just a little. But once it slides down and around my hips, the dress feels like it was made for me.

I hide Dr. Leyva's handscreen behind the painting of Aribella Palafox. Then I close the bomb collar around my neck.

Click.

When Col is brought here, I'll be waiting. Ready to free him, to fight for him. To take him back to his brother and whatever's left of the Victorian army.

It will be okay.

The Shreve commandos come crashing down into the trophy room a minute later. Twenty of them in full armor, with stun guns and a dozen screaming battle drones.

They find me fixing my hair.

"You're late," I say in my best Rafi voice. "Our visitors have already gone."

FATHER

"Your father will see you now," Dona Oliver says.

I give her a bored sigh as I stand up and smooth my dress. He's kept me waiting for two hours outside his office.

How petty. Just because I helped my sister make a little speech. What was I going to do—let her pretend to be *me*?

Dona watches as I walk past, but there's no suspicion in her eyes. Only fear of what he'll do to me.

I'm more worried about Dona than anyone else. The last time Rafi and I switched places, she was the one who caught us.

But it's one thing, telling twins apart when they're standing side by side, another when there's only one in front of you. And quite *another* to believe that anyone would snap a bomb collar around her own neck.

I can still hear that *click*.

The office door closes behind me.

For the first time in my life, I'm alone with my father.

From behind his desk, he looks up at me. His eyes travel across what I'm wearing.

I spent all morning in Rafi's closet, remembering all the times I've watched her get dressed. Trying not to get lost in the maze of materials, cuts, and biases, the rules of formal, casual, cocktail, creative. Trying to imagine that it all really belongs to me.

Only the *best* clothes for the first daughter of Shreve.

With Rafi's voice in my head, I stayed conservative—a buttoned white shirt and dark skirt, modest shoes. Like someone applying for a job.

My father looks like he hasn't slept. He flew straight back from the peace conference, of course. He must have spent the night trying to put his city back in order.

He gestures to a pair of chairs by the window.

We sit together, the city of Shreve spread out below us. The scars of battle blacken the farm belt, and the debris of protests fills the streets.

But nothing shows more damage than this tower, a gaping chunk blown out of my father's edifice. From my bedroom window, I saw people on the rooftops gazing up at it.

We've made him look weak, at least.

"Have you seen what they're saying about us?" he asks.

It takes me a moment to answer. The city feeds must still be churning after the revelations in our speech last night. Rafi would have read them all by now; choosing the right clothes would've taken her only seconds.

At the edge of her mocking voice, I ask him, "You haven't got the feeds under control yet?"

"In time. For now, let them talk, so we'll know who to deal with once the dust is back in the air."

I smile at his logic, my stomach churning. How many people has my call for rebellion put at risk?

My father leans forward in the chair, closer to me than he's ever been before.

"Do you finally understand?" He waves a hand at the city. "With nothing but a few rebels and Palafox diehards, Frey did all this. And she forced you to make that . . . *speech*."

His whole frame shudders with anger.

But not at me. At my little sister.

For a moment, I'm too head-spun to speak. A hundred excuses were ready on my tongue. How I had no choice. How it was better with me, Rafi, in front of the camera, to take control if Frey went too far. How I knew the battle was already won.

But my father has already made the excuses for me.

"We made your sister too well, too dangerous," he says. "Do you see now why I tried to kill her at the start of this?"

He's pleading for my approval.

After Col's diagnosis of Rafi's psyche, I almost forgot how formidable she can be. But this was always her job—making people feel she was on their side, no matter what crimes my father committed.

Maybe she's worked the same magic with him.

"Frey isn't my sister anymore," I say softly. "She killed Naya right in front of me. It was grisly, Daddy."

"Of course it was. I'm so sorry, Rafia." But he doesn't look sorry. He looks pleased, maybe a little surprised that I'm agreeing with him so easily.

Rafi would have made him work harder.

I run a fingertip along my necklace.

"Don't you think it's time we took this off?"

His smile fades, his eyes narrowing a little. He reaches over to take my hand, and a shiver travels down my spine.

It's the first time he's ever touched me.

"But without my little gift, she would've taken you away. It protects you from her."

He thinks I should be grateful for this collar.

Rafi's maxim rings in my head—*This is not normal.*

I give him a shrug. "I suppose. But maybe she'll stop bothering us, now that you've destroyed the Palafoxes."

"She won't. Not while we have him in our house." He makes a gesture.

The door to his private office opens, and two people step through. One is a soldier—not a house guard in a crisp gray uniform, but one of the commandos from last night, still in full body armor.

The other is Col Palafox.

COL

I turn, pulling from my father's touch, and give Col a bored look as my heart breaks.

"So *this* is the boy who's riled up my little sister?"

He's dirty, though they've wiped most of the blood from his face. His Victorian uniform has been replaced with a jumpsuit made by a hole in the wall. It doesn't fit right, like they scanned him with his hands bound.

Still I want to wrap my arms around him, to breathe him in.

My father chuckles. "Frey had nothing to compare him to. Our fault, perhaps, for not widening her education."

Col stares back at me.

For a brain-missing moment, I expect him to see through my disguise. As if he'll somehow just *know* who I really am.

But he looks horrified by me. Like I'm some uncanny plastic

replica of myself. I promised him that Rafia was on our side, and yet here she is, plotting with her father.

I stare into Col's eyes, imploring him to read my thoughts.

It's going to be okay.

But it isn't—he's wearing a bomb collar too. Not a necklace, like mine. A thick dark ring, like a dog collar.

"I was going to keep him hostage," my father says. "To make the Victorians behave. But what's the point now? Their army's gone."

"So we let him go?" I ask lightly. "A gesture of goodwill?"

My father lets out a roaring laugh. "I've missed your sense of humor, Rafia."

I nod, taking the compliment, as always. "Then what do we do with him?"

My father shrugs. "We show those protestors how we deal with our enemies."

I stare, not understanding.

"And think what it will do to Frey," my father says. "Watching him executed will finally break her spirit."

Executed.

For an awful moment, the room darkens around me. I see a portrait of Col hanging down in the trophy room, across from his mother's. My heart rails in the cage of my chest.

My father narrows his eyes.

"What is it, Rafia?"

I draw a slow breath, my mind racing for an answer.

"An execution, Daddy?" My voice is quivering. "On the *feeds*? What will the other cities think?"

He gives a tired sigh. "It's too late to worry about our reputation. Your sister's speech has seen to that."

"But what if there's a way to fix it? To make them accept your control of Victoria?"

He stares at me, his eyes bored and heavy lidded. Like he's made and discarded a hundred plans to rehabilitate himself.

"Like what, darling?"

I don't know what to say. I don't know how to save someone with words. All I understand is improvised weapons, finding weaknesses, and fighting with all my heart.

All I know is war.

I stand up and turn toward Col, my eyes pleading. He stares back at me, uncertain why I'm trying so hard to save him.

We connect, a slant of air kindling between us—

And I see the answer.

"What if Col Palafox wasn't your prisoner, or your enemy at all? What if he was your son?"

I turn back to my father, twisting my lips into Rafi's cruelest smile.

"What if instead of killing Col, you give him to *me*?"

There's a moment of silence. Thoughts scuttle across my father's face, too quick to interpret.

It feels like the tower is tipping around us, broken by last night's blast. Broken by all my mistakes.

At last my father murmurs, "An alliance of blood."

"No more Victorian citizens resisting. No legitimate claim to Victoria for Teo Palafox. The perfect excuse for the other cities to buy our metal again."

A low roll of laughter comes from my father. But he's shaking his head.

"No one would believe it, unless we put the wedding on the feeds. Are you going to hold a knife to his throat?"

I turn to Col and reach out, stroke his arm. He shudders at my touch.

It's going to be okay.

"I'll persuade him, Father. You know how persistent I can be when it comes to getting what I want. How steadfast."

A realization flashes across Col's face—then he drops back into character, turning away from me, defiant.

I lean closer to my father, like I'm whispering a joke.

"The two of us married. Think what *that* will do to poor Frey."

That's when he laughs the hardest, rising grandly from his chair to gather me into a hug. My first hug from my father ever. I've never felt this before—the heat of his body, the mass of him, the *greed*.

And that's when the rest of the plan comes clear . . .

The same night I escape this tower, my father will die at my hands.

ABOUT THE AUTHOR

Scott Westerfeld is the author of the Uglies series, the Leviathan trilogy, the Midnighters trilogy, the New York trilogy, the Zeroes series, as well as the Spill Zone graphic novels, the novel *Afterworlds*, and the first book in the Horizon series. He has also written books for adults. Born in Texas, he and his wife now split their time between Sydney, Australia and New York City. You can find him online at scottwesterfeld.com

Keep reading for even more from the world of

IMPOSTORS

In this exclusive bonus content for IMPOSTORS,

we get a glimpse of Rafia's side of her

and Frey's strange childhood.

My etiquette tutor is annoyed with me.

Sensei Noriko would never say so out loud, but I can see it in her pursed lips. In her crisp instructions to repeat my moves again and again. In her reminders that the First Family Ball is next week, and that my father expects me to be as perfect a hostess as my mother would've been.

The *best* daughter.

"Straighten your back," Noriko says. "This is a curtsy, Rafia, not a bow."

I learned how to bow last month—in case the family business ever takes us to Japan.

"Just a respectful nod," she says. "As if speaking to your father."

My stomach twists. When my father's in the room, I always stare at the floor. Not out of respect.

I force his image out of my mind. Concentrate. Be the best.

This is how you curtsy: Slide your right foot back. Shift your weight onto your left.

Take the corners of your dress between the thumb and first two fingers of each hand. Pull your dress wider, like gently opening a fan.

"Pinkies out," Noriko murmurs, even though they're out already.

Nod the head. Bend the knees forward, but keep the back straight.

All at the same time. Gracefully, like I'm asking someone to dance. When I come back up, my best smile is on my lips.

Everyone loves my smile.

But Sensei Noriko still isn't happy.

"A curtsy shows courtesy," she says. "The way you move shows something else."

I sigh. "How *bored* I am, maybe? We've done this a hundred times!"

Noriko doesn't answer at first. She steps closer, scanning my posture. Then she reaches out and flattens one palm on my stomach, like a doctor trying to sense something beneath the surface of the skin.

The twist in my stomach flinches a little.

Her eyes soften. "You move with anger, Rafia." I have to leave the lesson early.

On the way back to my room, my fists stay clenched until I cross the red line. Only in the secure area can I let go.

My father has enemies. The people who killed my mother, who stole my older brother before I was born. Here inside the red line is where I feel safest.

It's also where both halves of me slide back together with a *click*.

When I open the door to our room, my twin sister looks up at me, a little surprised. She's toweling her hair dry. Her skin is flushed with exertion, her eyes bright. Her knuckles look raw—combat training.

She smiles at me. It's such a waste. Frey has a smile like mine, and no one ever sees it.

"Rafi! You're early."

"Obviously." I fall backward onto my bed.

Frey sits down beside me. "What's up, big sister?"

"Just Noriko. She was being a pain today."

Frey has to think for a second. She's never met most of my tutors. "Your etiquette tutor?"

I nod. "She says I don't curtsy right."

Frey laughs like someone who never has to be a perfect hostess. Who never has to smile at people she doesn't like. She laughs like someone free, even if she's trapped here inside the red line.

"That's silly, Rafi." She leans back beside me on the bed. "You do all that stuff right."

I love the praise, but *you move with anger* still rings in my ears.

It was mean of Noriko to see inside me like that.

And I can't even tell Frey why I'm really upset. I have to protect her, like she protects me.

While I'm learning how to bow and dance and be polite all day, Frey is learning how to fight. How to shield me with her body. How to kill for me if she has to.

Frey is my anger, my violence. I'm not allowed to have my own.

It isn't fair. All that time I spend with language lessons, dance lessons, etiquette tutors, I'm squishing my feelings down into my stomach—and Frey is swinging her fists.

She jumps up and tugs on the sides of her sweatpants so they look like jodhpurs. Does a little bow.

"This is a curtsy, right?"

I have to laugh. "That's terrible!"

"Then show me. I'll have to learn eventually."

It scares me that someday soon Frey will start taking my place when I go out in public. In case of snipers, kidnappers, bombs.

And she'll have to know the basics of being a first daughter. Whose hand to shake. Who to ignore. How to wave to a crowd.

Sometimes it helps to settle the knowledge in me when I show her what I've learned that day. Frey's terrible with languages and etiquette, but she can imitate any movement. She thinks with her body. Her muscles, her fists.

I hold out my hands. "Okay. I'll show you."

She pulls me up from the bed, like I weigh nothing. We face each other, her in sweats, me in my formal dancing dress.

"Feet in third position," I say.

"That's ballet talk, right?"

I roll my eyes and show her. She becomes a scruffy mirror image of me.

Only one tiny thing is wrong—her pinkies are stiff. Like they're broken, in tiny splints.

"Relax your hands."

Frey tries, but her hands are never relaxed, never still—they always want to grab, to strike. Our hands are so different.

She always laughs at me when I make a fist.

Thumb on the outside! You wanna break it?

No. But most days I do want to punch someone.

Frey's first curtsy is graceful. In a feline way, measured and dangerous. But no anger in her movements.

"Is this right?"

I shake my head—it isn't fair. She's the trained killer. But I'm the one who wants to kill someone.

Frey tries again, and a low growl runs through me. This is so easy for her. "What am I doing wrong?" she asks.

"You have to be more . . . respectful."

She looks confused. Then straightens and bows from the waist, much lower than Noriko has ever taught me to.

"This is respectful, right?" I can only nod.

This must be the bow Frey gives her trainers. All at once, I see what's missing in my curtsy. Frey feels something for her teachers that I never have.

And suddenly I'm angry at her for being twenty-seven minutes younger. For getting to punch things. For living here inside the red line, away from our father.

And I'm mad at Noriko for putting her hand on my stomach. I want to punish her for that.

"You should take my next lesson," I say.

Frey's eyes widen. "With your etiquette tutor? Dona would *kill* us."

"She won't find out. No one can tell us apart."

"In a crowd, maybe. But this is your tutor!"

"One day you'll have to fool *everyone*, Frey—my friends, Dad's business partners, a million people watching on the feeds!"

She shakes her head, stepping back into the corner.

This is how it always is. I'm the one who makes my little sister break the rules. Like when we sneak out of the secure area and pretend to be adventurers in a dungeon full of monsters, making sure no one sees us together.

"Aren't you tired of hiding?" I ask.

Frey just stares at me. She doesn't know what hiding is, like a worm doesn't know what dirt is.

I switch to pleading. "I can't get this stupid curtsy right. But I bet you can. Then you can teach it to me!"

Thoughts flit across her face. She wants to help me. To protect me, like she was born to do. But she doesn't want to get us into trouble.

"What if your teacher figures it out?"

"How? Noriko doesn't even know you exist! If she looks at you funny, just say you feel sick and leave."

Frey stares at me. Maybe she's not allowed to walk out of lessons whenever she wants.

I take her shoulders. Dig my fingers in.

"Do this for your big sis, please?"

I'm going to get my way. But Frey has one last argument to make.

"Dona said if anyone sees us together, *they'll* get in trouble too." That's the whole point, little sister.

No one sees through me.

"We won't be together, Frey. And Noriko won't figure you out." I let go of her and turn away. "But if you're not up to it . . ."

The window is a few steps from me. It's late afternoon, and the shadow of our father's tower spills out across the gardens, almost to the forest.

"Okay. I guess." Her voice is small.

I smile, but my stomach twists tighter. I want to hurt Noriko, not Frey. I want to hurt me. I want my father's secret spilled into the world, just a little. I want to hurt him most of all.

As I turn to hug my twin sister, I move with anger.

7